# NANDIA'S CHILDREN

## Also by Ned Wolf

*Awaken Your Power to Heal*
*Sailing on a Banshee Wind*
*Floraporna*
*Nandia's Copper*
*Nandia's Apparition*

# NANDIA'S CHILDREN

## THE FINAL SAGA OF THE NANDIA TRILOGY

## NED WOLF

THE THERAPEUTAE

PRESS

Published by:

The Therapeutae Press
P.O. Box 23542
Flagstaff, AZ
U.S.A. 86002

Paperback ISBN: 978-0-9675575-8-8
Ebook ISBN: 978-0-9675575-9-5

TheTherapeutaePress.com

THE THERAPEUTAE

PRESS

# DEDICATION

*...to all who abandon hopelessness and
yearn to trust their unlimited power to heal.*

# NANDIA'S CHILDREN

# PROLOGUE

THERE WAS A TIME IN HUMANKIND'S future when the species populated planets within many galaxies. Some societies had evolved to the point where a few individuals were capable of telepathy, teleportation and effective healing. On these planets, the nurturing of individual talents and abilities was given the highest priority. These were societies where effective healing was commonplace — where the human lifespan usually exceeded three centuries.

And yet, most planets had not evolved in this manner. In these societies warfare was the religion. Much of their propaganda was devoted to idealizing war. Addiction rates were at epidemic level — mental, emotional and physical epidemics a way of life. Environmental degradation was the norm, species extinction rates were high. Education had devolved into preaching superstition and greed. Economies were based on competition, not cooperation. The divide between the haves and the have nots was extreme. Most of the civilizations on these planets self-destructed.

It was the purpose of the Galactic Grand Council to locate and train competent individuals to serve as delegates to these troubled planets. Their mission? To intervene during the vulnerable years when a society was most likely to self-destruct. The Council had neither military might, nor could impose economic sanctions. What it did have was a small cadre of dedicated delegates. Some of these unusual people died during their missions. A few of them were able to inspire civilizations to trust in the power of the individual and embrace life-sustaining lifestyles.

The Nandia Trilogy recounts the intriguing adventures of an extraordinary team of these Council delegates...

I

OK, SO I WAS BORED and impatient. My healing clinic was being handled by my students. In fact, several were treating new clients with far more aplomb than I'd ever mustered. There hadn't been an assignment from the Galactic Grand Council for years, and frankly, I was itching for a challenge.

I hadn't seen Nandia since our last Council mission, when we had helped King Sabre of the planet Aesir see his way through a rough patch or two. Since then, Nandia and I had remained in telepathic connection, but even that had waned these past weeks — for far too many weeks. It was unlike her not to touch base, to ask about my life and share hers. OK, it wasn't so much that I was bored and impatient. I was worried.

God knows I'd tried to telepathically reach out to her. But, whenever I made the attempt, it was as if I ran into some kind of impenetrable grey cloud that blocked all connection.

All right, truth be told, I was in a quandary. I've

always known Nandia to be quite capable of dealing with any kind of crisis. But since our Aesir caper, we had never gone even a week without at least a hello.

OK, so I was more than worried, I was afraid. And afraid to admit that I was afraid.

I stood up from the bench beneath a willow tree that had become my office these past troubled weeks and began to wander aimlessly through my garden. Lately, I hadn't even noticed the new blossoms on the magnificent mango and cherry trees. Their fragrance I sensed only in the dim shadows of my subconscious. As I ambled, I had to admit that I had been completely ignoring the beauty of my outer reality, which, given my love of nature, was unusual. Mentally grabbing myself by the shoulders, I insisted that I get a grip and make a decision — any decision — even if it was the wrong decision. Still, I worried and by the minute grew more irritated at my worry. If Nandia and her husband were going through some trouble, contacting her could exacerbate their problem. Or perhaps they were going through a sublime season and my reaching out could prove an embarrassing interruption.

Even though I could just as well imagine useful, playful ways that Nandia and I could reconnect, my mind, like a homing pigeon, came to roost on what else could be causing this break in telepathy. What if she was in pain and unable to ask for help? Suppose her planet had been subjected to an epidemic and her telepathic ability had become blocked? During our first Galactic Council assignment in planet Fantibo's city of Geasa, almost exactly that scenario had played out. That is, until we had found enough copper to neutralize the zinc deposits that were disrupting our dowsing, telepathic and teleporting abilities.

Rather than continue this useless debate, I finally realized that what I truly wanted was to attempt another contact with Nandia — even if I failed yet again.

Relieved, I returned to my garden office and sat down with renewed determination. I closed my eyes and began deep breathing in preparation for a telepathic connection. I recalled my mentor Agoragon's advice to imagine my target person engaged in some sort of activity as I sent my message. Of course telepathy is enhanced whenever a deep emotional connection exists. I remembered the time in the hallways of Aesir's palace when Nandia and I had playfully kissed, ran away, chased, captured and kissed again, our passions teetering on the brink of oblivion. A smile for these past love antics lit my face.

It was easy for me to picture Nandia's eyes, almond shaped, deep blue-green in color. After untold centuries of living, her eyes reflect a playfulness that reveals an ageless wisdom. Imagining her playing tag with me, I mentally probed her presence with a greeting and a question about her well-being. But, as before, damnit, I encountered a dark roiling cloud — as if a distant expanse of sparkling ocean had suddenly been eclipsed by a marauding thunderstorm.

While I brooded, an image of the cat Sirius leapt into my mind. As a young kitten, he had been gifted to us at the end of our Aesirian mission. After our last Grand Council debriefing, Nandia had asked to take him home. Handing him over, I knew I would deeply miss the black-furred, white-toed rascal. He was as full of vitality and as irreverent as Arcturus, his father. Both were capable of telepathy and teleportation and both enjoyed a respectable disregard for the conventions of the English language. Had he come to mind at just that moment because now was the time to connect telepathically with him?

It was easy to imagine Sirius at play, white toes flashing like strobe lights as he scampered about. Before relinquishing him, I had spent hours enjoying his exuberant vitality. Not one for squeak toys or catnip, he did enjoy mousing with a rubber ball that contained a tiny bell within its gizzards. I imagined him soccer-dribbling his ball while telepathing my message: "You dank, dizzy-eyed dogstar, how's Nandia?"

It was as if I were hearing a radio not clearly tuned into a station. Static surrounded the few words I could make out.

"Cxchsxsxsx...Need help....chxsxsxs...Get here..... xsxsxschcx........" It was Sirius, spitting clipped, concise words — quite uncharacteristic of him. Normally his language was laced with an alarming misuse of obscure Australian idioms — obviously learned at his father's knee.

But, double damnit all, my worst fears had been confirmed. I stood and again began pacing my garden. I knew Nandia lived on a planet called Praesepe. She mentioned a home located near a town called Warragin, explaining that its name had originated centuries earlier from the local indigenous people. It was the site of a battle that had led to the abduction of an entire generation of children — the conqueror's plan was to socialize captured youngsters into their new culture. A search of star charts could locate Praesepe, but not its city of Warragin. Damnation! If I was going to teleport there, I needed more information in a hurry. To effectively teleport, a traveler needs to accurately visualize his landing zone.

I decided to telepathically contact the Galactic Grand Council. There was an elder who sat on the Council whom I had nicknamed Liberace because of his outrageous sparkly outfits and outlandish gestures. Returning to my office bench I again calmed myself with deep, connected breathing. Liberace's fleshy, handsome face came to mind. I imagined him watching his own fingers fondle bejeweled rings — his habitual affectation whenever he puzzled a problem. I sent a message requesting an audience.

Liberace's startled face appeared vividly in my mind's eye. He looked as if he had been interrupted from a nap. "Thank God you've called," he exclaimed, rapidly blinking and shaking his head. "The Council convenes within the hour to address a crisis on Praesepe. Nandia is somehow involved. Stand by. We will teleport you to our chambers and share what little we know. Expect to be joined by Elli and Dunstan."

I stood and waited, continuing deep breathing as I sought to calm my troubled mind. With barely enough time to brush my brows and assure that my lockpicks and pendulum were in place, I once again found myself in the familiar Council chambers, facing the dozen Council Elders of varying species, sizes, genders and descriptions seated at an elevated semicircular table. Several were humanoid, a few reptilian, the others mostly alien species, unknown to me.

My mind returned to puzzle over a nagging mystery: How could the chamber's lighting, with its unknown source, illuminate only me and the Council, while leaving the rest of the immense rock cavern shrouded in darkness? An elder had informed me during an earlier briefing that the cavern provided failsafe shielding from not only electromagnetic but also telepathic eavesdropping.

"Welcome, Bernard." Their collective mental greeting appeared in my mind as a chorus of warm feeling-tones. I smiled in deep gratitude for these beings. Their lives were devoted to healing planets; respect for them reverberated to the ends of the inhabited galaxies.

"What news of Nandia?" I asked in the midst of meeting each Elder's gaze as I scanned the semicircle of beings. My worry over Nandia was interrupted, however, by the abrupt appearance of Dunstan and Elli. They arrived holding hands. Each was a much beloved ally whom Nandia and I had befriended during past Council missions, although, to my knowledge, neither of them knew the other.

El we had met just after beginning our second mission on Aesir. She is an immortal who has not only served many Aesirian kings as The Royal Chambermaid, but married several and even given birth to several during her centuries of devoted service. With a lightning-quick mind and agile wit, she proved to be an invaluable guide at court and quite adept at teleporting and telepathy.

A large and charismatic Scotsman, Dunstan is a talented healer and musician. Nandia and I met him during our mission to Geasa, where he had exiled himself to busking throughout its streets, for the sole purpose of lifting the troubled spirits of the city's inhabitants. With a rare talent for playing music that stimulates healing, Dunstan proved to be quite useful as we tamed the deadly Saragalla epidemic that had threatened Geasa's survival.

I was thrilled to see these dear friends again and turned toward the musician with the jibe, "Ya flamin, red-haired gudgeon, have you finally learned to play a decent tune on that shiny brass screech-horn you're still carrying around?" He grabbed me in a giant embrace that was quickly interrupted by an admonition from a Council Elder.

"Time is of the essence for this briefing on the Praesepian crisis. We ask that you forego your usual greetings." The message rang clearly in my mind and reminded me of Sirius's message. El and I smiled fondly at each other and turned our attention to the Council.

"What little information we have suggests that a besieging force has taken over the entire Praesepian government," Liberace began. "They have some type of shield that is preventing our telepaths from learning more. This shield is also preventing the Council from teleporting you to Praesepe. May we suggest your immediate departure on a starship scheduled to launch within the hour?"

Nandia and I had faced a similar crisis during our mission to Geasa. There we discovered, during our first meal in a streetside café, that copper-rich foods temporarily neutralized the city's zinc's disruptions to our dowsing. Further testing with our pendulums revealed that these same zinc deposits were interrupting both telepathy and teleportation.

"Have you checked to see if some type of zinc shielding is being used on Praesepe?" I asked the Council.

"It is quite possible," replied an extremely tall Elder

7

who looked reptilian. "We have no way of determining that, but perhaps you could make use of your dowsing skills to confirm your hypothesis."

From its nest on my belt, I extracted my pendulum and began dowsing. I always begin my practice with a few deep breaths to connect my body, mind and spirit/soul. Then I mentally affirm, "I dowse impeccably for the greater good of All That Is."

Dowsing is a tool that can be used to tap into the infinite library of information accessible within the inner dimensions of the Self. It trains the conscious mind to frame questions that must be answered with either a 'yes' or a 'no' response. Effective dowsing requires setting aside rational analysis and emotional attachments when exploring a problem. An ages-old discipline, it proves to be quite helpful when learning to merge the intellect with the intuition.

Standing in the Council chambers, I started with my pendulum hanging in its neutral stopped position. Then I mentally asked, "Are the disruptions to telepathy and teleportation on Praesepe the result of the presence of zinc?" My pendulum immediately began swinging in a forward-and-back motion, my 'yes' response that mimics the up and down affirmative nod we humans so often use.

My pendulum's negative response is a side-to-side motion that mimics our negative shake of the head. Early in my training, I had programmed my subconscious to settle on these simple signals, easy to remember. Other dowsers prefer different signals, but mine leave my conscious mind free to watch for any subtle expectations or judgments that may intrude and interrupt my accuracy.

So, my Inner Self had indicated that on Praesepe, telepathy was being blocked by some kind of advanced zinc-disruption field technology.

I puzzled over this news. Did our earlier discovery of zinc's disruption to telepathy and teleportation prompt Praesepe's besiegers to develop a zinc shield? Did they know of copper's effectiveness as an antidote? But even more disturbing was why they would even want to invade Praesepe.

Setting these questions aside, I pressed on with a final question. "Can we neutralize this disruption by broadcasting the frequency of copper to Praesepe using a radionics instrument?" Again, I received a positive response.

Agoragon, perhaps the most beloved of my teachers, taught me about radionics, a science based on the simple fact that every element, every type of life, every organ in the body vibrates to its own unique electromagnetic frequency. For countless centuries dowsing has been used to identify these frequency rates. Radionics instruments can be calibrated to different rates and then used to transmit frequencies or create remedies that can be ingested orally.

Science has yet to measure the subtle emanations of energy used in the practice of radionics. Agoragon helped me learn that ill health is a result of blockages to the body's natural flow of subtle energies. These blockages are caused by distorted thinking, trauma, or even suppressed desires or emotions. A radionics frequency sends an electromagnetic signal into the energy field, dissipating the blockage and restoring the body's natural, healthy flow of energy. As the energy field recovers its balance, mental, emotional and physical imbalances ease and healing is accelerated in the body.

I knew the radionic frequency rate for copper and knew we could radionically transmit it to Praesepe. My hope was that this would restore a telepathic connection with Nandia.

Agoragon used to say that while radionics is indeed a powerful healing tool, it cannot hold a candle to the unlimited power of the human brain when merged with the spirit/soul mind. But, until we as a species learn and trust the incredible creative power of consciousness, radionics serves quite a useful purpose.

Although I assumed that Council members had telepathically tuned into my testing, still, I verbally summarized my findings. "Testing indicates that the intruders are using some type of zinc shielding that disrupts telepathy. I also find that we can neutralize that shield by broadcasting the frequency for copper to the planet. I will need a radionics instrument and the celestial coordinates of Praesepe relative to where we are. I have the equipment and frequencies we need at my home."

"We can supply your needs from here," the reptilian Elder offered. "I recommend that we order what is needed immediately." The rest of the Council Elders readily agreed.

A young courier brought in a folding table. He was followed by a team carrying a radionics instrument, a power supply and a copy of a universal rate book. After setting up the equipment, I dialed in the frequency rate for copper. All that was needed were the celestial coordinates for Praesepe, which a second courier handed to me on a small slip of paper.

I placed the note listing the coordinates into the instrument's receptor-well and activated a series of switches that allowed it to transmit copper's frequency to the planet. I checked with my pendulum to determine the optimum broadcast time.

I addressed the Council. "After seven minutes, we will find out whether my dowsing was accurate. If so, the intruders' zinc shielding will have been neutralized."

As the minutes counted down, everyone agreed that I should be the one to telepathically connect with Nandia and find out what she needed to deal with the crisis. Several wanted to know the identity of Praesepe's besiegers. As the courier checking his watch nodded, I began breathing in a deep, connected rhythm. I closed my eyes and imagined Nandia waving to me from Praesepe's surface. I focused on her eyes and listened. Suddenly a surprised "Oh!" came back to me. It was Nandia's voice. I sent her the message that I was in the Grand Council chambers with Dunstan and Elli.

"What a relief that you've managed to penetrate the zinc shielding, Bearns," she responded, using the familiar nickname I'd been given at birth. I could make out a vague and intermittent mental image of Nandia, as if she were shrouded in banks of billowing gray clouds. "We're surviving a state of siege here, but only just. Could use your help," she said. "Bring Dunstan and Elli and a radionics instrument. These cretins from the planet Erylia have confiscated my copper. I'm in the city of Braeoon and will watch for you at the entrance to the Braeoon Gardens. How soon can you get here?"

I needed a suitcase, or preferably a backpack, to carry the equipment. This I requested of the Council and then asked, "Can you teleport the three of us together?" After a moment's consultation together, they agreed they could, although it would test the limits of their combined abilities.

"We've heard that the Erylians are suffering some type of epidemic that has hit their younger generations," Liberace said. "We can explore that further from here. Meanwhile, the equipment should be packed up and ready to go within the quarter hour. However it would be wise for you continue broadcasting the copper frequency for as long as possible. We can certainly feel the easing of the Erylian shielding."

"We can be there in fifteen minutes," I telepathed to Nandia. "Send a mental image of the entrance to Braeoon Gardens."

I looked to El and Dunstan to make sure they were telepathically tuned in and then closed my eyes. Immediately I saw a broad pathway spanned by a long, wrought-iron archway. It was overgrown with flowering vines bursting with bright orange blossoms. A few solitary people walked beneath this structure, despite the beauty of a day only occasionally shadowed by bright, cumulus clouds gently rolling across the rose and blue tinted Praesepian sky.

This rare color would aid us when visualizing our landing zone. Opening our eyes at the same time, El and Dunstan nodded that they had captured the target image and were ready to travel. I indicated to the Elders that we were prepared for departure.

Liberace telepathed that the Council needed only a few moments more to complete the gathering of our supplies. I turned to El and properly greeted her. As we warmly held each other, she informed me that she had once been a Council member many generations past. Then I recalled our time together on Aesir and realized that El's prescient wisdom and vast knowledge of the galaxy added up a connection with the Grand Council. I was about to apologize for my short-sightedness when Dunstan joined in our hug.

"Aye, 'tis grand ta lay me eyes on ya once again, Laddie, so 'tis," he crowed. "And what rancorous burdens have ya' been layin' on the fair Nandia's shoulders since our last troubles, ya malingerin' minnow?" We all laughed at the prospect of a new mission together.

Only years after our assignment to Geasa did Nandia and I learn that the Council had sent abundant funds and staffing to Dunstan who had chosen to remain behind. There he established school for young, homeless survivors of the Saragalla epidemic. It was only then that I finally discovered that Dunstan was also a former Council member.

El interrupted these musings to remind me that Nandia's copper had been confiscated. After I relayed this to the Council, Liberace informed us that they were providing half dozen copper amulets and medallions. The spare metal could come in handy, especially if we ran into the same kind of troubles we had encountered in Geasa. There we were unable to use our telepathic and teleporting abilities until Dunstan had discovered a hidden source of the rare and proscribed metal. And for that, he had been imprisoned in a foul dungeon until Nandia and I rescued him.

A courier rushed in carrying a backpack. I checked

that power supply, rate book, copper baubles and radionics instrument were safe and secure. There was also a bag containing a generous supply of gold coins — the Council's characteristic method of providing funds that could easily be converted into local currencies. After shouldering the pack, I turned to El and Dunstan and held out a hand to each of them. We formed a triangle and smiled at each other. I felt as worry-excited as a small child stepping onto a spinning merry-go-round.

Staring intently at the three of us, the Elders suddenly disappeared, replaced by a familiar spiraling of white light behind my eyes. The next moment a feeling of weightlessness overtook me, and I mentally heard Elli say, as if far off in the distance, "Let's be away to Praesepe and find Nandia."

II

Immediately a flow of warm air caressed my skin. I opened my eyes to find us standing at the base of a larger-than-life statue of a horse and rider at the entrance to a large park. Behind it stood the iron archway blanketed with orange blossoms that Nandia had transmitted. This was Braeoon Gardens.

Looking up, I discovered that the warmth I was enjoying emanated from two suns in the sky above me: one with a maroon tint, the other smaller and quite similar to Sol back home. The pair of suns was separated by nearly half of the sky's expanse.

"Look at those twin suns," I marveled. "Two in the sky must make for long days."

"Aye, and Praesepians must have an interestin' way of describin' the half-light of the single sun at dusk and daybreak," Dunstan added.

"And look here!" I said, waving my arms overhead to play with the suns' double shadows. "I've never seen daylight anywhere that does this!"

"Welcome to Praesepe," Elli said as we turned circles drinking in the surroundings. I was overtaken by the colorful variety of tropical plants — a lush and beautifully overgrown, yet peaceful place. Each vibrant orange blossom adorning the wrought-iron archway could have spanned a blacksmith's hand. Not a single soul waited or walked beneath the enchanting canopy. Disappointed that Nandia was nowhere to be seen, I looked further afield, hoping she had not run afoul of trouble.

Majestic, forest-green fig trees, similar to those of my home's Morton Bays, bordered wide, verdant, grass-carpeted spaces. With broad, elephant-hide trunks, they sprouted root structures tall enough to conceal whole families. Thick, leafy domes soared high above us and reverberated with songs of countless birds. The normal sounds of the city in the background were muted by this cacophony of unfamiliar bird calls.

"Shall we take a bit of a wander?" Dunstan suggested, as he nodded toward the nearest stand of trees. I appreciated moving away from the few pedestrians I now noticed passing the park's entrance. They seemed to be seeking refuge from the rigors of their workday. I thought it curious that none of them gave us even a cursory glance, despite our off-world garb.

We began our stroll. I used deep breathing to relax and begin focusing on the energy fields of the few passing people. Their aura colors reflected high levels of anxiety and fear. I realized that my own energy field would have reflected the same colors of muted browns, greys and muddy greens if my home planet were being subjected to an off-world siege.

"And where in heaven's name do ya suppose we

might find our fair lassie?" Dunstan loudly asked, hoping to find Nandia hiding amidst the nearby undergrowth.

"She said she would meet us at the garden entrance," El replied. "Let's watch for her there as we walk."

She lapsed into silence as we headed toward the nearest thicket of fig trees. Finally she said. "I've been trying to reach Nandia telepathically, but getting no response. Bearns, how long can the Erylian zinc shield be neutralized by your broadcast?"

"That I didn't test," I responded. "Obviously the shield is being neutralized by the copper we carry, but Nandia doesn't have that advantage. Let's find a secluded spot where we can broadcast copper's frequency to the surrounding area. If she's nearby, we should be able to tune in to her."

Carefully watching for any overtly curious passersby, we settled ourselves among the tall roots of ancient fig that were high enough to conceal us. There I set up the radionics instrument, connected its battery and dialed in the frequency for copper.

In the Grand Council chambers Praesepe's coordinates had been effective to locate the planet as a target for disseminating the copper frequency. But on Praesepe's surface, the celestial coordinates were meaningless. I decided that a spoonful of Braeoon Garden's dirt would serve as a witness to target copper's frequency, at least to the immediate neighborhood.

"We're now transmitting," I told my companions. "Time to see if we can tune in to Nandia."

"As I said more than once on Fantibo, Lad," Dunstan chuckled, "You does have your uses."

With that we each calmed ourselves and focused on our own images of Nandia. I visualized her lovely eyes and imagined her waving. Then I projected my desire to communicate with her. Suddenly, a picture of her face came into sharp relief. "Oh, I'm so relieved that you've found a way to reach me," she telepathed. "I had only just arrived at the garden archway when several Erylian proctors appeared. I escaped their attention by quickly befriending a young couple who were in a hurry to get back to Braeoon's financial center. The three of us scurried away together until I could get lost in a crowd. Where are you?"

We telepathed the scene of our fig tree refuge and within seconds, Nandia arrived. Relieved to find her safe and sound, we greeted each other with great fondness, oblivious to the risks of attracting unwanted attention. While waiting until El and Dunstan had released her from their warm embraces, I noticed that she looked a bit more tired and slender than when our paths had last crossed.

The intensity of our kiss as we came together caught me completely by surprise. Upon parting I found myself wondering how it was that each kiss felt as if it were our first kiss. Nandia's face was radiantly beautiful. The strain that had been apparent when she arrived eased as she breathed a huge sigh of relief.

Early in our Geasan mission, Nandia and I found that our individual talents and strengths melded together into an extremely effective team. During our assignments there and on Aesir there had been hardship and danger. We had survived attacks and helped each other heal. We always accomplished our goals using means consistent with our mutually held ideals.

We had a loving, playful ability to have fun together. And, despite this siege of her homeland, being together again with Nandia, El and Dunstan felt like I was being enfolded within the bosom of the most beloved of families. Any worries I had over unknown crises lurking in our future evaporated into the air.

"I think it's time to find out what we are facing," Elli said as Nandia and I untangled from our embrace. "Is it safe here to talk about Praesepe's problems?"

"For only a few moments, I'm afraid," Nandia said, standing tall to quickly survey our surroundings. "I am being hunted. We need to move further away from the garden entrance. Not only have Erylian proctors found a way to create a zinc shield, but they have devised sensors that let them locate telepaths. I can only assume their sensors somehow read the presence of copper. Speaking of which, where's mine?"

Dunstan lifted his medallion over his head and, as he kissed Nandia's brow, gently placed it around her neck. "We'll be needin' to secure a scug nearby where we can enjoy a quate confabble." His normally resonant voice strained as he hurriedly spoke of the need to remain one jump ahead of meddlesome proctors.

"I'm afraid by now the Erylians know all of my haunts," Nandia said. "My home is not secure. My family is now safely off-planet, except for my granddaughter, Gracie." A sharp, anguished sob only briefly escaped her lips before she wrestled it back in to some steel-plated inner cavern. Silently we waited, trusting Nandia's instincts about when she would share the turmoil she carried.

"The Erylian proctors will find us," she emphatically affirmed, maintaining her grip on her inner demons.

"When their scanners locate us, we'll have only the briefest of moments to teleport ourselves to safety. Their teams are lightning-quick in the arts of capture and restraint. If even one of us gets taken, this mission could end before it has begun. So, we need to select our next safe refuge right now.

"See those trees off to the left?" she asked, pointing her hand that direction. "Let's choose that spot for our next jump, should trouble appear."

I quickly packed up the radionics equipment. It was no longer needed now that Nandia had copper and could neutralize the Erylian zinc shield. I was lifting the pack to my shoulder, when a second sob escaped from her lips.

"My darling Gracie has been kidnapped," she cried. "And I don't know why." Her throat caught another sob. "I'm afraid the Erylians' plan is to get to me through my granddaughter." The flow of tears erupting from her eyes bespoke of a nightmare of fear and loss.

El immediately wrapped her arms around Nandia and held her. The two embraced in a way that only women can.

Dunstan and I watched in stunned silence, then gently joined in the women's embrace. The four of us held each other without speaking until the risk of nearby proctors intruded on our consolations. Untangling from the hug, Nandia smiled in gratitude and gave us the good news, "Sirius has Gracie's back. I heard him telepath once, telling me that they're both OK.

This news eased my worried mind somewhat. I knew Sirius could be trusted to keep Gracie safe. Once we found a way to get copper to him, we could communicate easily.

"We will get Gracie back, Nandia, please trust that." El's words exuded confidence. "I am so thankful for Arcturus's training of his son. Sirius will take good care of Gracie. But for now, tell us more. How the hell were they able to kidnap your granddaughter?" And how had the Erylians gotten past Nandia, I wondered.

"On the first day of the siege, a squad of armed proctors took over Gracie's school," Nandia said, calmer now after breathing deeply. "Most of us didn't know anything about the Erylian attack. They stormed her classroom and loaded more than a hundred of her schoolmates into buses they had commandeered. Where they've gone God only knows.

"We have little information about these besiegers," she went on to explain. "It is said that the word Erylia means 'tribal loyalty above all' in their ancient language. I don't know where their home planet is. Their attack was extremely well coordinated, with all of Praesepe's security centers neutralized at the same time.

"They are stealing our children!" Nandia cried.

Still cradling Nandia's shoulders, El asked, "And does anyone have a clue as to why?"

Suddenly Dunstan barked a warning, "'Ware right."

Off in the distance, a group of three proctors had just appeared. Wearing jet-black uniforms and high-peaked black hats, they were scanning their surroundings with small, hand-held black boxes.

Grabbing each other's hands, we teleported to the stand of trees we'd selected earlier. Upon arriving, Elli pointed to a distant hillside where stood another grove. We nodded, continued holding hands and projected ourselves there. This second location, with any luck, would put us well beyond the range of the proctors' scanners. After investigating our surroundings, we agreed it was safe enough to plan our next move. We settled on a landing zone even further from the proctors, beneath another grove of fig tree giants.

We hunkered down behind a tall root structure, and relaxed after a few deep breaths. Dunstan stood guard. Nandia returned to El's question. "I've no idea why the Erylians are stealing our youngsters. But I worry that they've taken Gracie in the hopes that now they can force me to bend the Grand Council to their wishes. That's all I can imagine."

"Aye, Lassie, it do make sense," Dunstan said after some thought. "And if true, they'll be sure ta see that Gracie stays healthy. Without her, they'll nae be able ta play their intimidation games.

"Which means, the bastards'll be most anxious ta throw a bridle on you ta bend you to their will. That's when Gracie'll be most vulnerable — they'll reckon, and rightly so, for you'll nae stand for her bein' hurt."

We all nodded, realizing that keeping Nandia free from Erylian clutches was our highest priority.

"But, even though Gracie is only thirteen," Nandia added, "she's making inroads as a telepath. Sirius is training her. If we can clear the intruders' zinc shield we should be able to learn more from them."

"Until we can get some actual copper to them," I said, "we'll need to broadcast the copper frequency to telepathically connect. Keep a sharp eye out and be ready to grab the gear if we're spotted." I said, already setting up the instrument.

Within a few short moments I was once again transmitting copper's frequency. I projected a mental picture of Sirius, feigning disinterest while grooming his tail — a perfect imitation of one of his father's favorite gestures. The others quickly picked up the image. Together we breathed calm into our bodies and focused on mentally greeting the black cat with white toes.

"G'day, mates," came his clear response. "Best be quick before the proctors' telepathy detectors lock on to us. Go ahead." His imperative made it obvious that we needed to be brief and be gone.

"Are you and Gracie safe and sound?" Nandia asked.

"Yes," came the reply. "Hurry."

"What can you tell us about where you are?"

"Four story, ivy covered brick building," came the cat's curt reply. "Soldiers everywhere. I think their scanners can detect the presence of copper. We're locked in a school dorm room that has been turned into a prison. Other youngsters in other rooms. Tall trees outside barred windows facing the direction of sunrise." Amidst static we heard mention of a Saint Someone's school.

"Any ideas of why you've been kidnapped?" Nandia asked.

"It's not much — one guard complaining that the Erylian Intelligence Division proved it was seriously lacking in smarts when they kidnapped us. Another insisted that the Council would never agree to their demands."

"Understood and we'll sign off now," replied Nandia. "We'll see what we can find out and report back. Stay out of harm's way."

"Will do. Tell whomever taught Gracie dominoes that they should be slapped," was Sirius's closing remark. "I owe the little sharper fifty gold reales."

"I'll teach you how to play, ya goatish, hedge-born apple-john," I telepathed and caught a glimpse of a raspberry cheer from my furry friend as his image faded.

We were all chuckling as Nandia signed off. After dismantling and loading up the radionics gear, I once again slung the pack over my shoulder.

"Aye, findin' a dorm at St. Somethin' or 'Tother — that's been converted to a prison," Dunstan remarked. "'tis a right fair puzzle. Hmmmm, I wouldn't mind stagin' a prison break. We'll first be needin' ta find just the right dormitory with windows facin' the sunrise."

I nodded and added, "It wouldn't hurt to find Intelligence Division headquarters either. At least it would be a start."

"We must find out where Gracie is imprisoned," Elli reminded us. "But there could be an easier way. How about if we have Sirius teleport himself to us? While Gracie couldn't join him, we'd at least get a chance to hear more of what they've learned about the Erylians, and the demands they mean to impose upon the Grand Council.

"And, Sirius can give us a target image so we can teleport to where they are imprisoned. He could even teleport copper back to Gracie..."

With my mind buzzing like a colony of beehives, I interrupted. "But first we need to find a protected spot where Sirius can teleport. A base camp that's secure enough to broadcast copper's frequency so Sirius can safely teleport to us and then back to Gracie."

"Aye, Laddie," Dunstan agreed. "'Twouldn't do ta risk Sirius arrivin' in the midst of another sudden appearance of a clutch of sticky-beak proctors."

Like a bolt of lightning, an idea struck me. "Wait a minute!" I proclaimed, excited with my realization. "I don't know why I've been such a chuckle-head. I'm always saying to clients that radionics is only an interim technology until we learn how to use our consciousness more responsibly and effectively. A radionics instrument has no capabilities beyond what our own consciousness can do.

"We don't even need the radionics instrument to reach Sirius and Gracie!" I crowed. "I think we can mentally replicate the frequency for copper and telepathically connect. It may allow us to teleport as well. We should be able to achieve the same shielding results we get while wearing the metal," I was so excited, I was babbling.

"8-3-4-1-0-3-7 ..." I quietly repeated the copper frequency, reassuring myself that I had the correct rate. "If this works," I added with growing confidence, "we now have a way to get inside the Erylian's defenses."

Dunstan let out a whoop. "If that's true, Lad, then we hold on to our copper, allow ourselves to be taken by the proctors, learn what we can about the Erylian plan and then focus on the frequency of copper and teleport ourselves out of harm's way."

Nandia and Elli laughed at the implications of Dunstan's idea. We all spontaneously reached for each other in an exuberant embrace. After a moment Elli refocused our energy saying, "Let's secure a hideaway and test Bearn's theory. Then we can let Sirius and Gracie know copper's frequency."

"It's too bad that the Erylians are searching for me," Nandia said. "We wouldn't be safe in my home, nor the homes of my friends. So, let's walk to the city center and find a safe haven in one of Braeoon's hotels."

"Aye, 'n once we're settled, we'll ken the kind of creature these Erylians are and what they're up to," Dunstan observed. "Perhaps a dreaming? That's sure to help us."

# III

I MUST EXPLAIN ABOUT DREAMING. Early in my training, Agoragon had taught me to use my dream-time to ask for specific dreams. I learned how to use healing dreams, creation dreams, conflict resolution dreams and dreams of growth. He taught me how to identify past dreams, future dreams, dreams of other dimensions, and those carrying clairvoyant messages for this reality.

For years he harangued me to record my dreams, and as I learned to remember them, my skills in the dreamtime grew. I learned how to use my creative power to consciously change outcomes in my dreams, which often changes outcomes in these physical realms.

Later, after I began working with my fellow Grand Council Delegates, I was delightfully surprised to discover that each of them had mastered the use of the dreamtime. In every one of our missions, our family visits to the dreamtime had been crucial to our success. Dunstan's suggestion of a Braeoon dream would be the first time the four of us had worked as a dreamtime team.

I eagerly anticipated the experience of dreaming together as Nandia guided us into the subdued bustle of the city's hub.

Pausing in the shadows, Dunstan brought up the rear, ever alert to proctor sightings. Fiercely piercing the summer sky, Praesepe's twin suns divided into thirds the rare, maroon-blue-hued dome above us.

A mild breeze sent majestic billows of clouds trundling across the sky. Their double shadows, briefly interrupted by the twin suns, cooled the air. As we moved toward the center of Braeoon, El asked about Praesepe's suns.

"The larger one to the west, slightly maroon in color, is called Njoror," Nandia said. "It was named eons ago for the mythological god who restored life after a planetary cataclysm. Njoror calmed the banshee winds, seas and fire. Female in nature, she is said to grant Praesepe easy recuperative powers and prosperity. Freyr is the name of Njoror's closer, smaller and brighter, golden twin, said to bring favorable weather for abundant crops as well as enhanced sexual vitality. He also is the bringer of peace."

I studied the unique light and shadows produced by these combined stars, and the obvious differences in their distance from the planet. Aside from vibrant plant growth, I wondered what benefits Praesepe enjoyed from its unusual solar geometry. I'd heard that it is rare for twin suns not to scorch a planet and render it unfit for life.

We continued marveling at Praesepe's sky as we

walked into the city, with its complement of half-built modern skyscrapers and half-demolished outdated buildings. While proctors were clearly in evidence, we saw none carrying the black box scanners we'd seen in the park. There was little civilian activity on the streets.

"Since the invasion three weeks ago," Nandia explained, "few people venture beyond the safety of their homes. I think we'll find the hotels eager to provide us rooms. Let's think about getting a second room in a second hotel as a getaway should the proctors come calling."

"'Tis better to be safe than sorry, so 'tis," Dunstan agreed as we milled about like a gaggle of indecisive tourists on a corner. "But why not get rooms in three or four hotels? I'm nae inclined ta trust that only one or two hotels will protect us from determined proctors. Each of us can check in at a different hotel. Less conspicuous than this mob a' four."

The more we all thought about the idea, the more we liked it. "Let's get crackin'," Dunstan advised. "Our escapes will be safer if we pick hotels far apart. Harder for these Erylian blighters to mount a coordinated sweep."

Elli pointed midway down the block to an elegant hotel marquee crowned in a bright cursive sign. "The Don" it was named, perhaps after some long past Latin influence. Nandia agreed to take some of our gold coins and register for a room. "I'll telepath the room number and you can join me there. Once each of us sees the interior of the room, we'll have all we need to use it as a hideout."

In the few minutes it took Nandia to get the room, Elli stood watch for proctors while Dunstan and I loitered at an antique shop window crowded with unusual implements. We were having fun speculating aloud about their uses when I recalled an unanswered mystery from our Aesir mission and turned and spoke to El.

"I had suspicions that you worked with the Galactic Council when we were together on Aesir," I said. "But we had never talked of it. When did you first begin your tenure as Elder Elli?"

"The early days, as the Council was just forming, Mister Sticky-beak," We laughed that she'd picked up from Sirius the Australian idiom for a very nosy person. Yet, she graciously continued. "I was enlisted because my mother had trained me in the subtle arts as a child, and my reputation had reached the Council through its ambassador to Aesir's court. At the time I was married to Aesir's third King and, with the Council's help, built the foundation for the royal family that has survived to this day."

Dunstan looked at the Royal Chambermaid with new-found respect. "Excuse me, Elli, but I thought you were much younger. I would love to hear more of that story."

"If you're lucky, you might get a chance to flirt with me, young man," she said demurely. However, at that moment we received a mental impression of Nandia's face and heard her telepath, "Room 213. Come on up, but one at a time. I'll leave the door open."

"Lass, let's you 'n I traipse to the Don's entry together," Dunstan suggested to El. "I want to look over any folk in the lobby who show an interest in you as you pass through to Nandia's suite. I'll follow after ye presently."

Dunstan's idea made sense, if only to learn who might be overly curious about newcomers to the hotel. As they set out across the street I watched people coming and going while keeping an eye out for proctors.

I wanted to be at peace so I could read people's auras as they exited the hotel. I breathed a series of ten connected breaths, a technique I had learned from Agoragon for entering the realm he called Inner Time. From there it is quite easy to tap into deeper inner realms. I focused on a group gathering beneath the Don's marquee and noticed that each of their energy fields was tainted with muddy, yet intense, dark browns and blues and streaked with the muted gold/yellows of worry and fear.

Auras, or energy fields, are individual's unique signature of physical, emotional, mental and spiritual well-being — sometimes called the weathervane of the soul. For years I had worked with Agoragon to consciously see auras — but to no avail. Then, early in our mission to Geasa, Nandia proved to be of great help. She taught me to first feel the person and then focus on their head and shoulder area, where the energy field is usually easiest to see. By watching people over time, I've come to realize that bright, vibrant colors are signals of strength, health and joy. Muted tones reflect imbalance. Whenever a person seeks to speak falsely, or evade a truth, a streak of lemon-green shoots across their energy field, just above their head. Whenever possible, I observe energy fields and have come to interpret auras more accurately.

Watching people outside the Don, I found a few whose energy fields were a curiosity to me. Their auras reflected azure blue colors, which I took to indicate some experience of satisfaction. I probed their minds and heard beliefs that corroborating with the Erylians provided them with a sense of well-being and security. A few others radiated darker blue colors indicating a true sense of purpose. I was surprised to discover they were intently confident of their work with an underground group of Praesepians. I realized then that there must be at least two networks of sympathizers, both supporting and opposing the Erylians. Troubling in itself, I telepathed this information to the family — it could prove to be useful when wanting to identify allies.

Dunstan telepathed, "On me way to 213 — be there soon." I knew I still had a short wait, so I scanned the streets and walkways again. As I noted the scant population moving about I wondered what civil proscriptions the Erylians were enforcing. Curfews? Identity cards? Restrictions to bank accounts? Had they seized commercial interests? They had to have expropriated a significant amount of real estate to house kidnapped children and provide billets for their legions of proctors.

I saw three proctors crossing the far end of the street, pursuing their unseen destination with determination. Thankfully, none carried a scanner. Dropping my gaze to my feet, I adopted the discouraged slouch of many Praesepians and huddled back into a shadowed doorway. Within moments the proctors passed without giving me a second glance.

Straightening up, I breathed deeply and resumed watching pedestrians' auras. Whenever I noticed a calmer energy field approaching, I took care to resume my downtrodden stance, focused on reading their political leanings, and remembering them after they had passed. Then I heard a welcome message from Dunstan, "Our room 213 awaits ya', Laddie. But take care through the lobby, there's many a hungry eye castin' about."

As I walked casually toward the hotel entry, two more proctors stepped onto the sidewalk. I slowed down and again assumed a distraught Praesepian stance. I was coming to realize that we needed to learn if proctors could sense telepathic messages — transmitted and received. As the pair ambled off down the street, I breathed another sigh of relief. I was growing more desperate by the moment to find out if mentally focusing on the copper frequency would replace the copper I was carrying. As I stepped into the hotel, I felt as vulnerable as a misplaced duckling in an eagle's nest.

The Don's lobby was lavish, with spacious areas to relax and read. An atrium was adorned with tall, exotic potted plants, expensive couches and comfortable stuffed chairs. Crystal chandeliers and gilt wallpaper encouraged a well-heeled clientele to believe that the Don would spare little expense when accommodating their desires. Toward the rear of the lobby a bank of elevators was flanked by stairways. I chose the stairs and quickly arrived on the second floor to find the door to 213 ajar. I telepathed my presence as I stepped inside and locked the door behind me.

Our suite was in keeping with the lavish hotel decor. Designers of an age gone by had generously appointed it with gold-embossed wallpaper, elegant fixtures and statuesque bronzed lamps. I rounded the corner into a large sitting room where I found the family resting on thickly cushioned couches, enjoying a round of hot tea. Somehow I had the feeling mine would be a quick cup.

"I saw several proctors leaving as I came in, any trouble?" I asked.

"It seems there are a number of Officer Friendlies bunking here," Dunstan said. "While sittin' in the lobby I watched several groups movin' from the hotel restaurant to the elevators. They seem relaxed. None of them carried sensors. Could be good news or bad news, but I suggest we find another hotel quickly. We'll not be safe here for long with all this copper, especially if their sensors can locate it."

"Give me a second to make a mental target of this room so I can teleport back here," I said. Gathering three gold coins from the backpack, I placed them on the mantelpiece. Now we had a handy target image for teleported returns. "Three coins to remember the Don," I quipped.

My friends nodded in appreciation. We decided to leave the room one at a time and meet across the street in front of the antique shop.

Our second hotel we found a half-dozen blocks away. Not quite as elegant as the Don, its marquee introduced it as 'The Vasantamos.' This time Elli grabbed a handful of gold and headed to the registration desk. As we waited, Nandia reported that the registration clerks at the Don had no difficulty accepting gold as a deposit — recently arrived Erylian administrators, programmers, and military used gold until a new Praesepian currency could be minted. "I helped them assume I was with the Erylians," Nandia explained,

"Still, I'm not wild about nesting in the middle of a pack of proctors. For us to rescue Gracie, we'll need to stay as invisible as mice in a cat's lair."

We soon heard from Elli and staggered our arrivals to her room, number 312. Dunstan was first to arrive, I followed, with Nandia bringing up the rear. There were plenty of proctors at the Vasantamos too — good incentive to find yet another hotel. I did relax a bit, however, knowing that we now had one escape hatch, should trouble arise.

"It's time to find out if we can teleport by mentally focusing on copper's frequency," I announced, as I lifted my copper medallion from my neck. "I'm going to experiment by teleporting back to Nandia's room at the Don. I'll leave this with you." I handed Dunstan the copper talisman he'd given me in Geasa.

"Remember the frequency 8-3-4-1-0-8-3-7." I said in a jazzy, syncopated rhythm, wanting to make it easier for all of us to remember. "I'll use it along with the image of three gold coins on the mantelpiece. Wish me luck."

Standing in the middle of our Vasantamos lounge room, I breathed deeply, closed my eyes, focused on 8-3-4-1-0-8-3-7 and started my teleportation process. I began by imagining a single atom of my body projecting to the mantle at our room at the Don. Next, within my body, I located the feeling of desire to teleport there and directed the energy within that intent to expand into a wave and follow the atom that I'd just projected.

Then I asked my Inner Self to intensify this wave of desire. A burst of energy flooded through my body as this feeling-wave suddenly grew into a broad expanse of sensation, an ocean's breadth of desire that I mentally lasered to my destination. Finally, it was simply a matter of asking my Inner Self to direct my entire body to room 213 at the Don.

The result was the familiar flash of spiraling white light behind my eyes, accompanied by a momentary sense of weightlessness. I opened my eyes, and danced a jig of delight as I found myself once again in the room Nandia had secured for us.

I brought the family to my mind's eye and telepathed a message: "Arrived safely. It's not as fun here without you. Before returning, I'm going to step into the hall, for another look around." Cheers of congratulations lit their faces.

I quietly opened the doorway and peered down the hall, first to my left, then to my right. And there my gaze froze. A proctor was pulling out his room key and opening a door near the elevators at the end of the hall. Useful info, I noted, as I ducked back into the room. I quietly closed and locked the door, hoping my furtive peek hadn't been noticed. Picturing the family back at the Vasantamos, I telepathed, "Heading home."

I stood in the middle of the room, breathing to calm myself and began my protocol. As I asked my Inner Self for help returning my field of being to the Vasantamos, I heard a message from Nandia, "Bearns, have you forgotten something?"

I drew a blank and asked my subconscious to bring any forgotten items to mind. 8-3-4-1-0-8-3-7 flashed in brightly lit numbers behind my eyes. "Many thanks," I said aloud as I added the frequency to a visualization of my brightly colored copper medallion dangling from Dunstan's hand. Then I returned to my Inner Self's presence and asked that my energy field and my body be easily teleported to room 312.

"Start over," came a suggestion from within. "Thanks again," I telepathed. But, at that moment, a deliberate rap resonated through the door. Whether or not it was the proctor I'd seen down the hall didn't matter. My anxiety soared imagining that it was the cursed Erylian. I shoved this disturbance into a holding closet within my mind. Visualizing my copper medallion, I added the frequency, and sent an originating atom from my body to our Vasantamos room. I continued with the protocol, only to hear a second, louder, more insistent knocking at the door.

Now my frustration was in a horserace with my fear, nose to nose as they raced toward despair. I wanted to reach through the door and soundly slap the proctor whom I imagined was pounding. Then Agoragon's face swept into view. I remembered his insistence that that I've never had any event thrust upon me. Begrudgingly, I conceded that lesson had to include this current crisis, damnitall anyway. So, somehow my Inner Self and conscious self were collaborating to construct this noisy, repeated rapping for some useful purpose.

He reminded me that I am a being with the innate power to hold myself above violation. He then reminded me that all energy is moving toward the fulfillment of its greatest value. So, the message was, I had all that I needed to deal with this damned irritating distraction.

I breathed deeply and asked my subconscious and Inner Self to transform the energy of my distress into a bountiful trust in my ability to teleport to the

Vasantamos with ease. I continued breathing deeply, mentally acquired copper's frequency and relaxed my body. I asked the intensity within the now insistent knocking to transform itself into a wave of desire to be with Nandia and family.

I felt my energy field instantly blossom with the force of a powerful ocean wave. I directed that wave toward their loving presence and sent my body's aura in hot pursuit. I saw white light spiraling, felt weightless for a moment and then opened my eyes to my beloved family.

"Have I got news for you," I whooped. "First, I never want to do that again, and second, I think we'll all need to practice. Thanks for reminding me of copper's frequency, Nandia. It was sure easy to forget in the face of such a frightening distraction. Without our deep, family connection, I would have come unhinged." They each hugged me, beaming with congratulations. I'd just demonstrated that all we needed was the frequency of copper — not the actual metal — to teleport here on Praesepe!

"Listen to this," I continued. "I checked out our hallway while I was there. There's at least one proctor staying on our floor — in the first room just shy of the elevators. I expect that it was he who was so irritatingly knocking just as I was about to teleport back here. Hopefully the Erylian sensors can't pick up telepathy. If they can, it's a sure bet they'll be able to sense teleportation as well. I hope that all their sensors can measure is the presence of copper. That pesky pipsqueak of a proctor probably considered my quick glance down the hallway to be suspicious enough to investigate. In any event, it was your loving support that kept me focused enough to get back here amidst all that foment and furor."

"Aye, Lad, we were watchin' as that kerfuffle unfolded," Dunstan said. "Other than short hops to slip away from a hot pursuit, about all the Don is good for is to plant copper, await proctors and let them escort us to Intelligence Headquarters," The Scotsman was way ahead of me — his idea also helped me see the value in the proctor's intrusion. We could perhaps use his suspicions about the occupants of room 213 to our advantage.

"You're quite right, young man," El applauded Dunstan. "Anyone knocking from housekeeping or maintenance would have announced themselves. The Don isn't going to be the safest refuge. We need to find a third hotel before we'll have a base camp safe enough for Sirius to visit."

We all agreed with Aesir's Royal Chambermaid. I picked up the backpack and we departed in pairs. Just outside the front door, El and Nandia suddenly pulled up short. "Watch left," Nandia telepathed. Dunstan and I, three steps behind, immediately stopped. At the intersection to our left stood a trio of proctors. They were focusing on their hand-held scanners.

It could well have been the copper we were carrying that had drawn the proctors this close. Then it suddenly occurred to me that zinc might shield the presence of our copper. I asked my subconscious for help in remembering the frequency for zinc. The 8-3-4-5-0-0-9 sprang sharply into focus.

"Focus on the frequency for zinc," I telepathed. "A bubble of zinc 8-3-4-5-0-0-9 surrounding us. Let's see if it will shield us from the Erylian proctors." I keenly hoped that my theory would work and render our copper invisible to their scanners.

They began drawing closer. Without missing a beat, Nandia and El turned right. Dunstan and I held back. I turned and waved to an imaginary friend inside the hotel and, after adopting my Praesepian slouch, crowded next to Dunstan. We followed several paces behind our partners. With the tall Scotsman's brawny arm across my shoulders, I ducked my head and furtively glanced back to see what was happening.

The proctors were stalled in their attempts to scan in our direction. One, his face puckered like a pine tree knot, was scouring the sidewalk, searching for anyone trying to evade them. Another was whacking his scanner with the palm of his hand, trying to clear whatever had disrupted its signal. Obviously our focus on zinc's frequency was having its desired effect. It wasn't long before the three Erylians were only interested in what was happening to their scanners and completely ignored those of us travelling the street.

We continued imagining the zinc bubble and, like mice skulking past a sleeping cat, made our way along several more city blocks. We stayed close to buildings and nestled in with other walkers whenever possible.

It was a gorgeous day; the sharp edge of heat that was generated by Praesepe's twin suns was blunted by a gentle breeze. The tree-lined streets were not crowded. With no proctors in sight, we relaxed, meandering with Nandia as tour guide. Open shops flagrantly displayed their wares as if desperate to make a sale. I studied the few vehicles that passed, which Nandia explained were all solar-battery powered.

We came upon a grand Victorian-style hotel that

stood at the apex of a large triangular plaza that served as the hub for several streets leading into different sectors of Braeoon. Memories of a bygone era graced the aging, yet beautiful building, whose marquis introduced the grand edifice as 'The Abyssinian.'

From the backpack, Dunstan grabbed a handful of gold coins. "I'll snag a scrug and sing out as soon as it's secure." As I watched him cross the street, I was warmed by my fondness for this man's unwavering loyalty, bravery and strength.

Nandia pulled Elli and me over to the display window of an upscale jeweler. While focusing on zinc's frequency, I asked my subconscious to alert my conscious mind should any trouble begin brewing behind us. Then I told El the tale of a similar store, The Opulatum, whose owner was the villain who had been siphoning off the city of Geasa's wealth. It was his avarice that had fueled the wildfire-like spread of the Saragalla epidemic.

While awaiting Dunstan, we pointed out unusual and extravagant baubles to each other as Nandia added color to my story. We had originally sought out The Opulatum's owner looking for copper, and laughed recalling how hard he had tried to herd us into a police-sting operation. We enjoyed reminiscing with Elli and shared a warm sense of déjà vu standing in front of this jewelry store.

I felt a mental nudge of alarm and turned to see our three proctors passing on the far side of the plaza, scanning a street perpendicular to ours. I resumed my Praesepian slouch, thankful that our focus on zinc's frequency was still protecting us. I pointed to a tiara of diamonds that were nestled in gold and asked El and

Nandia, "I wonder if we have enough money to get one of these for each of you?"

"Such nerve trying flirt with both of us just as proctors pass," El scolded. "I think Nandia and I need to plan a private slap session for you."

"I'm still focusing on our zinc bubble, despite your inducements to distract me," I countered in mock innocence. "By the way, we'll need to relax our zinc shield for Dunstan to get through." That said, his face jumped into sharp relief as he telepathed, "Been tryin' ta reach ya. Room 407. Door's open." I imagined his face and smiled in gratitude.

Shuffling over to the street corner, I watched the Erylian's progress. They were facing away from us, standing over a block away. As they milled about, one officer again smacked his scanner, looking irritated and confused. Passersby completely ignored them, as if this were a normal, everyday occurrence.

"Your turn to lead the way, Bearns," Nandia telepathed. I nodded, crossed the street and stepped into The Abyssinian's formerly elegant and now slightly shabby lobby. It was nearly devoid of people, not a proctor to be seen. I telepathed this news to Nandia and then asked the single reservation clerk for directions to the stairs. He pointed toward a bank of antique elevators. I gave him my thanks and made my way up to the fourth floor.

I found Dunstan peering through a gauze curtained window as I stepped through into room 407. Joining him, we watched Nandia and Elli as they crossed the street and disappeared beneath the marquis. No one on the street took any notice of the two beautiful women.

"Those stairs are a great cardio workout," I said. "What a wonderful hotel." We were standing in a large sitting room where luxurious warm-toned lounge chairs faced a tall stone fireplace. Tasteful antique faux-gas lighting fixtures cast gilded highlights across the dappled pastel green and gold wallpaper, elegant despite its age.

"Laddie, you stopped our hearts back there at the Vasantamos," Dunstan admitted. "'Twas a wee dark moment when I feared you'd come a gutzer. Had a right worry over that bane of a proctor wantin' ta break the door down. Thank the Lord El reminded us to be sendin' ya bales a' helper energy. I was right proud to see you standin with us again, Laddie, so I was."

"We all need to practice teleporting while focusing on the copper frequency," I said as I hugged Dunstan. "I had to sharpen my focus in a flash and certainly appreciated the helper energy."

"You can be sure that pesky proctor's rapping helped me to concentrate," I continued. "I knew I had to get out of there — we cannot afford to be recognized by the Erylians, nor reveal that there are teleporters in their midst."

"Aye, and we'll need to crack on 'n stash our copper quick smart," Dunstan added.

I wondered about getting a fourth room, perhaps one floor above or below 407. As I opened my mouth to speak, Nandia and Elli stepped through the doorway.

"Ah, Dunstan, you've always deserved to live like a king," Elli gushed between taking deep breaths.

"Did you two come up the stairs?" I asked, incredulous.

"Of course," Nandia replied, breathing heavily as well. "Why?"

"It took me twice as long to get here, and I was racing with my mountain climbing legs," I said, both envious and curious. "How did you do it so fast?"

"We projected from the first stair of each flight to the top. Took all of two minutes. But we decided to race up the last one. Elli won." Nandia's breathing was calming. "This is a lovely suite, Duncan," she said as she inventoried its furnishings. "Perhaps we might consider it our base camp?" We all agreed.

"Need ta practice projections without our copper bangles," Dunstan affirmed. "We need ta know we can scarper out a' the reach a' any danger. Problem is, wherever we stockpile our copper, you can bet Officer Friendlies will soon come a-visitin'."

"If we had scampered from the Vasantamos just a few seconds later," he added, "we could now be enjoyin' free room 'n board, compliments a' the Erylians. Me thinks those proctors we evaded on the street were gettin' a bead on our copper. Comin' up with yer zinc frequency, Laddie, was a spot a' well-timed genius, so 'twas."

"Yes, thank you, Bearns," Elli said. "It's plain we need to stash our copper in a place that draws proctors away from us. And if it takes perhaps another hour or two for them to locate our copper, we'd best get Sirius to join us soon. Does anyone doubt that we need to fly below the proctors' radar, at least for now?"

"Quite right," I replied as everyone nodded. "I was also thinking that we might want another room, in this same hotel, but on a different floor. We could hide the copper there. That will keep us safe long enough to meet with Sirius at least."

Everyone liked that idea. We all began relieving ourselves of our copper trinkets, piling them on the dining table. "What I'm wondering is," El added as she removed a copper-beset-with-emeralds bracelet, "if this copper is confiscated, could we find yet another place to squirrel away one or two baubles of copper, just in case we need them later?"

"That would require that we constantly shield them with the zinc frequency," Nandia observed. "We could risk losing the radionics instrument, or else one of us stays constantly preoccupied with the shielding job. Much easier and safer not to try, at least for now. But, it's a good idea. Can we let it marinate in the family subconscious 'till later?"

We all readily agreed and realized that a rest was called for, to eat and recharge. "Aye, even a cat nap would serve," Dunstan said. That reminded us of the urgency of Sirius's arrival. The Scotsman and the Chambermaid decided to round up a meal from the hotel kitchen. I grabbed a handful of gold coins and our copper baubles and set out to rent another room.

Nandia's voice stopped me at the door. "I'll connect with Sirius, and send him the target image he needs," she said. "And I'll let him know how to use the copper frequency. Hopefully he'll be here by the time you all return."

"Great idea," I replied. "And he can let Gracie know that it won't be long before the cavalry arrives."

"Aye, 'twill be grand ta have the wee one nestled safe in the fold of her family," Dunstan said. "The quicker we clear this suite of copper, the safer we'll be. Get along with ye now, Laddie."

"We'll have dinner ready by the time you get back," El called out as I scurried out the door.

I took the stairs down to the lobby, which again was nearly deserted. At the reception counter I asked if 517 was available for a few days, citing a family preference for the room. It was directly above our current nest and would be easiest to hear if proctors came storming in with their scanners. Shiny gold makes people friendly. The desk clerk happily crossed my palm with 517's keycard.

After climbing the first flight of stairs, I ran up the next four flights, anxious to be free of our copper and curious to find out how long it would take proctors to locate our stash.

Then I realized that if they found the copper, the nosy buzzards would be quizzing the desk clerks. Soon enough they'd be hunting me. At that point, I'd be a marked man and bouncing between the Abyssinian, the Vasantamos and the Don just to stay clear of their clutches. Unlocking the door to 517, I realized how a ten-pound osprey must feel trying to deliver a twenty pound salmon to its family nest.

The room was smallish, with twin beds, the usual Abyssinian décor and a noisy steam heating system. It had an unusual L-shaped configuration, as if the original architect had relegated one of its corners to be a storage closet with access elsewhere. Later I would investigate it more thoroughly as a possible hiding place. I opened a small closet and seeded our copper between layers of linens.

I imagined our suite one floor below and brought

to mind Nandia's beautiful smile. Focusing on copper's frequency I telepathically sang out to her. I wanted to make sure I could connect while she was copperless and again vulnerable to the Erylians' zinc disruption. Her smiling face appeared. We happily cheered at the clarity of our connection. "Our copper will be under pillow slips in the linen closet in room 517," I telepathed. Scanning the room, I passed the image along to Nandia, taking care to focus on the door to the linen closet.

"Thanks for the good news, Bearns." she said. "As of now, we're on heightened alert for proctors bearing scanners. Oh, and I got hold of Sirius. He'll be here soon."

"While you're watching for proctors coming through the front of the hotel," I replied, "I'll check around back to see if there's a rear entrance. If so, I'll stand watch there. If I spot any proctors, I'll teleport back to where you are and we can prepare ourselves for a jump to The Don. Keep the backpack within easy reach. Are El and Dunstan back yet with dinner?"

Both of them cheered and then touted the delights of the meal they were bringing home.

"Am I to presume there's no meal delivery service?" I asked.

"Ne'er ya worry, Laddie," Dunstan replied. "'Tis easy slather ta drop off a bundle, once we know where you're standin' post. 'Twill give me more practice teleportin' just by usin' copper's frequency.

"Thanks," I replied. "Keep in mind I'm going to be on the Erylians' most wanted list if they find our copper here in room 517. They'll probably try a room-to-room search, so we'll have time for a jump to our room at the

Don. They'll most likely leave officers on continuous welcome duty at here at 517, hoping for my return."

"Right, ya are, me gleekin' fly-bitten pignut." It was Sirius's voice I heard telepathing! "Right decent of ya to share your dinner — what passes fer food at our digs is dreadful," he exclaimed. My delight in knowing that he was now safely with us overshadowed my stomach's growling protest over another delayed meal.

"And by the way, ya bent flogon," he continued, "Nandia taught me your mental copper trick. Good work! I'll finish off yur meal here and then be on my way ta teach it to Gracie. Ta fer now!"

## IV

IT WAS REASSURING to know that we could now connect with Gracie through Sirius. I locked the door to 517 and with little trouble found the Abyssinian's rear entrance. An abandoned crate provided a useful vantage point for viewing both ends of the alley where it met the adjacent streets. I took a seat, breathed and relaxed my back to rest against the hotel wall.

It was past sunset for Praesepe's sun Njoror and nearing sunset for its twin, Freyr. The sky was a unique blend of vibrant pinks and violets painted across sensually sculpted cloud formations. In wide-eyed delight, I felt the beauty tingling through my cells, the sensation building. It reminded me of my elation of years past, when Agoragon had spoken of my own inner beauty as an individualized portion of nature.

The sky's colors danced toward the coming second sunset. I heard my teacher's voice speaking of the abundant resources that lie within each of us. Propelled by my elation, I moved into a deeper experience of trusting my own inner strength and power. I let my voice tone a musical note that harmonized with this joyful intensity and sang, marveling at this moment's lovely and peaceful contrast to the day's stress of feeling hunted.

With heightened senses, I inventoried my surroundings in the surreal light. Not far from me a freight elevator scaled the hotel's exterior. I studied the design of its floor's structure and decided that here was a better place to safely hide our copper. My imagination was piqued but I tabled further investigation until the coming of darkness. I focused on the street and took my time to carefully examine both alley entries for proctors. There was no one about so I breathed, relaxed, slumped a bit and felt the wall across my back. I dropped into a profound sense of calm.

Suddenly I had the playful thought to try an experiment. I slouched to let my body more deeply feel the energy of the building. Then, using what Agoragon called the inner, conceptual sense, I mentally touched the hotel's consciousness. I imagined my energy field's ions, electrons and atoms melding with the consciousness of the Abyssinian Hotel. As a student, I had resisted the idea that all energy is conscious — but eventually my teacher's wisdom pierced through my stubbornness.

I was curious to see if I could tap into the historical consciousness of this grand edifice. I imagined my energies merging with those of the hotel and closed my eyes. To my surprise, I immediately heard a male voice, friendly and deeply resonant.

"Hello," he said. "I am the being identified as The

Hotel Abyssinian." His tone conveyed an aged presence, at peace with the world. He telepathed a quizzical impulse about my presence.

"I'm named Bernard, called Bearns by my friends," I happily introduced myself and told of my need to be aware of any nearby proctors who might be scanning for copper.

"I'm quite a dutiful sentry, although sadly, most people don't accept that all matter and energy are conscious," said the deep, gentle voice. "The idea that a building is conscious even borders on intellectual instability for many people." A feeling of sadness, perhaps loneliness wafted through his message, but then I sensed a pride and passion for himself and his long accomplished history.

"I've long relished the time when I could freely talk with a human."

"I, as well, delight in discovering that I can talk with you," I replied. "I'm with three friends." I visualized them together, loving me. Suddenly all the family was part of the conversation.

"What a lovely surprise," Nandia telepathed warmly. "I am called Nandia. My friends here are Elli and Dunstan." Each happily greeted our new friend in turn. "I've a sense that your service to our kind has spanned centuries," she continued. "What a lovely warmth and generosity of spirit you have. We are quite fortunate to have found you."

"It is my great pleasure. As I'm sure you're aware, my marquee reads 'The Abyssinian.' In my prime it was quite handsome. I much favor the name." The warmth and caring within his consciousness vibrated through his words.

"We are here to recover a kidnapped child and find a way to disarm the siege the Erylians have imposed upon Praesepe." Nandia said. "May I call you Abe?"

"What a delight, a nickname. Never had one before. Funny thing. Thank you, and I like it. Abe it is."

"Abe, any warning you could provide of approaching proctors would be invaluable." The gently musical tone of Nandia's request reflected her growing fondness for Abe.

"We arrived with ample copper to neutralize the Erylians' zinc disrupter shield," Elli added. "But we've since learned that the proctors are using scanners to track us. We believe they can scan for the presence of copper. We seek a safe place to store our copper where it won't attract their attention."

"Upon your arrival earlier today," Abe responded, "I could feel the presence of your copper. It's a warming energy. Bearns, I noted you secreting it in room 517." His warm, deep voice was laced with excitement. "I have also noted your unusual mode of transport. It's quite rare to encounter people with teleporting skills. As for your copper caper, I believe I have a place that will serve admirably." We all chuckled at our newfound friend's playful nature.

"Hello Abe, I see you're both ancient and lighthearted. I'm Sirius," the cat telepathed. "A proper hiding place would ease my mission."

"Ah, a serious grimalkin — and one most clearly telepathic," Abe joked. "I do enjoy making close friends with nature's creatures. Hello friend Sirius, curiously named for the Dog Star."

Sirius telepathed a deep purr, which Abe matched

with his voice. "I do so admire an intelligent and vibrant spirit," he said.

"Abe, might we inquire ...?" Nandia asked, but her question was abruptly cut short by an interruption from him.

"Excuse me," he said firmly. "I wish to inform you that I've detected three proctors just turning onto this street and headed this way. They are eight blocks distant, on foot, moving briskly. Each carries a small black box. I'd say we have five minutes, perhaps seven, at the most."

"Perhaps the hefty Guardsman, Dunstan is it?" he hurriedly continued, "could gather up your copper and make his way to my outdated boiler room. It is located in northwest corner of the lower basement. I can provide directions when needed. Whenever you wish you can tune in to me by simply touching the nearest wall."

"Aye, I'll go collect our copper from 517 now," Dunstan said and suddenly fell silent. Shortly, he was standing next to me at the rear of the hotel, carrying a pillow case loaded with our copper. Holding the bag open, he asked, "Laddie, will ya be puttin' your medallion in storage or would you prefer ta be wearin' it?"

I hadn't been without that medallion since Dunstan had given it to me in Geasa. I was deeply attached to it. It was a powerful talisman that reminded me of Nandia and her ease of abundant love.

"Best let it go for now, Bearns," she telepathed softly. "It's only a symbol. You'll be safe without it."

Obviously Nandia knew me well enough to realize

that I was tempted to hold onto it as some sort of protection. Most likely a hidden fear of losing her again, was my guess. Her encouraging tone reminded me that I alone have all the power I need to hold myself above violation. After all, what is loss to beings who relate to each other in multiple dimensions?

"O.K., I'm getting the message," I telepathed as I removed the copper from around my neck. "I'll leave it in the boiler room."

"My, those rascals can tune in quickly," Elli said of the proctors. "Amazing technology. It would be interesting to study the energy frequencies they're using. Meanwhile, Abe, what do you say if we all teleport to your boiler room? That way, each of us will be familiar with our copper's new home — and able to retrieve it."

"Excuse me, M'Lady Elli. Please forgive my shortsightedness. Yes, of course, you all should come. And shall I assume that you all wish to remain unseen by the proctors?" Abe replied, already thinking ahead of us.

"Yes," we all chimed in simultaneously.

"I believe I can be of use. But let me take a moment to say that I am finding myself particularly drawn to you, Elli. From whence do you hail?" Abe sounded warmly curious.

"Aesir."

"Ahh, I thought so. Of royal lineage, I presume."

"And mother to many generations of the line."

"Do you mind if I address you as Queen El?" Abe asked, obviously quite pleased to be in the presence of royalty.

"I would be honored," El replied graciously. "I'm

quite pleased to learn that you know of the House of Aesir."

"Thank you. I look forward to learning more of your history. For now you must all teleport your way to my lower basement. You too, Bearns. Later on I'll want to learn the origins of such an unusual name. Watch now as I project a target image for your destination."

The image of a cavernous, disused utility room came to mind. Dunstan and I teleported there from the hotel's rear entrance, the rest of the family projected from upstairs. The Abyssinian's boiler room was indeed ancient, its central space generously open and surrounded by a tarnished forest of tubes, tools and tanks fashioned from copper. The silence was penetrating here, as if its last noise had faded away many years ago.

Dust, spider webs and small critters had decades ago developed suburbs among the aging equipment. Delighted to see that Sirius had arrived, I whooped with joy and plucked him from the floor. We'd not been together since I'd last passed him into Nandia's arms following the Aesir mission. My cry of delight startled me as it bounced off rock walls and metal boilers with a resounding echo.

Indulging in my reunion cuddle with Sirius, I hurriedly searched for my latest entry in our ongoing moniker duel. "'Bout time you showed up for work, ya probbling, plume-plucked moldwarp."

"Ah, ya mammerin', fen-sucked lewduster, I know ya missed me."

As his deeply resonant chuckle reverberated through the cavern, Dunstan, for the first time, welcomed the loudly purring Sirius into his arms. "Aye, yur purrfect singin', 'tis pure poetry to accompany us whilst we be hidin' our copper needles in the midst a' this haystack," he said, cradling the cat.

"Yes, it's a lovely minuet to our copper caper, courtesy of our new friend Abe," Elli smiled demurely and curtseyed toward us all.

"You are truly an esteemed family," Abe declared. "I am quite honored to be your friend and ally." To celebrate the end to our worries about copper and proctor scans we sang the Russian folk song we'd performed together in Geasa. With a harmonic yowl, Sirius leapt through the air and gently landed in my arms, settling down as he continued to purr.

"Brother Abe," Dunstan added as our song came to a close, "'tis far better that we have ya coverin' our backs, so 'tis. But, best use caution that we don't try ta make ya part of this whimsical Hydra-headed mob." There was enthusiastic applause to welcome Abe as one of the family.

"And, speaking of music," Nandia chimed in, "Most of you have not yet heard Dunstan play his horn, have you?"

"Best we find a safe place for these," Dunstan sang, holding up the bag of copper. "Then I'll play 'til yer all as happy as bastards on Father's Day."

"Proctors just coming through the front doors," Abe said. "Two minutes, three minutes tops. They well know of this boiler room. Once while hazing a raw recruit they sent him here to retrieve copper, but I'll warn you in sufficient time if tonight's such a night. Meanwhile, it is quite safe to perform music here — ample soundproofing was originally designed into this boiler room. I do so hope for some live music."

Searching for a new home for our copper, Elli clambered around the boilers. She soon called Dunstan over. Together they turned a latch handle to a large copper tank, revealing a nesting site obscured by darkness.

"No proctor has ever thought to open that hatch," Abe said. "Well chosen, Your Highness." After securing the copper and offering a hand for El's safe landing, Dunstan returned to my side and hung one of El's gemstone-studded copper bracelets around Sirius's neck.

"It occurs to me that your new necklace just might come in handy," I said to the cat. "I envy the fun you'll have fun staying one jump ahead of the police." Sirius nodded and resumed his tail grooming, again reminding me of his sire, Arcturus.

During our Aesirian adventures, Arcturus had protected Nandia and me by luring several soldiers away from their post at the resident warlord's bedchambers. Without Arcturus, we never could have succeeded in building the alliance between King Sabre of Aesir and The Tabir, as the planet Fusium's tyrant warlord was called.

"Aye, Dogstar, seein' you wearin' that piece a' jewelry has put me heart at rest," Dunstan said to Sirius. "'Twill well serve Gracie's needs at least until she learns the copper frequency and can master teleportin'."

"And it seems to me we've found a safe place for Gracie as well," Nandia said as she surveyed the boiler room. The idea hit us all at the same time and we applauded at how effortlessly another problem had been solved.

"Might you enlighten me as to whom Gracie is?" Abe asked.

"My apologies, kind sir," Nandia said. "It is Grace, my granddaughter, who has been kidnapped by the Erylians. Sirius has been her companion in captivity and is only visiting us for a more few moments before he rejoins her."

"With your amazing abilities, I have great confidence you'll soon have Gracie back," Abe said. "I've never before met a cat capable of teleportation. What a rare wonder, indeed."

"Good on ya, cobber," Sirius responded. "Unless someone cruels the pitch, I reckon I'll be back here faster'na Bondi tram. I have high hopes ya'll guide me to yer high-yield mouse hunting range upon my return."

We heard a warm baritone chuckle. "You may depend on it, Sir," Abe replied. "Until then I will be spotting for you. Count on latest updates for only the finest morsels."

"Abe, it seems to me that your hotel will also serve as a sanctuary for Gracie," Nandia continued. "By the way, what news of our proctor friends?"

"They have been scanning each floor, occasionally banging their scanners to make sure they're working. They grow increasingly more frustrated and are now grumbling as they make their departure from the lobby.

"And, speaking of a sanctuary for your granddaughter," Abe continued, "may I suggest that you register for room 419 at the end of your hallway? There you'll find a hidden panel, unknown even to hotel security that opens onto a small, well-concealed nest."

"How wonderful, Abe. I could kiss you," Nandia said, leaning into the wall and planting a beauty. She put her back into it, and I can tell you from personal experience how memorable that is.

"And now I believe it's time to go rescue a child," Nandia stated. "Abe, Sirius has described the school where he and Gracie are being held by the Erylians. Would you know where in Braeoon there is a Saint Someone-or-Other's that faces the sunrise and is surrounded by trees?"

"It sounds like St. Bernadette's along the river," Abe said. "I know a bit about these Erylian officers, but can little imagine why in God's name anyone would want to imprison children."

"And that, my beloved Abe, is what we're about to find out," Nandia said.

V

THE REST OF THE FAMILY teleported to our room to make preparations to rescue Gracie. I made my way to the front desk and asked to have my reservation changed from room 517 to 419. I complained that someone had been fiddling with the door recently and wanted a room that was a bit more secluded. The clerk gave me a beady stare, as if looking for signs of depravity, but handed over the keycard.

Once out of sight from the lobby, I teleported back to our room on the fourth floor. Nandia, Elli and Sirius had teleported to St. Bernadette's after confirming that Sirius's image of the school coincided with Abe's. Dunstan and I walked to the end of the hallway, went inside our new room and began exploring the elegantly appointed, yet smallish suite. Softly, we began knocking on paneled walls to see if we could locate the false one.

"The lad who engineered this hidden lair," Dunstan mused, "did a bloody fine job. I'm nae seein' any shred a' evidence of a concealed cranny."

"That's what I like about it," Abe telepathically interjected. "The last mortal to know about it lived over two generations ago. Notice the andirons in the fireplace?"

We crouched down and inspected each of the poorly polished antiques. A dusty, wrought iron ball perched atop a braided brass support. I looked to see if there was a hinged member but the entire structure seemed quite rigid. Dunstan reached down and pushed the iron sphere, hoping to find some manner of movement. I reached for the other andiron and began poking and prodding, hoping to coax it into revealing its secret.

Finally Dunstan twisted the ball itself. A creak sounded from across the room. Adjacent to the short hallway that led to the bathroom, a wall panel slid open to reveal a closet large enough to sleep one person. Next to the sleeping bench stood a small cupboard with an aged candelabra, bereft of candles. Muted daylight streamed through a narrow window, smudged with decades worth of grime, that peered dimly across an alley to a solid wall of brick.

"I must apologize," Abe said. "The meticulous arm of The Abyssinian's housekeeping does not reach quite this far. However, I believe you will find candles in the cupboard."

"Aye, the perfect proctor hugger-mugger," Dunstan crowed. "And is there a panel release from within this hidey hole?"

"I don't often get to make the acquaintance of Scotsmen," Abe said. "Your language is decidedly colorful. Try turning the candle holder. And don't forget, you owe me a musical performance."

Dunstan stepped into the closet, faced me and followed Abe's instruction. The panel slid closed. After a moment, it reopened.

"Could you hear me shouting?" he asked.

"Not even the slightest of sounds," I replied, grateful he had thought to test its soundproofing.

I was anxious to show the rest of the family this wonderful secret and said, "Let's see if we can connect with Nandia and Elli." I visualized Nandia's face breaking into a smile, focused on the copper frequency, imagined the rate highlighted in a bright copper color, and transmitted my desire to be together.

Nandia quickly responded. "Not quite done here, Bearns. With Abe's directions we've found Gracie. She's doing well. Right now we're rifling through the warden's office, hoping to learn more. We'll be back to 407 in a tic."

"No need to interrupt their shufflin' 'n bustlin', Lad," Dunstan noted. "They'll get the twenty-five cent tour later." He then asked Abe, "Is this room quiet enough to favor you with a tune?"

We were assured that the room was as soundproof as the closet. Dunstan untangled from the horn case that was perennially strapped diagonally across his back. After extracting the brass instrument he set its reed.

Suddenly a three-note trill loudly resonated throughout the room. Pure, crystal-clear notes bounced off the walls.

"Ah, delight," Abe said as I settled into an elegantly cushioned setee to listen to the master musician at work. Three times Dunstan repeated a long, bell-like tone, followed by a clarion trill that extended for many seconds before it disappeared into a delicious fade. All this was the troubadour's way of simply introducing my favorite bluesy number. It was the same intriguing heart-warming tune that he'd played at our concert in Geasa, the event he'd created along with hundreds of homeless youths. That was how we introduced the city to our radionics remedies — the ones we discovered that did prove to be the answer to the fatal Saragalla virus.

Here in 419, Dunstan began dancing as he played. His tunic, quite similar to his Geasan concert attire, swirled about keeping time with his bluesy tempo. At times he bounced and bended notes off the room's ceiling. Suddenly the music loped into a jazz tempo and I began clapping to the syncopated rhythm. I heard Abe's voice adding a deep baritone to the beat.

We were enjoying our improvised trio when Nandia's voice pierced our minds. "We're home. All safe and sound, and with good news too."

With that, Dunstan brought his performance to a tender close. As I applauded we could hear Abe cheering, punctuated with an enthusiastic wolf whistle. The minstrel bowed, saying, "Aye, 'tis a rare pleasure to play for you again, Laddie. And an honor to perform for such an esteemed being as you, Abe."

We left the room and made our way down the hall to 407. Upon entering, I touched the wall and mentally asked, "Abe, what more have you heard about these Erylians? Do you have any better idea why they are kidnapping Praesepe's children?"

"Since we've met, I've been engaged in a bit of eavesdropping on the proctors," he replied. Waiting in the sitting room, the family noted my look of inner focus, and telepathically tuned in. "Erylian proctors are a dedicated bunch," Abe continued. "They share a grave concern for the future of their own world. I have listened to a number of them worry about the fate of their own children, seething with resentment toward the ineffective medical treatment on their planet. I cannot possibly imagine what benefits the Erylians might realize by stealing our children."

"Have you heard anything about the fate of the kidnapped children?" Nandia asked.

"From the tone of the proctors' chatter, it seems they are being well taken care of," Abe replied.

"One last question, Abe," Dunstan interjected. "Do ya have any idea where Erylian military command is for their operations here on Praesepe?"

"The proctors staying here are mid-level officers," Abe replied. "They all report at least weekly to a military installation they've seized near the spaceport."

"Well, at least we've a startin' point," Dunstan said. "We've learned more from you than we've been able to find out since our arrival. Many thanks."

I turned to find a young, blonde Nandia standing nearby, staring at me. "Gracie," I proclaimed, opening my arms. "I'm Bearns. Believe everything Nandia says about me."

As we embraced, I saw she was wearing El's copper bracelet that Dunstan had bestowed upon Sirius. After being introduced and hugged by Dunstan, she took a hand from each of us and said, "Last Spring, when Gama Nan was teaching me Reiki energy healing, she told me much about how you two helped Geasa with its epidemic. I wish I could have been there with you."

"'Twas your nana made it all happen," Dunstan

declared as I nodded. "And, 'tis grand, Lassie, to have ya on this caper."

A beautiful, younger version of her grandmother, Gracie stood only a bit shorter, youthfully slender and perhaps a bit awkward. I mentally asked her if she could hear our telepathic messages. Suddenly startled, she then smiled and said out loud, "G'ma has been teaching me to hear such messages, but I'm not very good at sending them yet. But, I am finding it much easier since Sirius gave me this copper."

"And, Lass, there's nae to worry about there," Dunstan responded. "With this mob, you'll be transmitting your thoughts afore ya' know it."

"Abe led us to the secret panel in room 419," I said. "It's a wonderfully secure spot for Gracie if necessary, with sleeping space as well. Grace, we must make sure that whenever you're there, you're free of any copper. We don't want the proctors breaking down walls because their copper sensors are setting off alarms."

"It is a pleasure to welcome you, young lady," Abe telepathed. "My name is Abe. I am the being who embodies this hotel. Today is a red letter day, for I've been allowed to become a member of this family. Please consider this your safe home, for as long as you need one. You can speak to me any time. All you need to do to contact me is simply touch the nearest wall and think my name."

"How wonderful!" Gracie was excited. "A telepathic hotel! And I've heard that your boiler room is just the place we can safely store my copper and also hide from the proctors if we need to."

"Yes, Your Grace," Sirius said. "I'll stay within cooee range so if the crabs show up you can toss me your necklace. I'll make it vanish to the boiler room. Meanwhile, I think we all need to ogle Bearn's new haunt and learn its secrets."

Everyone agreed. I cautiously checked the hallway to make sure it was vacant. Dunstan led the way and quickly we were all crowded into our new room.

"Gracie, have you had time to memorize the copper frequency?" I asked as soon as we were safely behind 419's closed door.

"8-3-4-1-0-8-3-7," she repeated three times using her sing-song voice. "Thanks for discovering that, Bearns. One less thing to worry about.

Dunstan demonstrated the hearth's andiron that opened the room's secret lair. All were delighted to see how cleverly the mystery was solved. Gracie stepped inside the refuge as soon as the door slid open. I thought I'd test her telepathic ability and twisted the brass head of the andiron, imprisoning the youngster within the hidden cubby hole.

"Would you like to know how to open the door from the inside, Gracie?" I telepathed.

"Yes," we all mentally heard her message quite clearly.

"You're telepathing very well now," I said. "Notice the intensity of the sensations of your focus as you think. That will aid in sending clearer messages."

"Thanks, you rat, now get me out of here." Gracie's thoughts were tinged with a feigned irritation at being teased so.

"You might try setting your copper aside in the room and see if you can focus on its color and frequency. Let's see if you can still telepath without it." I replied.

After a moment's hesitation, we picked up the message, "Can you hear me now? And you're still a rat."

"Loud and clear. Good work, Darling," Nandia said.

"Well done, Lassie," Dunstan chimed in. "Now, if you were to be about designing a way to open door from inside the closet, what would you imagine it would be?" As he asked the question he mentally sent the image of the candelabra.

After several moments the door slid open, to reveal a broadly smiling young lady, obviously proud of herself. "G'ma did mention that you like playing tricks, you double rat," she said. "I won't forget that again. But it wasn't rocket science once I realized that the image of the candlestick was being telepathed to me."

"I'm proud of you, Gracie," Nandia said. "Your telepathic messages were quite clear. I think that, despite Bearn's trickery, you'll find it easier to send messages now."

"He'll always be a rat," she said and threw her copper my direction.

As the rest of us laughed, Dunstan plucked it out of the air. "Aye, Lassie," he agreed, "We've all known that from the very beginnin'." He shifted his gaze to take us all in. "But me thinks 'tis time ta hear what was learned springing this wee treasure from her gaol. Abe, ya'll warn of proctors approaching?"

"Of course," he said. "And you may want to deposit Gracie's copper in the boiler room until you need it again."

"Easy slather, I've got it," Sirius said. He leapt onto Dunstan's shoulder and grabbed the bauble with his teeth. Gazing ahead with the copper bracelet dangling from his lips, he closed his eyes and disappeared. He was back within seconds without the jewelry.

Arcturus had once bested me in a teleportation race on Aesir. Obviously his son had learned the same techniques. On Aesir I'd promised myself to ask Arcturus to teach me the technique, yet never seemed to find an opportunity to do so. Still quite keen to learn how to project with such speed, I made a mental note to ask Sirius for a tutorial. Then remembered I was deeply curious about what was discovered at St. Bernadette's.

"Before we escaped with Gracie," Elli said, after hearing my thought, "we rifled through the warden's offices. There we learned that the head of Erylian Intelligence Command is one Marshal Everen. He's the senior officer on Praesepe and reports to a General Haplydean on Erylia. All we need to do now is find his office at the Intelligence Center near the spaceport."

"That must be the facility Abe told us about," I offered, "Remember? While eavesdropping on mid-level officers, he learned that they attend a weekly meeting somewhere near the spaceport. It must be the Intelligence Center."

"So Marshal Everen oversees the abduction of Praesepe's children," Nandia added. "He has an entire division commandeering schools, jails, hospitals, and other public buildings where he can confine large numbers of youngsters."

"Any idea why?" I asked.

"No. That has us mystified."

Abe spoke up. "When eavesdropping on proctors' conversations, I heard several expressed dismay over the declining health of their children. I've since learned that Everen has mobilized an entire company of proctors to identify the most capable of Praesepe's young people. They are planning a return to their homeland, very soon, with over fifty percent of our kidnapped youngsters in tow."

"There's nae a ray of hope in that news, to be sure," Dunstan said. "Nandia, Praesepe is your home. Be there many people here who know of your unusual talents?"

"Yes," she replied. "I've been teaching healing and telepathy now for several generations. Certainly hundreds of families now practice healing in their communities. That number has grown steadily. I've become even more of a public figure since our missions to Geasa and Aesir. Our news media milked those stories for months. As a result, my connection with the Galactic Grand Council is widely known as well."

"Aye, 'n that could be why the Erylians chose Praesepe to invade," the Scotsman added.

"Well, it suggests that they're looking for a healthy breeding stock to replace some defect within their own people," Elli suggested.

"Charming," Nandia replied sardonically.

"What?" Gracie shrilly protested. "They want me to make babies for them?"

"We're just imagining possibilities right now, Darling," Nandia responded. "But that idea fits with what we know. We need more information about what's motivating the Erylians. It seems to me we need to come up with a plan to meet their intelligence chief, Marshal Everen. A private meeting like we had on Fusium with The Tabir would be a good start." She nodded toward me as she referred to our strategy on Aesir.

"'Twould be grand if we knew where he lived,"

Dunstan said. "That way, we'd nae have to negotiate our way through his guards and minders."

"Abe, can you tell if any of our resident proctors have a directory of the Erylians' top command lying about in an unoccupied room?" Elli asked.

"Not so much, I'm sorry to say."

"Sounds like open slather to me," Sirius said and leapt to the top of an antique bureau to begin his next, in an endless round, of grooming ablutions. "Get me their room numbers and I can have a quick Captain Cook. But me belly's hopping like a frog in a sock. Time ta boil the billy."

From my time in Aesir, Arcturus had taught me that a 'Captain Cook' was originally Australian convicts' rhyming slang meaning 'to take a look'. Boil the billy means it's time to prepare tea, which could be a full meal. Of course open slather expresses an admirable ease of accomplishment.

"Right as rain," laughed Dunstan. "Seems like it's been days since El and I set about supper. But first let's figure what's next. Ya' know, now might be the time for a few of us, with the fair Nandia, ta go roamin' the streets. Be carryin' copper. Won't be long afore we'd be arrested. Capturing her will sure ta put yards a' feathers in some proctor's cap. They'll want to quiz ya about Gracie's escape, and sure to deliver ya ta Everen's office."

"Yes, and there's a chance we could get wrapped in zinc chains and be unable to escape," I said dourly.

We mused over that possibility for a few moments until Elli came up with another plan. "Why not borrow a proctor's uniform and blend in with a group headed for the Intelligence Center near the spaceport?"

I liked that idea and asked, "Abe, any proctor's rooms nearby that are empty?"

"Two. One just down the hall, room 401, and another upstairs, 808. But, if I may suggest, how about a visit to the hotel laundry where proctors' uniforms are being cleaned? They shut down over an hour ago and won't resume operations until first sunrise tomorrow."

"Lovely," Dunstan said. "Bearns, let's you and I go acquire a new wardrobe."

"Now wait just a minute there buster," Elli objected, smiling through her bluster. "Seems to me we could all use a new wardrobe. Why not plan to visit Marshal Everen en masse? The sudden appearance of a group of proctors at Everen's office would not be seen as unusual. And if the four of us go together, we could split into teams if trouble arises."

"And one a' ya garish pretenders needs ta be totin' a cat," Sirius added. As I listened to everyone's enthusiasm for being included, it occurred to me that we needed to learn how to make the best use of our combined talents. And Sirius was right. Who would ever suspect a group of proctors, when one of them was carrying a pet?

"Abe, how do you feel about keeping an eye on Gracie while we investigate Everen's stronghold?" Nandia asked.

"Set your minds to rest, my friends," Abe's tone was soothing. "I'll see that Gracie is secure in room 419. If danger comes near, she knows how to access its secret compartment. I'll alert you to any trouble. And it will be a rare pleasure to get to know you better, Gracie."

"Excuse me," she loudly protested. "While I

appreciate your care and concern, Abe, I'm wondering which of you think that I wouldn't look good in a proctor's uniform? You're planning to exclude me because....?"

"If we run into trouble," Nandia explained, "it would take some finesse to spirit you to safety. Elli and I were able to provide a teleport assist when we sprung you from St. Bernadette's dormitory-prison — but we weren't under attack and had plenty of time. This mission would be safer, sweetheart, if you remained here."

"Now I'm feeling really hurt and disappointed," Gracie said petulantly. "And, for the moment, G'ma, I think that's all your fault."

We all waited in silence. It was impressive that the young girl knew herself well enough, and felt safe enough, to honestly disclose her hurt and her impulse to blame.

And then Gracie demonstrated an even deeper wisdom. She abruptly sat in the nearest chair, closed her eyes and began breathing deeply. After a few breaths, she began musical toning, trying first one note and then another.

Once Gracie had selected the note that accentuated healing her hurts, Dunstan picked a harmonizing tone and softly joined her, soon followed by Nandia and El. After listening for a moment, I added my voice, having picked a note an octave above Dunstan's. The combined toning was beautiful. Gracie's face became radiant, her contagious smile spreading to each of us. The music swept from forte to pianissimo several times until her volume began to fade. When she opened her eyes, we were all grinning like Cheshire cats.

"Gracie, that was quite a gift," El said. "Thank you for allowing us to be a part of your healing," Her warm expression of gratitude spoke for us all.

The immortal stepped closer to the youngster, took her hand and pulled her into a warm embrace. We all melded into the hug as El said, "This young lady has wisdom beyond her years. Obviously she's been in training with her grandmother."

We slowly unwrapped ourselves and stepped back. "How wonderful that was," Gracie said quietly. "I really loved it when you all joined me. There was a moment of toning together, when a cloud lifted from my body, a fog lifted from my brain. At that moment, I realized that I blame other people when ever I feel disappointed. And then I start feeling sorry for myself and get preoccupied with what I don't have. Up until today I've been afraid to admit that. Oh, thank you! I now feel so much lighter, like I'm being suspended in the air. Thank you, thank you, each of you." Radiant, she twirled, beaming her gratitude toward each of us.

"You know, Nandia, I have a sense that Gracie will add something useful to this upcoming adventure," Elli said. "Need I mention that there would be risks leaving her here that we wouldn't encounter by staying together? And, you'll have to admit that when we all do go out, it will be much safer if each of us were garbed as a proctor."

"Yes," Nandia smiled briefly, then turned serious again. "But I would hope she could more effectively teleport before we next leave the hotel."

"True," Elli responded. "Yet you and I easily got her here from St. Bernadette's. We need to practice tandem jumps until we've mastered them, so why not sooner rather than later? Gracie picks things up quickly — notice how easily she telepathed a message when stuck inside that closet. I suspect she'll learn faster in our presence than being isolated here."

Nandia momentarily bit her lip, lost in worry. After an awkward moment she looked up and said, "Gracie, we have no wish for you to be recaptured. So whenever we go out, you must stay with one of us, especially since you'll not be able to carry copper. We'll need to practice focusing on the copper frequency and teleporting in tandem. If you and I are both satisfied with your progress, then you're part of the team. Do you agree?" The youngster loudly cheered and bounced about gleefully before stopping to hug each of us. Then she turned and caught Sirius as he leapt into her outswept arms.

"No worries, she'll be solo teleportin' soon," Sirius offered. "She's already working with Bearn's copper frequency, an'becomin' such a big problem we won't be able to take care of her much longer."

Gracie swatted at Sirius, scolding him. "I just might get to be a bigger problem for you, you furry rodent." We all laughed as Sirius leapt away and began grooming a paw.

"I wonder how loudly the alarm has been spread since Gracie's disappearance," Nandia remarked, bringing us back to reality. "Everen and his gang must be foaming at the mouth like rabid dogs. That means more proctor overtime and should make our disguises even more helpful."

"Aye, and I'll go bail some officer's head is already on the choppin' block," Dunstan added thoughtfully. "But they know of you, Nandia, and they'll figure you're behind this mischief, so they'll be puttin' a pretty price on your pretty head."

"Everen's smart," I noted. "He's probably doubled his scanner teams and trying to figure out our next moves."

"Which we don't know very much about ourselves," El observed. "Gentle Abyssinian, might you please direct us to the laundry?"

Abe and Sirius guided us through hallways, down stairways and along several detours to avoid being seen. We arrived to find the laundry doors locked, which I made short work of using my lockpicks. Within seconds we had stolen our way into the anteroom of the large cleaning facility which smelled strongly of detergents and pressed fabrics. I closed the door and switched on some lights. To keep from advertising our presence, Dunstan piled several nearby towels along the base of the door. Inside, large rooms were loaded with washers, dryers, industrial pressing machines and a maze of clothes on conveyors awaiting delivery. Most of the clothes hanging on the conveyors were uniforms.

"Aye, I do love shopping with the ladies," Dunstan crowed as he began pulling down uniforms and passing them to us.

"Abe, are you there?" I asked.

"Yes, I'm having fun watching you," he said. "Nice touch with the door locks, Bearns. Remind me to hire you as a security consultant."

"Keep watch for us, will you?"

"No problem. Have fun."

Sirius was scouting beneath machinery and around corners. "Place smells so bad, no self-respecting meal would ever consider livin' here." He lifted his nose in disgust and found a throne atop a warm dryer.

We stripped to our underwear, shy as schoolchildren on the first day in a locker room. I worried that we might not find a uniform slender enough to fit Gracie, who had chosen the modesty option and taken several selections to try on behind a cupboard. Nandia and El occupied one corner, while Dunstan and I stood in the middle of the room. Stacks of bagged uniforms surrounded us. I couldn't keep my eyes away from Nandia as she undressed, and was delightfully captivated as she and Elli peeled to nearly naked. El surprised me with the youthful allure of her splendid form. The two ladies certainly captured Dunstan's broad-smiled attention as well.

"Focus, Lads, focus," Elli chided.

"Aye, lass, that's precisely what I'm doin'," Dunstan laughed. "But you're quite right; admirin' you lovelies won't get the job done any quicker, now, will it?"

He was rewarded with a feminine sounding raspberry from behind Gracie's cupboard as an airborne proctor's cap came sailing toward his head. He plucked it from midair, found it fit and laughed, "Just the right size, Lassie. Me thanks go out ta ya."

We played like kids preparing for a costume party as we searched for uniforms that fit. At one point, Nandia waltzed around the room in a vastly oversized officer's jacket. She was carrying Sirius in its huge front pocket. For that moment she transformed into a lovely little girl. "I'd hate to have to eat what this giant must feed on every day," she quipped as she dug around in the empty pockets of the tent that enfolded her.

"Oh! Look what I found," she exclaimed, as she

pulled a name badge from the jacket's top pocket. Each of us checked our uniforms and also found a nametag in the same place.

"Must be their way of making sure they get the right uniform back," I mused as I fastened a nametag to my jacket.

"Dunstan, you're looking a bit shaggy beneath that cap," El observed. He growled and barked — a very realistic canine reply. Sirius rose on his hind legs, hissing and swinging out with claws poised to attack. Dunstan sailed his cap that direction and the cat skittered back to his warm throne.

After settling on uniforms, we returned those we didn't need to the conveyor. Just before hanging the last one I saw a bright, star-shaped battle decoration dangling from a golden ribbon beneath a collar. I imagined it hanging from Sirius's neck and so stuffed it into my pocket.

We practiced goose stepping around the laundry and saluting each other. Dunstan issued commands. Gracie's giggle switch was set on 'constant.' She was the only one not wearing dark shoes.

"Abe," El asked, "Is there a housekeeping closet nearby where we might find a pair of shoes for Gracie?"

"Right down the hall," came his welcome reply. "However, Bearns, you'll need to work your magic on the lock."

After gathering up our clothes, I showed off the medal I'd found for Sirius and was rewarded with delighted applause for my efforts.

"I'm so hungry me stomach thinks 'tis been banded," Dunstan said. "Let's get Gracie's shoes and then quick launch back to our room and see what we need ta add ta the meal that's still waitin' there. Room service could well do."

"Or, if you'd rather," Abe offered, "there's an all-night grocery down the block where you can fill your own larder."

Gracie was thrilled to hear that. "Oh good, an outing. Let's go shopping and see how well these disguises work."

The young lady's enthusiasm was infectious. "We'll need to stop by the room to pick up some gold and drop off our clothes," I said. I liked the idea of going out during the quiet of the evening to see how much these uniforms would render us invisible.

A quick stop for shoes at housekeeping was delayed when Gracie had to choose between three different pairs that fit. "But these make me look old," she haughtily complained as she tried on the last pair.

"Aye, Lassie, that's the point," Dunstan said gently. The light dawned in the girl's eyes, and within moments we were headed for our room. At Abe's direction we navigated several detours — no one wanted to be seen carrying armfuls of clothes and uniform bags.

Once safely within 407, we dumped our civilian togs and gathered in a circle to admire each other. Gracie's uniform was tailored for a slightly built male, but her height made her believable as an Erylian. "We may need a dab of ash 'n grease to age yer mug," Dunstan teased and then went about straightening everyone's ribbons and medals. For some reason, he needed an extra a bit of time with those adorning El's jacket. Nandia adjusted Gracie's hat, who then marched around executing sharp turns and mock salutes.

"I think you've got talent for the stage, young lady," Nandia said. "But don't get too cocky in that uniform. Don't forget we'll all be much safer once you've learned how to teleport effectively. In the meantime, stay close and only minimal eye contact with any proctors we encounter."

"Oh, yes," she said, "I'm OK with that. What else do I need to know?"

"Carry me on our way to find cat food," Sirius suggested. "I've got more ideas that will help." Gracie gathered up the cat. I sized the ribbon for the medal I had borrowed from the laundry and suspended it from Sirius's neck. It dangled slightly below his chin, giving him a ceremonial look that I hoped would render our disguises more believable.

We traveled in two groups to the grocery store. Nandia, Dunstan and Gracie with Sirius took the lead. Elli and I stopped at the hotel's front desk and exchanged gold for Praesepe's local currency. I was happy to note that our uniforms did not arouse any suspicion with the desk clerks. The few pedestrians on the street all averted their eyes as we drew near. We arrived at the shop without incident.

While roaming the aisles I listened as Sirius telepathed to Gracie the idea of mentally projecting a single atom of her body to a desired destination. She liked the idea and was eager to practice it, telepathically asking if she must always begin with the copper frequency.

"Only when there's the presence of zinc nearby," Nandia telepathed in reply. "All that was needed during the Geasan mission was to be wearing copper. In some ways that was easier because we didn't need to remember the frequency. Here the proctors can scan for the presence of copper so remembering 8-3-4-1-0-8-3-7 is necessary. It's something we all need to practice until it's second nature."

It turned out Sirius was quite finicky while making his selections at the pet food aisle. After a prod from Dunstan to be quick about it, we made our way to the checkout counter. Again, our uniforms gave us anonymity. Elli made small talk with the store's young clerk, who responded with short, polite and distant dismissals.

A pair of proctors wandered in as we headed out the front door, draped with bundles and bags. One commented on Sirius who was quietly nestled in Nandia's arms. She paused, letting the proctor scratch the cat's chin. We held our breath as he fondled the commendation around the cat's neck.

"I've always thought that it looks better on him," I quickly commented as I nodded to the proctors. Their smiles were interrupted by Dunstan.

"Let's get this food back to our rooms before we starve out here on the street," Dunstan's loud complaint was a protest completely devoid of his usual accent. The proctors formally wished us a good evening and stepped into the store. We all breathed a sigh of relief as we proceeded safely along the sidewalk.

"We each need to develop a proctor persona." Nandia telepathed. "The last thing we need is to stumble over our stories if we get drawn into a conversation. And Sirius wearing that commendation medal might attract more attention than we'd like."

Her words made me realize that our uniforms would not end all risks we would face at the Erylians' intelligence headquarters tomorrow. Nandia was right, we needed to polish up our disguises if we were planning to go out and find a way to meet Marshal Everen.

# VI

I AND MY STOMACH were quite happy when Dunstan and El finally set about preparing dinner. The rest of us changed into civilian clothes. Nandia and Gracie began talking about their proctor personalities. I took two armfuls of stolen uniforms to 419 and secured them within its hidden closet. Upon returning, I overheard Gracie complaining, "But I don't want to pretend that I'm a proctor-in-training. Having been imprisoned around those fools for the past few weeks, I know I can be a very convincing adult."

"The less attention you draw to yourself, the better Gracie," Nandia countered. "Don't forget, you're probably the most wanted person on the planet at this moment. If you're going to join our foray tomorrow, we'll need you to be as invisible as possible."

"But, I can do it, I know I can," the youngster insisted.

"Darling, this is not an excursion to demonstrate our acting abilities," Nandia patiently explained. "It is vitally important that our appearance and behavior arouse no suspicion. We've decided upon this high-risk excursion to help us find the key to ending the Erylian siege. We must find out why the Erylians are kidnapping Praesepian children and who their decision makers are. I know how anxious you are to show that you are capable of taking an adult role in this venture, but you must remember, if you're to join us you need to minimize the risks to the entire group."

While still looking petulant, Gracie nodded thoughtfully.

"There is one inner skill that aids teleportation that Sirius has yet to mention," Elli had stepped out of the kitchen and sat on the couch next to Gracie. "There is an innate power that each of us has, and you must come to trust it if you wish to teleport." Gracie listened intently as El continued.

"You must accept that you are solely responsible for your own approval and well-being. Your thoughts, beliefs and choices alone determine your state of mental, emotional and physical health. You must come to accept that you are revered and respected as the unique individual you are. There is nothing wrong with you. There is nothing you must prove about yourself.

"Being the unique individual you are is justification enough to be in this world. You have a right to work on any lesson in whatever way and in whatever time you choose. As you come to accept and trust in such power you will find your impatience dissolving. Tomorrow's venture is a good opportunity to work on that."

The last shadows of resistance eased from Gracie's face. She was beginning to understand the need to proceed slowly and cautiously. "OK," she offered, "I'll work my persona as a young male trainee, whose name is Greg. I will maintain only minimal eye contact with any proctors we meet, and will stay toward the back of our group. If we have to escape quickly I will grab the hand of the person I'm closest to and begin breathing deeply. And I'm sorry, G'ma, that I've been such a problem."

"Thank you, Darling," Nandia replied, her voice gently tender. "I know you are anxious for the freedom to express yourself as a responsible adult. I also well know of your respect and love for me. Let's talk more about this as we eat, so that everyone has a chance to share their views. Any decision we make must be made by all of us. That way we can trust that our collective consciousness will guide us toward this mission's most ideal outcome."

El returned to the kitchen and joined Dunstan in laying out the meal. "Let's eat," she prompted. Tired and hungry, we sat down around the antique dining table with its silver candelabra and sterling cutlery. I mentally blessed the meal, after which everyone said "Amen." For the next few minutes each of us concentrated solely upon tasting our food. Sirius was perched atop a tall sideboard, making quick work of a plate of salmon. In the growing chorus of soft tones and grunts of approval, it was obvious we were all delighted with the fare that had been prepared.

"El, your kale, cashew and avocado salad is delicious," Dunstan offered.

"And your rice and lentil dish is sublime with the rosemary you've added," the Royal Chambermaid replied. All in the family nodded as they chewed. None of the rest of us were about interrupt savoring flavors to indulge in conversation.

It was only after we'd finished our first servings that talk resumed. "We do need to discuss our outing tomorrow," Elli began. "If we are apprehended while dressed as proctors, we'll have much more to answer for than simply carrying copper."

"Too right," I said. "And if Gracie the imposter is recognized as Gracie the escapee, we could find ourselves sailing some very stormy waters. That said, we must find out the reasons for this Erylian siege."

"Aye, 'tis true enough," Dunstan agreed. "'Tis sorely troublin' that we risk puttin' this wee lass in harm's way if we get nabbed." Nodding with the Scotsman, we all fell soberly quiet. "Until we learn how to navigate the risks, 'twill be touch and go," he continued, "nip 'n tuck. I'll make bail there are proctor secret handshakes 'n passwords that we'll be needin' to learn before we can safely sail these seas."

"Yes, there are these risks and more," Elli said, "but, we mustn't underestimate our abilities. Mentally using Bearn's copper frequency gives us tremendous advantages — we're invisible to Erylian scanners and can telepath and teleport. We've safe havens here at Abe's, the Vasantamos and the Don. We're fast and we're agile. Our combined talents produce a gestalt of creative power that is greater than all of us combined. We work well together and should be able to stay ahead of any pursuit."

I appreciated El's reminder and shared an idea that had occurred to me earlier. "How would everyone feel if Dunstan and I reconnoiter Marshal Everen's headquarters tomorrow? Everyone else can be dressed as proctors standing by as a backup. We'll be in telepathic connection and you could be there in a thrice if we need help."

To my surprise, everyone, including Gracie, readily agreed. "I like having a voice in making our plans," she explained. "I know I get impatient and want to be accepted as an adult, but the fact is, there are sides to this mission that I've never encountered before."

"Yes, there are many pieces to this puzzle," Nandia agreed. "I've been wondering just how the Erylians could overthrow our planetary government so quickly. They've also done a good job minimizing disruptions to Praesepe's economy. All I can assume is that they've had their own people working unseen within our government for quite some time." I recalled watching Praesepians' auras outside the Don and discovering that there were Erylian collaborators.

"'Tis hard ta imagine otherwise," Dunstan added. "We'll do well rememberin' to nae be trustin' Praesepians 'til we know who's butterin' their bread." It was a useful caution to keep in mind for tomorrow's mission. Nandia and Elli decided they would take Gracie and Sirius out, dressed as proctors. They would practice teleporting with Gracie while shopping for shoes that were more suited to their uniforms.

"We need to exchange more of our gold," Elli said. "And we should practice visiting our rooms at the Don and the Vasantamos, so both Gracie and Sirius are familiar with our escape routes."

I tuned in to Abe and asked if he knew of how proctors travelled to the Intelligence Center near the spaceport.

"There's a rotoplane shuttle that takes off from the roof here and takes our guests directly to the space-port. A taxi to the Erylian Intellegence Center — the I.C. — can be hired from there," he replied. "I'd recommend you catch the little-used early shuttle that leaves at five a.m."

"Aye, there's a sound plan," Dunstan said. "We'll need to have our wits about us lad. Is there a barber working in the hotel this late, Abe? I need to get these locks shorn, or I'll stand out like a bloody warnin' beacon."

"I'll be happy to take care of that problem," Elli said. "Sit yourself here in the kitchen and we'll have you as handsome as a proctor in no time."

We all finished our preparations for the morning's early departure. After making sure we had ample cash, Dunstan and I practiced focusing on the copper frequency when telepathing. We also memorized our proctor identity badges that were pinned to our uniforms and created a cursory cover story about our presence at the I.C. Exhausted, we settled into the three rooms of the suite. Dunstan and I bunked together in light of our early departure.

I asked my Inner Self for a constructive dream with Marshal Everen that would help us easily resolve any of tomorrow's difficulties and quickly fell asleep.

I found myself on a beach and, by the bright rosy-pink color of the sky, knew immediately that I was dreaming. The hue was unlike any of the skies above planets I'd ever visited. Although unusual, it wasn't unpleasant. I set off to my left, barefoot along the water's edge. I enjoyed how the sky and the distant ocean met in a rosy-hued horizon. The warm, dark line separating the two was a pleasing contrast to my memories of seascapes, and a pleasing contrast to the water's many shades of maroon.

Breathing the rich air coming off the ocean's waves, I reminded myself of the healing available while walking along nature's transition zones. I'd long known that the energy at the edge of a forest or along a beach is highly regenerative. Here the air is thick with oxygen ions. Playfully I splashed my feet through the water, warm sand delightfully massaging my toes.

In these energy-transition places I always feel physically vitalized and more deeply at peace within myself. It's easier to appreciate myself as an individualized portion of nature. I had the feeling that I was personally being recognized by the consciousness of this planet, and celebrated for being my unique self.

Allowing my body's energy field to recharge, my peaceful musings were abruptly interrupted by the sound of wailing. The rhythm of the waves was being accented by a song of at least two poor souls grieving.

Looking up, I saw a dark-haired girl about Gracie's age sitting in the sand. Facing her was middle-aged man, kneeling in the sand, water lapping at his feet. Both were in tears.

Not wanting to be an unwelcome intrusion, I telepathed the gentle message, "Hello, dear people." I know that in dreams telepathic communication is the norm. Seeing the two in turmoil, I sought to offer assistance, if requested.

"Would you mind some company?" I asked softly. I had stopped a fair distance away and was looking out to sea as I waited. It was not a moment in which to hurry, so I satisfied myself with the sound of the waves and the beautiful blend of rosy-pink and blue colors.

After a long moment, the man stood and called out, "Please join us." I turned, waved and walked toward them.

"I'm sorry to intrude on your sadness," I began, "But I wondered if you might appreciate talking about it. My name is Bernard, but please call me Bearns. May I ask what is troubling you so?"

"I am known as Marshal Everen." He stood tall and erect with greying highlights in his otherwise dark hair. His severely handsome face was streaked with tears. "And this is my daughter, Hyldie. Please join us." He invited me to sit next to them just back from the water's edge.

"We've just found out that Hyldie has an incurable disease," he explained as his daughter watched the ocean's waves. "Doctors say there is nothing that can be done. My only child has lost her ability to have children." In the midst of this heart-rending explanation, a sob escaped his lips and tears again began flowing down his cheeks. After a time, he wiped his eyes with his sleeve and turned back toward me.

"We've known that Hyldie was unwell for a while now, but we both kept procrastinating about visiting a doctor. I blame myself for not challenging her to look squarely at her problems. I stayed distracted, thinking that preparing for our invasion of Praesepe was more important. It was only after Hyldie became so exhausted that she rarely left her room, that I grew alarmed enough to seek out help."

"But, Papa, it's not your fault," Hyldie replied. "I was the one feeling so sorry for myself that I not only shut myself off from you, but from everybody I care about."

"Ah, my darling Hyldie, as your father, I have failed you," he lamented. "I should never have neglected your health as I did."

I listened while they proclaimed their sorrow and their shame. They reminded me of the countless losses I had suffered and the decades, even lifetimes that I had waited before realizing that I was wallowing in self-pity. It was only after meeting Agoragon in my youth, that I learned that self-pity blocks the natural process of healing.

"Thank you for so openly telling me of your pain," I said. "Perhaps I can offer another perspective that may aid in your healing. Would you like me to continue?

Hyldie wiped her face on the back of her hand, while Everen pulled a tissue from his pocket. During a moment's reflection they dried their tears, and then both nodded.

"Right now, I think you're both feeling great sadness, shame and guilt," I said. "But may I remind you that you are beings of tremendous power and energy. You originate from and have a home within the many worlds of spirit. That we are in this dream together attests to that.

"I am simply reminding you that you've not left the domains of the spirit even though you've chosen a temporary stop-over in the realm of time and flesh. I want to suggest that, at some inner level, you trusted there would be many opportunities to grow and express greater talents and abilities in the physical domain."

They looked at me as if wondering why I was speaking of such things. "I'm saying that you are both beings of unlimited strength and power," I continued. "None of these experiences were thrust upon you. I would like to suggest that you both placed this challenge on your path, using your creative powers, for some constructive purpose."

"You're saying that whatever we get in our lives we get because that's what we've been concentrating upon?" Hyldie asked.

"Well said," I replied, "Since you created this challenge, you must have the power to heal and restore balance to the troubled areas of your life. It always takes far less energy to heal a problem than it took to create it.

"I firmly believe that the only reason we beings of power create such suffering is to ultimately learn that there is absolutely no reason for suffering. And I am suggesting that by changing your attitudes of self-pity and blame you can move through the remaining sadness and hurt that has hindered you from accepting this loss. Once you've accomplished that, who knows what else you could heal, or what else you could create together?"

Everen and his daughter looked at each other and, with a renewed burst of tears, fell into each other's arms. The brighter blue and yellow colors in their auras showed me they knew the value of what I was saying. I sat down in the nearby in the sand and looked out to sea as they continued to hold each other. Finally their tears abated. They looked toward me with bright faces smiling.

"Thank you, Bearns," Hyldie said. "We needed to be reminded that the power to heal resides within us.

Everen stood and stepped toward me, extending his hand to shake mine. I stood, reached out, and with another step discovered that what had begun as a handshake had become a heartfelt hug.

"My deepest thanks," he said in my ear. "I see now that Erylia's plans for Praesepe are a bit shortsighted. Perhaps a way can be found to convince our leaders of the sheer folly of trying to replace our ill children with Praesepe's healthy ones."

And then I knew the reason for the Erylian siege of Praesepe. With that realization, the dream faded. I awakened to sun streaming into the room and the sound of a Scotsman snoring.

# VII

I HURRIED TO 419 to collect our uniforms. Upon returning, Dunstan and I dressed and decided to forego eating until we had reached the spaceport. There we would further test our disguises and perhaps pick up some useful information while eating breakfast at one of their restaurants.

Before leaving, the family agreed to telepathically check in with each other at the top of every hour for the duration of today's adventure. If anyone was more than ten minutes late we would all immediately teleport back to 407, prepared to face a crisis.

Abe had suggested that we take the elevator to the rooftop shuttle landing pad. There we encountered a small group of proctors, each standing silently in the early morning sunlight. Dunstan and I took up positions at the group's periphery, and telepathically confirmed that each other's uniform had passed inspection. I mentally passed along my appreciation for how military he looked since Elli had shorn his locks.

Within minutes the rotoplane arrived and began loading passengers.

Onboard we took seats toward the rear of the passenger cabin. I examined the energy fields of the proctors in the forward rows — their auras featured subdued dark grays and browns. Proctors slouched in their reclining seats, withdrawn into themselves.

I mentally called out to the family eavesdroppers, deciding now was the time to recount last night's dreaming with Marshal Everen and Hyldie. I passed along the success of my blame and self-pity talk. "Good work, Bearns," Gracie said. "I'm still working on that one."

"As am I, Sweetheart, as am I."

"Several proctors waitin' for the shuttle were worryin' about their wee ones back home," Dunstan advised, just at the end of my dreamtale. "Maybe Erylia truly is plannin' ta use Praesepians to seed their next generation, Lad," he added. "Could account for why these proctors seem so weighted down with worry."

"Right. Just yesterday, I caught a faint whiff of worry from proctors remembering their children back home," I recalled. "And wasn't Abe saying something about it as well?"

"Aye, so he did. Let's hope our eavesdroppin' at the spaceport sheds more light on that puzzle."

Minutes later, the shuttle slowly vertically descended into a spaceport berth. While disembarking, I stopped to admire the rotoplane's design, recalling how handy it was through the air while needing scant space for takeoffs and landings. With propulsion ports fore and aft, it was about the size of a small bus and yet carried at least fifty passengers quite efficiently.

We fell in with a group that strolled through the spaceport. A large, modern structure, it was built to berth dozens of intergalactic starships at the same time, accommodating countless thousands of passengers. Its design tastefully integrated marbled ceilings with soaring glass panels that were beautifully accented with tall trees and colorful floral beds. The air smelled fresh and cool. The muted roar of launching starships was not at all disturbing, evidence that Praesepian engineers knew effective soundproofing. This early in the morning there were only a few dozen travelers occupying the pedestrian conveyors.

We stopped at the first diner we found open. Amidst the steady stream of hungry, mostly proctor patrons, we managed to find a table that overlooked the launch pads. We nursed steaming cups of tea as we awaited the hearty breakfast we had ordered.

Dunstan and I telepathically eavesdropped on neighboring tables, shifting our focus from one to the next to see what we might learn. Mentally using the copper frequency had become second nature. From time to time we commented on what we heard — mostly that proctors hoped this siege would end soon. It seemed that very few of the Erylian troops had their hearts in their work. Most seemed quite anxious to return to their families, with many expressing unusual concern for their children's well-being.

"'Twould be grand to ask one of these blokes what's troublin' their wee ones," Dunstan observed. I nodded and then concentrated on a table where I overheard Marshal Everen's name.

"Everen will not be a happy chappy when he hears

we've not found that young girl who escaped from St. Bernadette's." An older, grizzled officer was speaking to several younger proctors a few tables away. "You can bet he'll ask how she and her cat managed to wriggle out of our grasp. Then he'll come to three conclusions: One, we're incompetent; two, someone from the outside sprung 'em; and three, we're incompetent. And you can bet he'll want us to tell him who it was that had helped them." I watched as the pale red colors of the aura surrounding his head and shoulders grew murkier the longer he spoke.

An eager young officer enthusiastically put forth a theory. "It seems very likely that her grandmother, a Galactic Council member, masterminded the escape. It is known that she has taught telepathy and teleportation to many here in Braeoon. We've got people watching her home and her usual haunts, but so far no sign of her."

"Have you circulated photos and her identity papers to the hotels and transport terminals?" Officer Grizzled asked.

"Just finished the job yesterday. All around Praesepe. But teleportation is the most likely way she would have managed to spirit the youngster and her cat out of a locked and guarded room. And for that to have happened, the grandmother must have discovered that copper would neutralize our zinc disruptor shield. Yesterday, on three separate occasions, our copper sensor teams picked up measurable copper readings. Yet, when investigated, all readings proved to be futile. We've picked up no further readings since then, despite trebling the number of scan teams on the streets."

"Were the readings located near each other?"

"One was in the Braeoon Gardens, the other two in the heart of the city."

"You know what Everen will say to that," the veteran officer remarked.

"He'll want us to check every flophouse, round-house and public house near where we picked up those readings looking for anyone matching the girl and her grandmother's description," the younger officer looked pleased to have anticipated his superior's question.

"And have you?"

"My team is starting on that project this morning."

"Very good." The senior officer nodded toward his subordinate and went back to finishing his breakfast.

The good news was that early in our eavesdropping, Dunstan and I had telepathically alerted Nandia and Elli to listen in. "Not to worry, boys," Nandia said cheerfully. "We'll have Abe watching our backs and we've always got his hidden closet if we need it. Before we set out on our shopping spree, we'll practice teleporting there with Gracie."

"Aye, Lass," Dunstan said, "You'll be safe enough, so you will. But you'll not be wantin' to visit our room at the Don — too great a chance their front desk staff'll remember ya. Proctors could already be waitin' to ambush anyone goin' into that suite. Gracie's escape set off a bloody crusade."

"You boys take care to keep a low profile," Elli warned. She was right, of course. The longer the proctors had no idea what we looked like, the longer we were free to accomplish what we had come to do. "And now we're sure that it's the proctor's uniform for Gracie whenever we go out," she noted.

Dunstan and I picked up bits of other conversations while we sat nursing our final cups of tea. We discovered that most people walked to the I.C. — a ten minute jaunt about three city blocks distant. I listened to see if I could get details about Everen's office, but learned nothing more. On nearby tables, we noticed tips left for the waitresses and followed suit before making our way toward the spaceport exit.

We passed an information booth occupied by a bored looking matronly woman. I mentally nudged Dunstan and we returned to its counter.

"We've just arrived for our first assignment here on Praesepe," I smiled, putting on my friendly charm. "We're late, and sorry to say, missed our escort to Marshal Everen's office. Could you point us in the right direction?"

"Certainly, young man," she noted our uniforms and responded coolly. "We've had a lot of you proctors arriving from Erylia. I imagine you've heard that you may not receive the warmest welcome you could have hoped for."

"We understand that, Madam," Dunstan replied, without any trace of his accent. "Frankly many of us here find this assignment quite distasteful — absconding with other peoples' children and the like. I'm sure that our mission troubles most Praesepians. How do you feel about our presence here?"

The woman, whose name badge identified her as Midge shrugged. "Well, you know, I must do my job," she conceded. Sighing, she slouched and leaned in closer. "But, somehow I've got a rare feeling about you two. You seem to be different than other proctors.

Would you mind if I spoke openly about my family?" she asked lowering her voice.

We both nodded for Midge to continue. "My own granddaughter has gone missing," she confided. "Every day our family grows more desperate not knowing what's become of her. The police don't even respond to reports of lost children."

"Perhaps we can be of help locating her," I quietly suggested. Midge's face lit up. I smiled at her and asked, "Have you heard any rumors about where the children are being held?"

"Well, by the holy suns Freyr and Njoror we must celebrate your arrival," she exclaimed. Laughing, Midge thrust both her hands across the counter and warmly shook ours.

"Finally someone shows up who refuses to kowtow to this madness and has at least a lick of sense," she exclaimed. "The Praesepian government has all but disappeared — they've gone underground.

"These Erylian malfastards are seizing as many schools and prisons as they can get their hands on," she continued. "The teachers and guards who have lost their jobs have been offered financial compensation, but we Praesepians are getting angrier and angrier as more children go missing. There's a group of underground dissidents, to be sure. We consider anyone working for the Erylians to be traitors. Unfortunately, we've had little success trying to bring an end to this siege."

Tears were welling up in her eyes as she finished speaking. I mentally asked Dunstan what he thought of making this woman an ally. He readily agreed. While speaking more honestly about her true feelings, her energy field had grown brighter, a vibrant blue color washing through her aura. Midge was growing to trust us. She must have recognized our compassion, for she smiled broadly at each of us before grabbing a tissue and wiping her eyes.

I leaned in close to her. "Midge," I said quietly, "despite these uniforms we wear, we are part of a group of five people who are here to help end this siege. It's a godsend that we've met you and learned there is a Praesepian underground."

"Aye, Lassie, set aside ye worries," Dunstan reassured her, returning to his natural brogue. This did more to comfort Midge than his words. "Yer family will come together again, ne'er ye fear." Our notorious telepathing eavesdroppers, Nandia and Elli, sent along their cheers of support.

Midge smiled broadly and reached out as if to hug us both. But then remembering where she was, she quickly dropped her arms and glanced around to make sure that this display of affection had not been noticed. Instead, she leaned toward the red-haired Scotsman as he pushed back his proctor's cap.

Dunstan smiled as he also moved closer. "'Tis great good fortune that we've found ye, for we're needin' to learn fast the lay o' the land. Would ya be havin' a photograph of your granddaughter?"

She pulled a well-worn print from an inside pocket and handed it over. "Her name is Mary-Ann Olgivie, but she goes by Annie."

"Do you mind if we keep this for now?" I asked.

"If there's any chance it will help, please do," she replied.

"I hope you don't mind my asking this," I added,

"But I have the feeling we can trust you to keep our presence here confidential, unless of course, you see us on the vid news. Am I right?"

"Oh, yes," she replied sincerely. "Like I said, I've had a good feeling about the two of you since you walked up. How can I help?"

"Aye, Lassie, you're a breath of fresh air, so ya are," Dunstan said quietly.

It was time to reveal more of our plans. "We are here helping another Praesepian family whose child was also kidnapped," I said. "Wearing these proctor disguises, we want to visit Marshal Everen's office to find out the reasons for this Erylian siege and how to thwart it. We promise to stay in touch with you and share what we learn."

After impatiently waiting to speak, Midge interjected, "Later we must talk of our local underground community. We have an effective communication network and have managed to locate most of the prisons and schools where our children are being held."

"That's the best news yet, fair Lassie," Dunstan said as he took her hand. "And hear now that there are others in our group who will help the bringin' of wee Annie home." Dunstan sent me an image of Sirius. We both knew he would come in very handy for that job.

I telepathically picked up a loud protest from Sirius. "Yeooow, thank Holy Felicia you blockheads finally listened. Are ya deef? I'm on it, I tell ya." I suddenly realized that he might be able to eavesdrop into several conversations at once.

"You two can find me here by first light any day," Midge said. "But it's best if you go now to avoid attracting attention. Know that I am a forward observation post for the underground.

"Everen's office is on the top floor of the I.C. He's well guarded. But today, you're in luck. There's an intelligence briefing beginning in an hour in the main conference room of the building. I'm told they're expecting dozens of new soldiers to be there."

"Do you know if we need a special pass to get in?" I asked.

"I'm to direct any officers who are having trouble finding their way," Midge said. "I've been told to watch for uniforms with the same inverted blue triangles on their right shoulders that both of you have."

"Cheers, Lassie, for that added bit o' good news," Dunstan remarked. "But we could use different identity badges. Less chance a' runnin' into someone who recognizes our names but not our faces."

Midge nodded quickly. "As you leave the building, watch for a bright yellow taxi bearing the number 714 at the taxi stand. Tell Joseph, the driver, that Midge says you're OK. He knows several cabbies who have found proctor ID badges in their back seats, apparently overlooked after an evening's carousing with one of our local entertainers. Remember, cab 7-1-4.

"And new identity badges should baffle anyone looking for these uniforms," I agreed. "Many thanks, Midge. We'll let you know of our progress."

"Best of luck to you both. For the first time since this damn siege began, I see a ray of hope." Flashing a beautifully radiant smile, she briefly, yet firmly grabbed both our hands. We set off in search of Joseph's taxi.

# VIII

WHILE MAKING OUR WAY TO THE taxi stand, I
telepathed Sirius and asked if he'd caught the image
of Midge's granddaughter Annie.

"Too right, mate," was his measured reply. "She'll be
apples. Finding that youngster should be open slather.
Fact is, Gracie and I think we may have seen her at St.
Bernadette's. Give me a day or so. We'll let you know."
It was a relief knowing that Sirius was on the job.

Dunstan and I were scanning the cabstand when
cab 714 rolled up. Midge's name was like magic. We
quickly folded into the back seat and told Joseph of
our mission. Even more quickly, he reached into his
glove box and produced two proctor identity tags.
Dunstan offered him a generous tip, which Joseph
refused by explaining, "If Midge sent you, you're part
of the solution, not part of the problem. There's a
good sized group of Praesepians working with me and
Midge. Here's my card, I'm yours any time."

He offered us a lift to Everen's headquarters and

gave us a brief tour of the area before delivering us to the I.C. There were several nearby buildings that had been commandeered by the military. Joseph identified them as the offices of logistics, intelligence and administration.

"The conference room you're wanting is on ground level, to the right," he pointed as he drove up to the tall, sleek Intelligence Center whose exterior featured countless shale-tinted glass windows framed in dark blue, anodized metal. The cab stopped next to a wide portico that was bustling with groups of proctors climbing its broad-staired entry.

"The meeting is an orientation for new intelligence officers," Joseph continued. "I've been ferrying them in all morning. In the past few weeks I've listened to many new arrivals from Erylia, several of whom have mentioned their home cities of New London and New Pittsburgh. I've learned enough to know that there's an epidemic among the children on Erylia, which is believed to have compromised their future ability to reproduce."

We were grateful to have a new ally, especially one offering this latest gem of news. Joseph had just confirmed last night's discovery in the dreamtime. We both shook his hand, and left him with a generous tip. Setting out toward the entry of the I. C., we had our caps pulled low and our mental antennae on high alert. Passing through the foyer we fell in step behind a group of proctors funneling into a conference room that occupied an entire wing of the ground floor. Stepping inside, I was surprised to find how large it was. It must have had room for at least two hundred people, and was nearly full.

We were each handed a folder of information. Calmly taking two seats on an outside aisle near the back, we removed our caps and began reading. Before long, I was scanning the energy fields of officers nearby, searching for any signs of alarm. We had entered the conference virtually unnoticed. Our eavesdropping family raised a telepathic cheer over that success.

As Marshal Everen entered the room, the normal din of hundreds of people suddenly hushed. He was exactly as I'd dreamed him but in Erylian military dress. This morning's uniform sported a gold braided epaulet on his right shoulder, with his collection of pips, metals and stripes the most impressive array in the room.

Dunstan and I rose briskly to our feet as the entire room stood. Everen strode to the podium and loudly said, "Welcome. Please be seated." He was all business, introducing himself as the Erylian Intelligence Commander. He stated that we had forty minutes in which to understand the importance of our mission on Praesepe.

"We are here... to assure... the continued survival... of the Erylian culture," the tall, middle-aged officer stated in a loud, flat voice. He paused between words, apparently for dramatic effect. "Nothing more ... nothing less."

"I know how distasteful it can be to forcibly take young Praesepians from their families.," the Marshal continued. "I am here to clarify for each of you that our planet faces a crisis. Our government has sought to keep this news from our population, for fear of its profoundly demoralizing effects." Many in the audience bowed their heads as sense of gloom settled over the room.

"For the past two generations, many of our offspring have been born with two distinct disabilities. The first is that their hormonal systems are not maturing. In addition to this unfortunate fact, their mental development seems to stall around the age of puberty. Our best scientists have said they believe an environmental toxin to be the cause, however they have been unable to isolate it."

"I know a number of you men have families that are experiencing these problems first hand." Some men nodded, others groaned. Dunstan telepathed a sense of excitement to me and to the family listening back at the Abyssinian. "Looks like we may have more allies in Braeoon than we could have imagined," he said.

"Yes, Dunstan," Nandia replied, "It's great news to see how many disturbed proctors there are. It appears that quite few object to their government's plan to assure future generations of Erylians. They've instituted a program that dismisses two generations' health problems! We need to be careful, however, not to befriend those who are hoping to replace their own children with kidnapped Praesepians."

"Aye, Lassie," he replied. "There's a worry I'd not considered. Which leaves me wonderin'— what is to become of the wee troubled Erylians back home? Degraded to second class citizens, at the very best. Your wisdom, Nandia, always gets me ta thinkin'. 'Tis good to have ye along."

After a moment of proctors grousing, Marshal Everen asked for silence. The audience soon calmed down. "Let me continue. Our intelligence research departments have been working on finding answers to these problems for the last ten years."

"You may have heard rumors that some Praesepian children have propensities toward telepathy and teleportation. Previously, such abilities were relegated only to members of the Galactic Council or members of a few rare planets' noble families. Here on Praesepe the Grand Council Elder Nandia resides. She has been teaching these skills to a select group of Praesepians for the past decade. Those children who possess these extraordinary skills also exhibit extremely high levels of physical vitality. They seem to be able to easily transfer these traits within their peer group.

"Our scientists believe these traits can be passed on to future Erylian generations, insuring the survival of our race."

Everen went on to describe their development of their zinc shield to thwart telepathy and teleportation. Without these abilities, the intelligence chief suggested, Praesepian youths should be quite easy to detain and transport to Erylia.

"Here at Intelligence Headquarters, we believe taking Nandia's granddaughter Gracie into custody to be a major coup. She is said to be telepathic and capable of teleportation. Through her, we may have access to a possible teacher of these extraordinary skills. We also believe that holding the girl would improve our negotiating stance, should the Grand Council make the mistake of meddling in Erylian affairs.

"Gracie is young enough to be socialized into our culture," Everen's tone was persuasive. Then he elevated the intensity of his voice. "Unfortunately, today...," he paused, sternly scanning faces in the room. "Today,

I am here to inform you that, as of thirteen hundred yesterday afternoon, Gracie went missing."

Everen waited a moment for the implications of that news to percolate into the minds of his audience. "This means that either the young lady found sympathetic Erylians who helped her escape, or that Nandia, perhaps with a group of allies, has found a way to neutralize our zinc disruptor field. Be most assured that if this action was due to a traitor in our midst, that traitor will be identified and executed.

"We have corrobating news that several copper-scanning teams have briefly identified the presence of copper moving, both within Braeoon Gardens and within the city itself. After following their scanners, however, our people have run into dead ends. This news is enough to alert us to the presence of an underground rebel terrorist force that is operating beyond our abilities to detect their presence."

Subdued murmurs arose sporadically across the room, begetting a wave of conversation and questions. Watching energy fields I noted that some reflected worry, a few reflected relief. Once again, Everen asked for silence.

"So, we will have to resort to our time-honored methods of methodically examining every hotel register, searching every room, every vacant apartment, and looking under every rock where Nandia and her people could be hiding Gracie. I want every one of our copper sensors immediately manned and on the streets until we find her.

"These people are smart. They are capable. They are more than capable. Photographs of Nandia and Gracie are included in your information packets."

Throughout Everen's diatribe, I'd failed to see any evidence that last night's dreaming had penetrated to his conscious mind. Unless it was completely my fabrication, his experience of the dream had to be stored in his subconscious. I mentally sent a request asking him to recall his dreams of the previous evening and hoped that it wouldn't take too long.

"We must recover the missing child, Gracie," he continued. "Once we have recaptured this young lady, we will immediately remove her to Erylia. As of now, and until she is safely imprisoned on Erylia, this is priority one. The success of our mission demands it. The success of our society demands it.

"Please now stand with me. Erylians, hear me. Hear me well. We must recover our ability to seed new generations on our planet. Our very bloodlines depend upon it; Erylia's future depends upon it." Here the Marshal stepped from behind the podium and stood rigidly at attention before the roomful of proctors. First one proctor, then another came to his feet and mirrored their commander's stance. Soon the entire room had followed suit.

"We have the opportunity to restore our civilization to its future," he loudly decreed. "It is a future that now includes the ability to telepath and teleport. Otherwise, we are a lost civilization. The future of Erylia rests in your hands, gentlemen."

Marshal Everen proudly saluted the group, hand rigidly glued horizontally above his right eye. He maintained this pose, waiting to drop his hand until everyone had returned his salute. Hands snapped to foreheads as eyes stared directly ahead. Less than ten minutes earlier I'd seen proctor energy fields showing discomfort with Erylia's Praesepian strategy. While few of these dissenters were hesitant to return Everen's salute, his steady, unwavering gaze convinced them otherwise. Dunstan and I were among the first to comply.

It was as slick a piece of salesmanship as I'd ever seen. I sent a message to the family back at the Abyssinian, "Did you get all that?"

"Yes," Elli responded. "How to make stealing another planet's children sound heroic," she added. "A textbook case of flaunting apparently patriotic ends to justify barbaric means and then elevating that to a religious experience."

"Erylia's problem," I added, "Is that they have no effective means to address the cause of their difficulties back home. They've completely abandoned any idea that they have the power to heal. It sounds to me like they're using toxic medications, or some other poison in their food chain or water supply. I expect that, with half a chance, we could help them heal this problem. Perhaps a visit to Erylia?"

"Aye, Lad, you're sounding spot on," Dunstan agreed. "But, first, let's sashay into Everen's office 'n offer our help."

"I'm wondering if the five of us, with Sirius, might want to appear at his doorstep and show him that kidnapping Gracie is no longer possible," I offered. "Once he realizes his strategy is doomed, perhaps then he'll be open to listening to other options. That might be the time to propose a visit to Erylia to see what healing support we can provide."

"I like it," Nandia admitted. "But it's risky. Give us some time here at the Abe to consider your idea. I'll get back to you. Can you lads remain anonymous for a few more minutes?"

I looked around the room. Proctors were milling about in groups, some excited and determined, but even more were hesitant and doubtful. It was obvious that many were concerned for their own families. After mentally eavesdropping, I could see that anxiety over Erylia's future had grown. Dunstan's earlier question over what was to become of a generation of sterile Erylian youngsters was a growing concern for this group of proctors.

"Dunstan," I telepathed, "we need some time away from this crowd. Let's teleport to Midge's kiosk at the spaceport. It's safer there, and now that we've seen this place, we can easily get back."

He readily agreed. Unobtrusively, we made our way through the crowd of officers. Once in the hallway, we decided to teleport individually. Dunstan walked ahead of me, as I watched for prying eyes. After I telepathed the "all clear," I saw him breathe deeply and then he disappeared. I took another look around, visualized Midge chatting at her kiosk, added the copper frequency, and soon found myself standing next to the information booth.

Our Scotsman was already walking away from the booth. I surveyed the area, and seeing no alarm caused by our sudden arrival, followed him to the restaurant we had visited earlier. We settled down with a cup of tea.

"So..., what do we hope to accomplish by visiting Everen's office?" I asked. "He's marching to the beat of a military bureaucracy and has little to say about the Erylians' mission on Praesepe."

"Aye, Laddie, that's surely how it sounds," Dunstan replied. "But then again, he's the lead bull in this stable. Ne'er forget there's more than one way to lead a lead bull. I've one of me feelin's that we can encourage him t' be singin' a tune beyond the range o' his superiors' music."

"Do you really think we can get him to stop kidnapping Praesepe's children?" I asked, raising my voice. As I heard my tone of irritation, I had to admit to myself that I was feeling cranky, and taking my anger out on Dunstan. I breathed deeply and asked myself if I was feeling cranky toward myself. That hit a nerve and suddenly I realized that I'd been trying to hide my self-hate because I felt powerless. The siege of Praesepe was feeling more and more hopeless and beyond our power to change.

With the voice of calm reason, Dunstan responded. "I'd like to learn how Everen personally feels about his mission here," he said. "I'd like to hear him talk about his wee lass back home — the one you met in your dreaming. I'd like to watch his face as it dawns on him that you know how to help those Erylian children heal their sufferin'."

"Right," I said. "But I still wonder if it wouldn't be wiser to go to Erylia immediately."

For one long moment, Dunstan just looked at me. Then he patiently responded. "We don't know how soon Everen plans to ship the Praesepian nubbins to Erylia. If we can convince him to let us experiment with some Erylian children here, then as soon as they arrive, we can begin testing and treating them. If successful — and I seem to remember that we do have some ability in these matters — 'twould be an easy skate convincin' him to delay plans for transportin' our Praesepian kids to Erylia."

As I listened, I breathed deeply. My fears of feeling powerless drained away, my anger evaporated. I appreciated my friend's gentle approach and his voice of wisdom. "Thanks, Dunstan," I said, and sent him an image of me hugging him, in the midst of this restaurant full of proctors. He smiled, and laid his massive hand over mine.

"Let's see if the rest of the family is on board," he suggested.

"Too late for that boys," Nandia's voice chimed in. "We're way ahead of you. We've got some new ideas that should make this a much easier job. Let's reconvene soon so we can compare notes.

"But before coming home," she added, "how about if you take a quick stop at Everen's office? That way we'll have a visual/feeling-tone to target-in on in case we want to teleport there later."

"No problem," I responded after Dunstan and I had nodded to each other. "We'll meet you back at our suite in The Abe right after the fly-by."

We decided to teleport from the restaurant to the hallway outside the I.C.'s conference room and find our way to Everen's office from there. "If we're questioned," I said, building a contingency plan, "we can say we're there to thank the commander for this morning's briefing. As to our assignments, we can suggest that we might be useful investigating the disappearance of the child who had formerly been in custody. And, our ace in the hole, will be volunteering to locate Nandia and bring her in for questioning. At that point let's set up a meeting for later and get out of there fast."

"As I've said before, Lad, I do like how your mind works," Dunstan replied. "At least it's a start."

There was no problem teleporting to our destination. On the off chance we might find Everen there, we ducked into the conference room. We planned to offer to escort him to his office, however, the room was vacant. Our problem was, we knew nothing of the location of Everen's office other than it was on the top floor of the I.C.

Neither of us wanted to field unwelcome questions that might arise while poking our heads into offices asking for Everen. Once, during our Aesirian adventure, the cat Arcturus had solved a similar dilemma by unexpectedly teleporting to us. After scouting a warlord's headquarters building for Nandia and myself, he easily led us to The Tabir's bedchambers.

I telepathed Sirius and asked if he would join us. He was delighted to be of use, so I sent him a mental image of the hallway outside the conference room. Within seconds he was there, calmly gliding figure-eights between our legs.

"We need to find Marshal Everen's office," I told the black fuzz-ball with the white toes. "Somewhere on the top floor. Guide us there?"

"She's apples, mate," Sirius telepathed. "Easy bludge for me to be a Sticky Beak. Boil the billy while I'm gone." This last comment was his way of saying that since Dunstan and I would just be waiting around during his scouting mission, we should use the time to prepare a meal for his return.

Sirius skittered along down the hallway and then disappeared up a stairway in the distance. This would be an easy job for him, no one would think to question a cat who was poking his head into the top-floor offices of the Erylian high command.

I was about to ask Dunstan if he had any other ideas for our cover story when Sirius meoooowed and, once again, was making figure eights between our legs.

"Sirius," I said, "I want to learn how to teleport outside of time as you and your father apparently do."

"Right, but not before these proctors pass." A covey of female proctors carrying beverages and clipboards went by, ignoring us and chattering away like songbirds. One finally noticed Sirius and lagged behind to caress his chin. He shamelessly leaned his weight into it, closed his eyes and revved up his motor. Satisfied, she nodded to us and hurried to catch up to her group.

As soon as they were out of sight Sirius telepathed, "807, gentlemen, middle of the top floor. Light traffic, let's get crackin'."

Dunstan scooped up the cat and we hurried toward the end of the hallway. Nearing the stairs, I suddenly remembered Midge's daughter, Annie, and placed my hand on Dunstan's shoulder, stopping him. I pulled the girl's photo from my jacket pocket and showed the image to Sirius.

"This is Annie, the girl we promised to help find," I said. "Do you remember her from St. Bernadette's?"

Sirius looked at the image, scratched his head with a hind paw and said, "Does look like one of the shielas we met while in prison. Show the picture to Gracie and see if she agrees. But no worries, mate, we'll see to it that Annie gets home."

We took the first flight of stairs two at a time. Looking up we could see the next two stairways were empty, so we teleported up to the second landing.

Repeating this maneuver, we quickly gained the eighth floor. The hallway was vacant. We strolled toward Everen's office and turned the corner into 807, our caps tucked snugly beneath our arms.

We found ourselves in an outer office, lined with bookcases behind chairs that faced a secretary's desk. Its uniformed occupant was a petite, graying, woman, who calmly looked up and asked, "May I help you, officers?"

"Yes, Maam," I offered. "We were hoping to catch Marshal Everen for just a moment. We do not have an appointment." I looked around, implanting the scene in my mind. The chest-high book cases were laden with law books and a number of potted plants. Behind the secretary's desk was an open doorway leading to an even larger office, where stood an imposing dark wooden desk, empty at the moment. The bank of floor-to-ceiling windows behind Everen's desk looked out over the spaceport.

"I'm sorry, young man, but the Marshal is in a meeting. What a lovely kitten you have there, what's its name?"

"Sirius, we're calling him," I responded. "He's a stray we found just today in Braeoon Gardens." I was hoping he would distract her from questions we weren't pre-pared to answer. The secretary reached up to scratch Sirius's ears and was rewarded with a loud purr. She then stood and reached out for him. He chirped and stepped deftly into her arms. I was proud of this cat. In addition to the subtle arts, he'd obviously learned charm from his father. He nuzzled her chin and settled in, seducing her with a full-throated purr that only got louder.

She was hooked. "Isn't he a love?" she chimed. "He doesn't look as if he's missed too many meals. Can you imagine anyone abandoning such a creature?"

"No, Maam," I replied. "We've just arrived from Erylia and unfortunately have no place to billet the creature. Would you happen to know of anyone who might give him a loving home?"

"Yo, Dogstar," I telepathically teased him as he was affection-basking. "Care to be forward scout for a while longer?" Who knows what he might learn? And he was so damn good at teleporting.

"I thought you'd never ask, ye fuzzy-headed flap-dragon," he mentally chided. "Not to worry, Mate. Just don't expect me to spend the day in this drooling dame's clutches."

"I'd be quite happy to take him," Everen's secretary replied. "If my daughter objects, I'm sure someone in our building would love to have him. I'll find a box for him to nest in until I can take him home this evening."

"Many thanks. That's quite a relief to know he won't be subjected to living a proctor's life," I said. "Would you object if we call back in a day or so, just to make sure he's doing well?"

"Of course not, young man," she said and handed me a card with Marshal Everen's details on it. "My name is Gladys, and you can reach me here any time during the day." Sirius gave her chin a second nuzzle, in response to her constant ear scratching. I could see Gladys was going to be getting much less work done this day.

"I must again say, we quite appreciate this, Gladys," I said. "Please relay our thanks for this morning's briefing to the Marshal. It clarified our work here on

Praesepe and was quite helpful. And please let him know we're sorry we missed him, but perhaps our duties will allow us to visit at some other time."

Grace glanced at our name badges as she struggled to maintain a comfortable platform for Sirius while shaking our hands. Dunstan had remained thankfully silent during this exchange — in size alone he was memorable enough. He nodded his thanks as I exchanged goodbyes several times. Backing out of the office, we stepped into the hallway and headed in the same direction from which we'd arrived.

"Let's go home," Dunstan telepathed. I nodded and we each visualized our suite at the Abe. By now it was becoming second nature to evoke the frequency of copper, and in a thrice we found ourselves standing between Nandia and Elli, snugly safe-havened. Relieved to be done with our masquerade, I flipped my cap onto the couch.

## IX

"GOOD WORK, BOYS," Elli said. "Having Sirius stand post in Everen's office was a stroke of genius. I just hope he doesn't lose too much fur, with Gladys trying to cuddle him into a coma."

We all laughed as Dunstan added, "Aye, he was about to turn green from an overdose of mollycoddle, but he'll find a way to stay out of harm's way. That cat has a wealth of untapped inner resources."

I telepathically tuned in to the cat and asked how he was faring.

"Soft collar job here, mate," he replied. "I'm in a box 'neath Gladys' desk, picking up on a conversation she's having with Everen. Bugger off, I'm needin' to listen."

Nandia, who had listened to this exchange, told the family, "Sirius is monitoring a chat between Gladys and the Marshal. That should help us stay one jump ahead of his proctors. Speaking of which, I think we need to return our uniforms to the laundry. Their absence will surely be noticed before long, and the news that five uniforms have been misplaced by laundry staff will soon find its way to Everen's desk. Now that we know there's a concerted search for us and Gracie, we need to cover our tracks as much as possible."

"A wise suggestion, young lady." It took a moment to realize that it was Abe who had telepathed that message. "You can always return to the laundry if you need uniforms again."

"I'll take them back," I offered. "But first we need to decide if we want to meet with Marshal Everen. At the moment it looks to be a forlorn hope — by rescuing Gracie, we made a certain enemy of Everen."

"Good point, Bearns. For this mission to succeed, we must build an alliance with him," Nandia said. "And he knows that I'm behind Gracie's escape — especially since she's the only kidnap victim who has disappeared."

"Aye," Dunstan added. "Should have rescued a dozen 'a the ankle biters. Missed that chance to cover our tracks. Ya can be sure we'll be needin' a convincin' olive branch to mollify the chap."

"A bit of kronk mozzle here mates," Sirius telepathically interrupted, alerting us to bad news. "Everen, the blighter, just suffered a right scaldin' over Gracie's disappearance. His Erylian commander demanded ta know how it happened, which our bodger was at a loss to explain. But have no doubt Everen's a clever cove. He didn't get this high on the food chain without knowin' how ta play the game."

As Sirius continued, his tone grew worried. "So now Everen's talkin' with Gladys about movin' up plans to transport Praesepe's kids to Erylia, soonest. That's his strategy to distract the brass from Gracie's disappearance. He's wantin' Gladys to file the paperwork needed to prove that they're running outta places to house the scudders. It's a right Big Barney back on Erylia over Gracie's scarper."

Gracie had been silent since our arrival. Watching the colors of her aura, I could see that she was puzzling over some dilemma. The vibrant blues and golds that normally surrounded her head and shoulders had turned muddy and gray. Suddenly, a streak of violet washed across her aura.

"I've got an answer to that problem," she happily asserted.

"Yes?" Nandia responded.

"How about if I surrender myself to Everen?"

The rest of us roared in a simultaneous howl of protest. I was first to voice my disapproval. "Why is it that you and your grandmother are always offering yourselves as sacrificial lambs to the bad guys? Is this some genetic disorder?" I was angry and frustrated that I might, once again, have to face losing someone I love.

"Bearns," Nandia soothed, "You're forgetting that my captivity during our Geasan mission, while risky, was the key to untangling the problems on Fantibo. Of course I wouldn't let Gracie go back to the proctors without me, but it's a very good idea when you think about it."

Elli dove into the fray, "But, it's a safe bet that Everen will anticipate Gracie and you escaping at will. He knows of your ability to teleport."

"I've got the answer for that too, El," Gracie said. "He wouldn't suspect us of being able to teleport if we let him confiscate the copper we're carrying, now would he?"

The brilliance of that idea stunned everyone into silence. At the very least, it would end the all-out manhunt that Everen had demanded during his conference this morning. And Gracie was right. Everen had no idea that we no longer needed copper to neutralize their zinc disruptor field — surely none of us were about to divulge that cherished secret.

So if Nandia and Gracie relinquished their copper, Everen would believe them incapable of teleporting. Gracie's plan was the olive branch Dunstan pointed out we so urgently needed! Having both Gracie and Nandia in custody would clean the egg off Everen's face, appease the tensions that Gracie's disappearance had sparked on Erylia and pacify his senior commanders — all in one fell swoop! Meanwhile, Nandia and Gracie would be free to escape from captivity whenever they wanted to shop, take a walk or return to the Abyssinian.

"Aye, Lassie, you've a mind as fine as pure gold, so you do," Dunstan congratulated Gracie. She ducked her head in embarrassment, yet her smile showed she was well pleased with her ideas.

"Nandia, how effectively can you tandem teleport with Gracie in an emergency?" Elli asked.

"Well, you know we did improve during our practice earlier today," she replied. "And we'll have more opportunities to work out the kinks. Right now I'd say we can safely teleport as long as we stay together."

"Aye, that's welcome news, so 'tis," Dunstan remarked. "And if the bastards try to separate you?"

"Well, until Gracie can safely teleport solo, she's at risk."

"Then we make sure Everen understands that

a condition of surrendering yourselves is that you remain together," Elli said.

"And once we're locked up, we can telepath our location and Sirius can join us. He always keeps us safe." Gracie added. "I know I can do this, Nana, I just know it." I believe it was this suggestion that tipped the scales.

"I'm all in for this ride," Sirius telepathed from beneath Gladys's desk. "Now that we can use copper's frequency without the metal, 'twill be a piece a' cake ta keep Gracie out of harm's way. Best I make sure to stay out of Everen's sight in the meantime. Why add to his suspicions?" It was this sharp insight that reminded us all how much we trusted this feline's abilities.

"Well, Gracie's plan does give us more options," I conceded. The more we talked about the idea, the better I liked it.

"If Everen's growing more indignant about Gracie's absence, we need to move quickly," Elli said. "I wonder, if we turn Gracie and Nandia in, might we propose to Everen that he keep the kidnapped kids here on Praesepe?"

"Aye, with a bit a' fair wind, that could happen," Dunstan mused. After a moment's further consideration he added, "If the cretin won't budge on trying to export our kids, we can all simply teleport back here and start over. There will always be new options. Why not give it a go?"

The chill of our protests over Gracie's idea hadn't taken long to thaw. My mind was in high gear as I continued brainstorming. "I could tell Everen about our success with Geasa's epidemic. Then I could outline a plan to begin working with a dozen or so afflicted

Erylian youths." I talked quickly as more thoughts raced through my mind. "Perhaps we can convince him to bring some of the Erylian kids here so I can begin testing them. We should be able to identify the pathogens that are undermining their health. Working with them for a few days should show Everen that there are vibrational remedies that will help each of them restore health to their bodies."

"If we can convince him 'a that Laddie," Dunstan said, "then we might just get his help convincin' his government to re-think the desperate measures they've taken."

And, in that moment, we all had a glimpse of the light at the end of this tunnel.

✕

WE IMMEDIATELY SET TO WORK. Dunstan projected to the boiler room and returned with a copper bracelet each for Nandia and Gracie. Elli tuned into Sirius.

"We appreciate your decision to return to lock-up once again," she telepathed to the cat. "We know you'll not fail to watch Gracie's back." A loud, telepathed purr came back in response.

"We'd like to get Gracie in to Everen's office as quickly as possible," El added. "Can you let us know when it's best to do that?" None of us wanted Everen to proceed any further with his plan to dispatch Praesepe's children to Erylia.

Sirius agreed, signed off, and promised to get back to as soon as he knew more of Everen's plans. Nandia and Gracie began preparing a midday meal. I rewrapped our proctor uniforms and, with Abe's help, made my way unseen to the hotel laundry.

I walked in, laid the five uniforms on the countertop

and said, "These were delivered to our room by mistake. But don't worry; the correct uniforms arrived a few minutes later. I thought you'd probably want to return these to their rightful owners before they were missed."

Looking greatly relieved, the clerk quickly reached out and shook my hand. "Thank you, thank you, Sir," she gushed. "I don't know how it happened, but you've certainly solved this morning's mystery. Everyone here has been searching high and low, trying to figure it out." She set about hanging them on her conveyor rack and was checking her inventory log as I smiled, waved and stepped out the door.

"Incoming proctors to your right," Abe telepathed. "Due any second."

I didn't stop to consider options, I simply imagined our suite upstairs, breathed, recalled copper's frequency and was standing in our sitting room faster than Sirius could snatch a fly from mid-air.

"Those lads you just missed are right now picking up the uniforms you returned," Abe informed us. "I have to admit, you folk do have a lovely gift for timing."

After I was warmly congratulated for that near miss, we all sat down to eat. Gracie served a lovely pumpkin soup, crowded with brown rice and lentils, steaming hot and adorned with fresh herbs and a dollop of cream.

"You have Abe to thank for this food," Nandia told us. "Somehow he had the kitchen deliver it from stock that had arrived just this morning from Braeoon's outlying farms."

"You know, Abe," Elli said, "If you keep treating us

like this, there's a chance we won't leave. I'm feeling loved, safe and well taken care of."

"And, Your Royal Highness of Aesir," he replied, "I would be more than delighted if you chose to make this your second home."

Elli visibly softened upon hearing that invitation. "I shall always remember your generosity, Abe," she replied. "It's a great comfort knowing that you so wonderfully look out for us."

"And that, my Queen, is my great honor."

Talk carried on as we dug into a vibrantly colored salad gleaming with live vegetables. Butter and orange marmalade adorned newly baked multigrain rolls. There was enough food to feed our group twice over.

"I trust you'll rectify the fact that I'm not being fed to my usual standards," Sirius telepathed, interrupting our table talk. "But meanwhile there's news. Everen just asked Gladys to hold all calls and cancel all appointments for the rest of the afternoon. He's secluding himself in his office to finalize the plan to export Praesepe's kids to Erylia.

"His ego's taken a beating. One of his sources on Erylia called to say there's a move afoot to send a fact-finding mission to Praesepe, led by Everen's commander. The Marshal was a bit gun shy before taking on the siege and now even more worried that a failure could cost him his career. Seems like the right time to be puttin' a knot in yer bluey."

Tension flashed across everyone's face hearing that now was the time to return Gracie to Everen's clutches. "But I'd hoped we could take another stroll through Braeoon Gardens before going back to work," Elli objected. "I yearn to feel the grass under my feet and sunlight on my face. Sirius, do you think you could join us?"

"Aye," was the cat's telepathic reply. "I'm fer that, boots 'n all. I'll be a sticky beak here for another tick, then there with ya."

"Yes," added Gracie. "A romp in the park would be fun. And can I practice teleporting while we're there, Nana?"

"Wonderful idea, Darling," Nandia replied. Dishes were cleared as we debated whether to carry the copper Dunstan had just retrieved or return it to the boiler room.

"We know Everen's lit a fire under his troops," I said. "It seems just plain foolish to travel with copper. Especially when we don't need it."

"True enough, Bearns," Nandia answered. "That is unless we feel like letting ourselves be taken by the proctors while we're out."

"There's pure poetry in that idea, Lassie," Dunstan mused. "But there's the chance some over-eager young officer with a patrol of copper scanners will be wantin' to make a name for himself and isolate us in separate vehicles. We'd be forced to teleport in order to escape. Trouble is, we'd show our hand and reveal we don't need the copper any more. Best not to risk being arrested."

"So right you are, Dunstan," Nandia replied. "For my penance I shall tandem teleport with Gracie and return our treasure to the boilers." After quickly gathering up the copper bracelets, the pair disappeared.

It was then that Sirius appeared. He leapt up to a counter stool and began grooming. He had not much to report, other than that Everen was still sequestered in his office and on the phone with trusted officers, hoping they would reassure him that his plans were sound. Nandia and Gracie returned, and we projected en masse to the grove of fig trees where we had first taken refuge yesterday.

We were the only people around as we stood beneath the trees' thick canopy of leaves. Breathing deeply of the fresh air, we relished the view before us and the feel of the ground beneath our feet. A vast parkland opened in front of us, wide enough to accommodate an interplanetary soccer game and thousands of spectators. It was carpeted with a lush blue-green lawn, flanked by majestic fig trees. Although the sky was mostly grey, it was a warm day. Low clouds parted periodically to reveal one of Praesepe's two suns.

Prying off her shoes, Gracie ran up to Dunstan, tagged him and shouted, "You're it." The game was on just as a cloudburst began. We ran through the rain in the open space that bordered the trees, laughing like children. Dunstan began chasing Elli. I projected myself, landing flat on the ground in front of him, and entangled his feet. He tumbled over me, laughing as he fell to the ground.

"Grand move, Laddie. But now you're it," he crowed. I jumped up, shook my head to clear my eyes of rainwater and took off after Nandia.

I teleported to where she stood and easily tagged her. "You wanted to get caught," I accused her as she laughed, kissed me and sprinted away. Sirius appeared and darted around each of us, tempting taggers and then racing easily out of reach. Despite posing as a sodden, black sponge, he seemed oblivious to the rain and was the only one not out of breath as we slowed to a stop a short while later. We gathered at a sheltered spot beneath the giant fig tree.

"So, Gracie," I asked as we dried our faces, "would you like to practice teleporting here?"

She was eager for more instruction. Nandia began with several short tandem leaps, between our fig tree and another one on the opposite side of the playing field. Next, Gracie took a few tandem hops with me, then Elli, and finally Dunstan. She was quickly mastering the ability to mentally focus on her destination, recall copper's frequency, and then project expanded bits of her consciousness, from a particle to a wave and finally a field.

"Try projecting yourself while holding Sirius," Nandia suggested.

The cat leapt into her waiting arms and asked, "Where to, Princess?"

"Over there," she nodded at a tree across the clearing. The pair imagined their arrival, used 8-3-4-1-0-8-3-7 and easily arrived at their destination. We cheered their success, clapping and whistling and then teleported over to join them.

"You're a grand Lass, so ye are." Dunstan hugged the youngster who stood happily in our midst, beaming at her accomplishment. "Now we know that the two of you can continue practicing even if Everen imprisons you alone."

For a while, Nandia had been lost in thought, but now added more to our plan. "I'm wondering if only Bearns, Gracie and I should visit Everen," Nandia said thoughtfully. "Bearns and I can easily make the case for treating the Erylian youngsters. Once that's done, Bearns, you can excuse yourself. You're more useful being free from Everen's custody. Gracie and I will offer ourselves as prisoners. Sirius can come and go as we need him, once he knows where we're being held. If Everen doesn't associate Dunstan and Elli with us right now, you'll both have more freedom to maneuver."

"True enough," Elli said. "And if you need us, we can be there in a flash."

We projected back to the Abyssinian to clean up. Sirius quickly licked himself dry and then announced his need to teleport back to Gladys's office. "I'll see you, I pray, sooner than you think," he said, feigning sadness, and was off.

"Bearns, you'll be wantin' ta take a bit o' copper while escortin' our fair maidens to Everen's office," Dunstan advised. "It could come in handy as a bargainin' chip. Or you might decide to inform Everen that you have it, just in case you want him to know you can teleport yourself out 'a there in a hurry."

"Good idea," I agreed.

"And we had better plan that you'll be followed once you leave there," Elli added. "If possible, leave on foot. Don't tip your hand about teleporting unless absolutely necessary. I think you should head for our room at The Don. Let me know when you're about to arrive and I'll watch from that hotel's lobby to see if anyone's tailing you. Once we're sure you're clear we'll be able to return to the Abyssinian safely."

"It's great to have you both watching my back," I said. "Thank you." Then I recalled what I'd heard at Everen's morning briefing and another worry emerged.

"Abe, can you let us know if Everen's proctors begin showing more than their usual interest in your boiler room?" I asked. "After we've surrendered our fair maidens and their copper, some proctor might begin to wonder why our copper wasn't picked up by their scanners. It's not much of a mental leap for them to suspect we're keeping our reserves hidden in the outdated copper infrastructures of older buildings. How many hotels do you think still have copper boilers in their basements?"

"That's a very good question, young man," our trusted elder replied. "There are only two other buildings in Braeoon ancient enough to house such antiques. I'm not sure if their management ever spent the money needed to remove their outdated copper boilers. So three hotel boiler rooms, along with a few aging industrial plants, will the first places proctors search once they get wise to the idea."

"Right. So we need ta find another place ta hide our copper, or else let the proctors find it," Dunstan observed. "But if we're willing to let the proctors confiscate it, it would be better if they found it anywhere but here in the Abyssinian. Abe, do ye know if the Vasantamos or the Don are among the hotels with copper boilers?

"Now that you mention it," he replied, "I'd forgotten that the Vasantamos may well have an antiquated boiler room."

"We'll investigate." Dunstan said. "Bearns, leave the problem with us. We'll have some ideas by the time you return from Everen's office."

Each of us was a bit nervous about taking the next step. I muttered to myself, trying to think of anything I might have overlooked, prior to teleporting to Everen's office. Gracie worried that she might not be coming back to the Abyssinian; until Nandia reminded her they would be projecting themselves back whenever they wanted.

"The proctors will most likely patrol our cell on a regular schedule," she explained to her granddaughter. "Once we know their schedule we'll be free to teleport as long as we return in time. Sirius will be watching as well.

"But, we do not want the Erylians to discover that we can teleport without the use of copper," Nandia added. "We'll need to be very careful about how we talk about our copper to Everen. The less said, the better. It definitely needs to be visible when we arrive."

"I'll keep mine concealed, you two can wear your bracelets," I said. "If a scanner locates mine, well, I'll surrender it. I've always got copper's frequency. Shall we stop by the boiler room and pick up what we need and then teleport to the Intelligence Center?"

I begrudged all the time it took us to hide and then chase after our copper, but still wasn't ready to surrender it all quite yet. It was time, however, to surrender Nandia and Gracie to Everen. El and Dunstan travelled with us to the boiler room. My medallion from Geasa went over my neck and under my shirt. To Dunstan I said, "Send a message to Sirius that we're on our way."

Nandia, Gracie and I held hands, smiled at each other and breathed deeply. I chuckled at the irony that, for this trip, we needn't remember the copper frequency. I focused on my image of Everen's office and then telepathed it to my travelling companions. Together we each imagined projecting a particle, then a wave, and finally a field of our individual energies to the space in front of his desk and quickly we were there. We dropped hands and formed a line facing the Erylian commander.

He was bent over a print-out ledger page, completely unaware of our arrival. His black uniform jacket hung from a coat tree in a corner beside large picture windows, his black tie swung loosely from the open collar of his starkly pressed white shirt. He was checking a long column of figures, his free hand mussing his tousled graying hair.

"Excuse me, Marshal Everen?" Nandia spoke quietly.

He looked up, surprise registering in his eyes. He slowly parked his pen next to the ledger and then examined Nandia and me — several times. Suddenly a flash of great relief washed away his otherwise tired and worried face as he realized Gracie was standing in front of him. He took another look and then recognized Nandia.

"Well, this is quite a welcome turn of events," the Intelligence Chief said, sitting back in his chair with a sigh. "Might I enquire as to what you're doing here?"

Nandia introduced both of us as Council Delegates. She used her soft, melodic voice as she reassured him we had come hoping to create an alliance that could be beneficial to us all.

"And what do you propose, young lady?" he asked.

"We would like to return my granddaughter, Gracie, to your protective custody," Nandia said, "in return for several concessions."

"And why I might want to consider such an idea?" he said. His tone had suddenly grown a suspicious edge, as if wanting to impress upon us that he was not about to be seduced into giving up Erylia's dominance of Praesepe. Yet, I saw that the otherwise muted blue and gray colors of his energy field were now streaked with bright reds of hopeful excitement.

He turned his gaze toward me and said, "You, Sir, seem familiar. Did I not see you at this morning's proctors' briefing?"

I had hoped that being out of uniform would change my appearance enough to avoid being recognized. Now, however, that cat was out of the bag. "Yes, Sir, I was there," I admitted. "And I do apologize for not introducing myself prior to this morning's briefing. In my defense, I must say that the misstep did allow us to learn about the problems on Erylia that have led to your invasion of Praesepe. Our only desire for being here today is to initiate a mutually agreeable resolution to the conflict between Erylia and Praesepe." I was hoping that Everen would overlook my diplomatic faux pas when Nandia intervened.

Leaning forward, she said, "I'm not sure if you're aware, Sir, that Bernard and I were the team of Galactic Council envoys who helped Geasa on Fantibo recover from the Saragalla epidemic. We have some skill as healers and perhaps could be of assistance with the problems on Erylia that have led you to make captives of so many of our young people."

"Yes, now that you mention it," he replied, his tone softening, "I do recall your names being associated with that amazing feat of recovery." He paused, examined Nandia and Gracie again and, with a sudden note of suspicion asked, "You mentioned concessions?"

"If we leave my granddaughter in your custody, I must be allowed to remain with her to assure that she is properly treated," Nandia stated in a steady, even tone making it clear that she considered this condition to be non-negotiable.

"I would be an idiot to agree to such a condition, when it appears you are able to teleport out of any confinement I could impose."

"But, Sir," Gracie interjected, "As a measure of good faith, we will relinquish our copper." That said, she and Nandia removed their bracelets and placed them on the desk in front of Everen.

The Marshal looked surprised and nodded. "I'm impressed," he said. As we had hoped, he clearly regarded Gracie's return to custody as a means of restoring his sagging reputation.

"And what of you, young man?" he asked me.

"I ask that I remain free to come and go as I choose. I also ask that you allow me to examine a group of your Erylian youths. I wish to test their health for the causes of the seemingly incurable malady that has precipitated this siege upon Praesepe. Testing will be done using an intuitive, non-invasive method to determine whether we can create effective remedies for the healing of the Erylian condition."

After giving Everen a moment to digest that opportunity, Nandia returned to the matter of their voluntary incarceration. "Another concession we seek for surrendering to your custody," she added in a warm, conciliatory tone, "is that, for now at least, the Praesepians you are holding remain on Praesepe.

"And, with all due respect," she straightened before continuing, "we ask that you cease and desist from any further removal of Praesepians from their homes. Please know that if our methods prove successful at improving the health of your young people, we will be asking that you return your hostages to their homes."

"I see," he said as he now leaned forward, planting his elbows squarely in the middle of his desk and steepling his fingers. "You seem to be quite well informed of what has been happening in this office," he said accusingly as he dourly considered Nandia's offer.

His energy field had shifted from suspicion, to excitement, then caution, and back again. I watched as bright blue and green colors now suddenly became muted and muddy. A streak of lemon-green shot across the top of his aura but, with a strong force of will, he suppressed a powerful inner impulse to somehow deceive us.

"And if I don't agree to these conditions?" Everen asked after a moment's hesitation.

I slowly and carefully picked up the two bracelets sitting in front of him. "Well in that case, Marshal Everen," I paused for effect, "we shall be on our way.

"But before we decide upon that option, may we...?"

Placing her hand on my arm, Nandia interrupted me. "Marshal," she began, "many of the healing modalities we used in Geasa are well suited to serve Erylia's needs. The Grand Council selected us to deal with both the Geasan and Praesepian crises. We tell you of the Geasa mission to encourage you to trust our motivations." She paused while both of us telepathically encouraged him to know it was safe to us.

"If you decide you cannot trust us," she continued, "we would pursue the more difficult option of travelling to your homeland to offer a similar proposal to your leaders there. That choice would cause an unfortunate delay in resolving this matter and would be quite costly to both Erylia and Praesepe. Be assured, however, Marshal, that we are quite capable of making that happen."

From the thoughtful manner with which Everen turned away to stare out his window, it was obvious that the consequences of not taking Gracie and Nandia into custody were becoming clearer to him. As I listened to his inner thoughts, I realized that he was worried about the high-level fact-finding delegation that could be on its way from Erylia. What would their conclusions be after they learned he had refused our offer? And, what repercussions would befall his command if our testing proved to be successful, as it had been in Geasa? The news media would have a field day with either story. His aura reflected a clear desire to agree to our proposal, yet I also sensed, as I had earlier, that he was stubbornly hiding some strong, inner desire.

"Very well," he said turning back to face us. "In return for holding Gracie and Nandia in custody, along with their copper, I will allow you, Bernard, to remain in Braeoon undisturbed by proctors. I will have a dozen of Erylia's youths transported here. They will be available to you in the ground floor conference room, within a day, two at the most. You may schedule whatever time you require to complete your examinations. However, I cannot agree that I will not transport Praesepian youths to Erylia. That will be decided by my superiors there. Should your work prove successful, I will intercede on your behalf and request that our government return your kidnapped children to their homes."

"And your forces will leave Praesepe," Nandia sternly added.

After only a moment's consideration, he replied, "Again, that is an agreement I cannot make, for the decision rests with my superiors. However, if your means prove successful, I will do everything I can to influence that outcome with the Erylian Imperial Council."

"Thank you, Marshal," I said. "And may I be informed of where Nandia and Gracie will be held?"

"It is my intention to keep them in this building. I believe it to be most secure facility on Praesepe."

I was relieved to hear that. I decided to press my luck. "And, Marshal, may I also request that Nandia and Gracie be allowed to join me for tomorrow's testing session? Their assistance with the details will be invaluable."

"Under the watchful eyes of a team of proctors, yes," he said.

"That is acceptable," Nandia responded, and turned to Gracie.

"OK?" she asked. Gracie smiled and nodded. Nandia repeated the question to me. I nodded as well.

"Then I believe, Marshal, as of now, Gracie and I are in your custody." She held out her hand to seal the deal. Marshal reached out and shook hers, mine and Gracie's.

"Very good," he said, suppressing the look of delight that was just beginning to dance across his face.

I turned and hugged Gracie. "Don't forget to call, Darling," I telepathed. "Remember, that you and you alone have the power to hold yourself above violation. But for now, how about a little theater? Let's put on a sad face for Everen's benefit shall we?"

We parted with tears in our eyes. I turned to Nandia and gave her a deep hug, hearing her message, "I like the sad face idea, Bearns. And let's get to the bottom of what this man is trying to hide, shall we?"

I mentally agreed and wiped an eye as Everen stood and escorted me to the door. There, he shook my hand. "Please return at 0900 tomorrow," he said. "I believe I can arrange for your work to begin then."

I nodded, turned and, with a final wave to Gracie and Nandia, stepped into Gladys's outer office. It was in that moment that a sudden, dark doubt-cloud cast its shadow across my mind.

# XI

I HAD HOPED TO FIND SIRIUS waiting for me in Everen's outer office. Instead, I found myself alone. I wondered where he was and called out to him telepathically. I wanted his help keeping track of Nandia and Gracie. And I wanted to hear his thoughts about what Everen was hiding.

"Relax, ya, fawnin' crook-plated maggot-pie. I'm at the moment condemned to Gladys duty." I smiled at his latest moniker creation and wondered about the nature of his current distasteful duty. "Her granddaughter is wrapped in the throes of ecstasy, ravaging me fur," he complained. "I'll scamper back soon to Everen's office. No need to flog the cat, I'll see that our girls are looked after."

In Siriusian, flogging the cat meant that I was reproaching myself. I was surprised that he'd picked up on that, and was suddenly aware of feeling quite alone. I questioned the wisdom of leaving Nandia and Gracie in Erylian custody — my fear of losing them welled up within me. I began breathing deeply. It took a few deep breaths for me to recover my trust that they could take care of themselves. Much more at peace, I stepped into the hallway, appreciating the success we'd had with Everen.

Remembering El's warning that I would most likely be followed, I put my mind on alert as I ambled along the hallway, down an elevator and out the building's front door. I walked casually, watching people's energy fields for any undue attention being directed my way. Initially I had thought to take a taxi to the Don, but as I started toward the space port I changed my mind, deciding instead to check in at Midge's information booth. She might have news that could shed light on plans to export Praesepian children to Erylia.

It wasn't long before I noticed a brightly colored aura amongst a crowd of pedestrians across the street. It was Dunstan! "I've got your back, Laddie," he telepathed. "Thought it best ta spot anyone tailin' ya early in the hunt."

I was reassured knowing that he was there and telepathed my new plan to visit Midge. I began to relax and enjoy the walk.

The cloudless sky was intensely bright, as if the twin Praesepian suns had challenged each other in a race to chase away all hint of a shadow. The walkways, however, were well shaded beneath ample tree canopies and brightly colored awnings. While most people were moving in the covered areas, it was still easy to study their auras. As I passed a flower vendor I noticed a tall, slender, young woman who was trying to disguise her interest in me behind a selection of roses.

"I don't think she's merely charmed by your good looks, Laddie," Dunstan telepathed from across the street. We both focused on her thoughts and realized that, via a hidden communicator, she was sending a message that I was headed toward the spaceport.

"Aye, she's got friends, so she does."

"Given that bit of news, I think I'll forego my visit to Midge and find a ride to the Don instead," I said. "No need to expose her to unwanted suspicion."

"'Tis a cannie plan, Lad. I'll pull up for a chat with her after you've found a ride. But, d'nae worry, I'll be watchin' the entrance to the hotel when you arrive," Dunstan said. "I'm wantin' ta see who else the Marshal's got shadowin' ya."

There was a taxi waiting in line outside the spaceport. I nodded to the driver who jumped out and held open the back door. I mentioned the hotel's name and sat back to enjoy the ride. Although keenly curious, I refrained from looking back to see if I was being followed. No need to tip our hand, especially with Dunstan on the job.

Then I visualized Nandia's smiling face, added the copper frequency and telepathed an inquiry asking how she and Gracie were faring. Her face lit up in a beautiful smile as she replied. "All's well here, Bearns. Bleak accommodations — little more than a prison cell with two gorillas outside. We're on the building's eighth floor, room Eight-Seventeen. Gracie and I are practicing solo and tandem teleporting to the Vasantamos while Sirius, the love, stands watch. I'll tell you, Everen's monkeys aren't having any fun growing more bored by the minute. Look forward to seeing you soon."

As the western-most, maroon-tinted of Praesepe's suns dipped below the horizon the afternoon heat began to wane. A few people strolled the nearly deserted sidewalks. Most, however, were hurried and withdrawn, intent upon their destinations. The auras of some carried the dark, muddy shades of green and gray, reflecting a deep fear of loss. As we passed, I telepathically sent them helper energies knowing that, at least on the subconscious level, they could use this energy constructively.

The subdued light of first sunset painted the surrounding clouds in warm hues of golden maroon. I couldn't recall if it was Freyr or Njoror that set first. Overhead the second, smaller sun shone brightly golden. I grew mildly irritated with myself and realized that the unusual light seemed strangely disquieting, as if my body was unsure whether the day was ending or not.

"Driver, I'm new here." I said, interrupting our silent ride. "I've forgotten the names of Praesepe's suns. What is the western setting sun called?"

"Njoror," came his curt reply.

"And do you recall, is Njoror considered the male or female of the pair?" I asked.

"Damned if I know." The driver sounded as if my questions were unwelcome. I was happy to let it pass for we were just pulling into the hotel's valet entrance. I paid the fare, tipped the cabbie and stepped out onto the cobblestoned entrance to the Don.

It was Dunstan's melodious voice I heard in my mind as I headed toward the front door. "You've picked up a couple a' parasites, Laddie. Looks like out-of-uniform proctors with copper scanners gettin' out a' the second taxi behind yours. El's inside. I'm sendin' her images a' the mongrels. See ya back at Abe's."

I slowed my pace as I led them through the hotel lobby. I wanted to give Elli ample time to examine the pesky critters. I telepathed a warm greeting as I passed her snuggled into a stuffed chair reading a newspaper.

"I'll follow these spooks for a bit and see what I can pick up from their thoughts and feelings," she mentally replied. "See you back at home."

I scurried up a full flight of stairs well ahead of my two shadows and then teleported to our room 213. It took only seconds to grab the gold coins I'd left on the mantelpiece. Then I projected to Abe's boiler room, depositing my copper medallion and returned to our suite. I was stowing the gold in our radionics pack when Dunstan and El arrived. Chattering away about the negotiations with Everen, we gathered up steaming cups of tea and headed into the sitting room. I telepathed Nandia, confirming everyone's safety and suggested that they eavesdrop on our conversation.

"Those boys who followed you are part of a clandestine intelligence network that Everen overseas," El said as we collapsed into comfortable couches. "They were talking about how they preferred these undercover jobs to other comparable positions within the I.C."

"Makes me wonder — is whatever Everen's hiding connected to this covert operation within his intelligence command?" I mused.

"He's quite fussed about being castigated by his superiors back home," Dunstan said. "Yer two shadows were told by Everen that he'd have their guts fer garters if they failed to find your hideout. He's countin' on 'em ta make sure he doesn't further let down his Erylian superiors. Imagine those boys gettin' all sweaty, flutterin' about after they lost ya at the Don." We all cackled at that picture.

"Yes," Elli then added. "And then they marched to the hotel's front desk to interrogate the staff about you, Bearns. Thank God they couldn't identify you other than a tall, dark haired, handsome man whose name is Bernard. No one at the front desk had a clue."

"That's great news," I said. "When he hears their report, Everen is going to know that I teleported away from the Don. He'll be cursing himself that he didn't check me for copper while I was standing there in front of him."

"Aye, but there's a bigger problem," Dunstan added. "I stopped in ta say hello to Midge. She says that Erylian intelligence is wantin' to find a starship that's returning to Erylia with extra passenger space. Everen musta lit a fire under 'em — they're desperate as starvin' rats — why they're even lookin' for starshuttles. Her source reckons Everen has pushed ahead his plans to export Praesepe's wee ones — whether 'twas before he made his promises to ya or not, I d'na ken.

"Well," Nandia telepathed from her lockdown at the I.C., "that could be what he was hiding from us."

"Wait, there's even more ill news," Dunstan said. "Midge said that a priority berthing slot for an inbound Imperial Erylian liner has been reserved." This came with a note of worry in his usually calm voice.

The afternoon light that streamed into the suite illuminated the growing bewilderment and worry tainting our faces like a quickly spreading rash.

"Right," Nandia dourly replied. "More indication that an Erylian delegation could be headed our way. If we have to, can we include them in your testing session Bearns?"

"There's a worry. I'll be prepared," I said. "If an Imperial Delegation is headed this way, you can bet Everen is going to be all spit and polish. We may want to visit him in the dreamtime and see if we can have a more honest conversation there."

"But, there is one spot a' good news I can offer," Dunstan finally added, "Sirius did drop in on me whilst I was talkin' with Midge. She's in love with the critter and will telepathically connect with him if she hears any news at the spaceport. We'll know if trouble begins a'brewin.'"

"Thanks, Dunstan, that is good news," Nandia said.

"Why don't Gracie and I rejoin you now at the Abe suite for a dreamtime session?" she then asked. "I'll ask Sirius if he'll stand watch for meddling guards. That way we're sure to be back before their next room check."

It wasn't long before we were reunited. Gracie looked excited being in the midst of this adventure, and was eager to talk of events since last we'd been together.

"The guards aren't mean or anything, but they sure seem cranky whenever they come to check on us," her voice was melodic like her grandmother's, but high-pitched and excited.

"The food they served was for carnivores, but they said they would see if the kitchen could offer something vegetarian this evening. Everen must have put the fear of God into them to make sure I don't disappear again."

"You're going to have an exciting tale to tell your

grandchildren," Nandia laughed. "And you've developed the ability to teleport on your own."

She then turned to us and said, "Let's lie out in our Haida circle." This is an indigenous cultural practice going back for many centuries that is used for group dreamtime meditations. Each of us found a spot on the circumference of a circle, laid supine and positioned our heads around its center, in line with each of Praesepe's cardinal points.

I remembered to ask Abe to keep watch for any approaching proctors. He informed us that a team of the rascals had just stopped at the front desk, inquiring as to whether Nandia or Gracie had been seen. "No need for worry," he said calmly. "Their curiosity quickly waned after finding that no one there could identify either of them."

Sirius telepathed from Nandia and Gracie's cell that no one had noticed their absence. "So, this latest inquiry must be related to Gracie's initial escape," he said.

"Aye, 'twas a good pull ta stay out a' the public eye," Dunstan observed. Then we settled down to dreaming together.

"Oh! Hold on please," Elli insisted and then leapt up to draw the window blinds. The afternoon light that so beautifully bathed our lavish suite suddenly dimmed and was replaced with an intriguing amber glow. I suspected our Aesirian immortal well knew which light would best serve our dreaming.

Nandia began the dreaming exercise with deep, connected breathing. She suggested that we each imagine Everen's face and ask for a dreamtime encounter that would reveal his true motivations and help him recognize ours. Then she began musical toning. We each joined in with our own harmonies and proceeded to sink into a deep state of relaxation.

Soon the only sound enfolding our group was the easy pace of each person's breathing. I closed my eyes to Elli's amber glow; feeling nestled in the bosom of a loving family. After a brief lapse into drowsiness, I entered the dreamtime and found myself sitting in a garishly appointed and dimly lit bordello from centuries long past. A bevy of scantily clad women bustled about, serving beverages. The scene dimmed and disappeared as I lapsed once again into that characteristic semi-conscious sensation of floating.

I mentally refocused on the bordello scene. An image of Everen appeared in the semi-darkness. He was wrapped in a dark robe and wearing a matching turban. Sitting cross-legged atop an array of brightly colored cushions, he was slightly elevated above a dozen or more people. Each of us was bathed in an amber-tinted light. A half-naked woman pouring drinks from an earthenware jug refilled a wooden cup sitting at Everen's side. He brought the rough-hewn container to his lips and began drinking.

Other than Everen, everyone there was unknown to me. They all seemed cowed by his presence. Like a peacock surrounded by a clutch of hens, he enjoyed exerting his superiority. After slamming his empty cup onto the table at his side, he licked his fingers and loudly belched. With piercing, beady eyes, he intently searched each of our faces, as if daring anyone to challenge his authority. An oppressive feeling of intimidation wafted through the room like a malodorous stench.

I was amazed at how this shade of Everen's personality contrasted with our earlier dream encounter. Even though I found his presence a bit daunting, I still wanted to learn more about the man's hidden motivations and encourage him to trust mine. I decided to speak up, knowing I might well be chastised for doing so. After a moment's reflection I decided to express some measure of solace for Erylia's predicament on Praesepe, in the hopes he would recognize me as an ally.

"Marshal Everen," I began, in a gentle, respectful tone, "I share your concerns for the future of Erylia's children. However, I believe that the causes of their illness can be remedied in ways that are safe and will restore their health. May I be allowed to explain further?"

His eyes flashed daggers in my direction as his lips compressed into a thin line. It appeared to physically hurt him as he attempted to bite back a spontaneous eruption of anger.

"And what are Erylia's problems to you, you off-world upstart?" he shouted. Clearly he recognized me from earlier in the day and had no compunction about expressing his distain.

"My daughter has been declared infertile by our doctors and spends her days in dark despair. She is my only offspring, you cretin. Her guilt and shame have left her in a depression that deepens with every passing week. I now fear for her very life. And you... you arrogant bastard...you presume to know how to help her?" Molten contempt boiled from within the pauses that separated his last words.

I took a deep breath, knowing that Everen was

trying to project his own guilt and despair onto me. His attempts to chase away his grieving over his daughter's illness were fueling his contempt and anger. A sudden insight flowed through me that Everen had all the power he needed to heal his pain. There was nothing for me to gain by lashing out against his attack. If I could help him abandon his denial and heal his grieving, his healing could well hold the keys to an entire generation of Erylians recovering their health.

"Sir, may I respectfully say that the conditions you face on your home planet are not insurmountable?" At least while he listened, he was setting aside his tirade long enough to consider the weight of my words. "And might I further suggest that individually and collectively Erylians possess all the power needed to resolve your dilemma? I firmly believe that there is a constructive purpose for the difficulties Erylia faces — and discovering that purpose will be most useful."

"Words, boy, that's all it is. Just words." Everen's contempt only grew more inflamed. He threw a nearby pillow at my head. I ducked as he yelled, with even more contempt: "You have no idea what you're talking about."

Nandia's face suddenly came to mind. In many past situations, her presence alone had been enough to open many a recalcitrant mind. I telepathically asked her to join me. I knew that despite being in her own version of our group dreaming, she would hear me.

At once, she was there beside me, smiling through the semi-darkness and din of my dreamtime bordello. She turned to Everen sitting upon his throne of pillows.

"Marshal, may I remind you that we are here at the request of the Galactic Grand Council?" she asked. Her sudden appearance did not disturb him in the least. She telepathed her question using a gentle tone, pitched to help him open his mind.

"But what do you know of Erylia?" his anger still pulsed above the noise of the brothel. "We're dealing with a genetic problem that has been fermenting in our blood for generations. Our best medical researchers say the problem is incurable. I should trust you because of some endorsement from the Grand Council? What twaddle. There must be some mischief you're up to, otherwise why surrender your own granddaughter? My superiors may well be sending an Imperial delegation to determine if I've allowed myself to be manipulated by you to sabotage the our military objectives."

"I know you are facing great risks, Marshal," Nandia acknowledged. "However, please listen. Sir, there has never been a disease that has proven to be beyond humanity's capacity to heal. In seeking to understand this, our scientists are exploring overwhelming evidence that it is consciousness that actually shapes form. If true, then soon we will see scientific validation that even genetic distortions can easily be healed." Throughout this inspiring message, I breathed deeply, seeking to nurture peace and healing within the Marshal.

"It was because of this truth that we were able to bring about such a miraculous recovery in Geasa," she continued. "We fully expect that by testing Erylia's children we can identify the electromagnetic frequencies that will trigger a complete reversal of their problems. May we visit your daughter to determine if we can help her healing?"

The dreamtime-Everen's severe demeanor softened slowly as he listened. He adjusted the pillows he was resting on and straightened his spine. "Very well," he said. "Let us go to my family home on Erylia and we will see whether or not your ideas have merit."

"And if you have no objection," Nandia continued, "I would like to include my granddaughter, Gracie, in this visit." The youngster suddenly appeared beside her grandmother, holding her hand.

Everen's eyes softened even further at the mention of Gracie. It occurred to me that many would consider her youthful beauty as magnetic as Nandia's.

"Yes, my daughter, Hyldie, might enjoy meeting her," he smiled at the thought. Arising from his cushions, he directed us to follow him to the spaceport. It was obvious that he had not realized we were dreaming together and so imagined that the only way to return to Erylia was via starship.

"Marshal Everen," Nandia interrupted his departure by gently placing her hand upon his shoulder. "In the dream realms, we can to travel to your home on Erylia instantly. If you will allow us both to place a hand on your shoulders and then focus upon your desire to return home, we will appear there in a twinkling."

Looking skeptical for a moment, Everen realized Nandia's suggestion was true and nodded his head. She and I stepped into position on either side of him, and with her free hand Nandia took hold of Gracie. "Ready," she announced.

After only the smallest spiral of white light behind my eyes, we were inside the entryway of a large, well-appointed home. Its most striking feature was a grand, curving stairway, carpeted in a plush golden wool that was decorated with an attractive wine-red design. Its elegant pattern danced up to an empty mezzanine balcony. Everen turned to us with a beam of gratitude lighting his face. "Thank you. Now I remember how easy that is. Let's go find my daughter."

He took the stairs two at a time, calling out for Hyldie on his way. I took in the style of the house as we followed him up the stairs. Of simple design, it was draped in colors of muted grays, taupes and pearly whites. Open wooden shades sided large windows that overlooked a lush lakefront. An ornate chandelier lit the foyer. Not a lavish spread, but tasteful.

Everen turned right down a wide hallway. Knocking at the first door he softly called out, "Hyldie?"

"Go away," came a muted response, sounding tired and angry.

"I have brought some people who may be able to help us," Everen said through the closed door. "At least let us come in. If you don't want them to stay, they won't." This gentle manner with his daughter was in stark contrast to the bordello-Everen. Somewhere in transit, his dark turban and robe had been replaced with his black uniform.

"Just a minute," Hyldie said. Sounds of shuffling and a closet being closed confirmed that she was preparing for visitors. "OK. You can come in now."

Everen carefully opened the door and stepped toward his waiting daughter. Hyldie was standing in the middle of a small lounge that was furnished with a desk, vid screen, couch and fireplace. Despite being in her early years of womanhood, she allowed her father to scoop her up in his arms. She was pale and drawn, too slender by half. Muted, muddied colors bled through her aura, as if some inner demon were gradually squeezing the life out of her body.

Gracie stepped forward, curtsied and said. "Hello, Hyldie. I'm Gracie. This is my grandmother, Nandia, and her friend, Bernard. They've been teaching me how to help others heal."

Hyldie warmed to Gracie immediately and signaled to her father to let her down. "My doctors say I can't heal," she said as she stood adjusting her gown and patting her hair. "It's so horrible to think that I can never have children. I feel so lost, so sad that I can never be a mother."

"That must feel awful," Gracie agreed as she gently took Hydie's hand. "Would you like to see if maybe I could help you heal? I could give you some Reiki healing energy."

"Oh," Everen's daughter responded. "I didn't think that it was even possible to heal what I've got."

Gracie nodded enthusiastically. "Oh yes, I've learned from Nana that there's never any illness we cannot heal. Why don't we try Reiki for a little while, and see if you like it? During the treatment we can talk more and get to know each other better too."

A smile spread across Hyldie's face to reveal the deeper beauty hidden beneath her despair. "Let's go into my bedroom," she said. "I'd like to hear more."

"How wonderful," Gracie replied. "Nana, would it be OK if you all left us alone for a while?"

Nandia looked to Everen, who nodded his assent. "We'll be waiting for you downstairs, Darling. Take your time."

We followed Everen down the stairway to his front parlor. He put off indulging his curiosity about Gracie's healing work by beckoning us toward several chairs and offering a choice of alcohol or tea. We asked for tea and got comfortable as he left the room.

"Bringing Gracie was inspired," I said to Nandia. "I expect Hyldie will learn a lot during her Reiki treatment, including what is happening on Praesepe. This visit could set her on the road to healing." I then telepathed the same ideas to Gracie.

"No problem, Bearns," Gracie mentally responded. "We're doing a fine job learning more about each other. Now stop meddling and go away."

Everen returned with a heated kettle and a selection of teas and biscuits. While helping ourselves, Everen said, "It's wonderful that you brought Gracie. I haven't seen my daughter smile like that for months. Thank you."

"How long has Hyldie known about her hormonal problems?" Nandia asked.

"Our medics began researching the problem several years ago," Everen replied. "About a year ago Hyldie's doctor completed the tests and told me of her diagnosis. The entire medical profession believes this genetic condition to be incurable, so I thought it best to tell Hyldie early to help her come to accept it. Unfortunately, the strategy backfired. Her health has been declining ever since we first talked about her problem. She has become more and more depressed. I never anticipated how much the inability to bear children would hurt Hyldie."

"It sounds as if the news hit her at a time when her identity as a woman was maturing around the idea of motherhood;" explained Nandia. She then decided on a new approach with the Marshal.

"Sir, might I continue and clear up some misunderstandings about the power to heal?" she asked. Clearly interested, Everen nodded. "I would like you to consider that the human body is an excellent healing machine capable of correcting any and all imbalances. This happens whether the condition is either acute or chronic; pathological or inherited.

"But health difficulties often arise because this amazingly powerful healing mechanism must first listen and respond to our thoughts and beliefs." She watched Everen to make sure he was following her. Again, he nodded. She continued with her explanation.

"Our thoughts and beliefs are therefore quite powerfully creative actions. Our ideas shape our experience of the world. If we focus on ideas of limitation or hate, then pain and illness are the natural result. This is not to punish us for misusing our consciousness, but to help us see the destructive consequences such misuse. Health challenges are meant to help us learn to use our thoughts constructively and responsibly.

"Often, widely accepted beliefs prove to block our natural healing abilities. For example, if we think we are powerless to recover from a genetic problem, we compromise the body's innate ability to restore health to its genetic structures.

"On Praesepe, for several generations now, we have been learning how the power of the conscious mind can block our natural healing ability. We have been learning ways to think that encourage the body's restorative powers. After investigating many amazing healings on our planet, our medical researchers have announced that they believe the conscious mind, all on its own, has the power to activate the repair of genetic imbalances."

Everen stared at his hands as he considered Nandia's message. Perhaps to distract himself from her radical ideas, or maybe because of a nagging curiosity, he asked, "I've heard rumors that you used some type of device to help Saragalla victims recover from the Geasan epidemic. What can you tell me about that?"

"We have been trained in a discipline called radionics," I interjected. "We use a radionics device, an energy-modulating instrument that produces specific electromagnetic frequencies. On Geasa, by dowsing with a pendulum, we were able to determine the frequency of the Saragalla virus. Then, using the radionics instrument, we were able imbue the Saragalla frequency into a remedy made from distilled water. Those suffering from the disease orally took the radionically charged water every hour.

"Within a short time their body's immunity was strong enough to begin healing the symptoms of the disease. After several days they were completely free of symptoms. We want to test Hyldie and others like her. We expect our research will lead us to discover a completely safe radionically made remedy that will help your young people recover from this condition."

In the dream, Everen's energy field was easy to see. The flashing colors of his aura were alternating from bright reds and yellows to muted greens and blues. I came to recognize that this was his characteristic energy signature when he was battling some inner demon. I decided to ask the obvious question.

"Sir, is there some force on Erylia that opposes this healing?"

From beneath furrowed brows, his eyes peered at me with mistrust and suspicion. Then Nandia intervened and reshaped my question. "Is there some force that opposes Hyldie's recovery?" Her question challenged Everen to look squarely at the conflicting beliefs that were plaguing him.

"Of course I wish only the best for my daughter," he began. "Since her mother fell ill and died when Hyldie was quite young, I've struggled to give her the best life possible on Erylia. I've thrown my heart and soul into my career to pay for this home, her tutors, vacations and health care. It devastated me when I learned that our doctors consider her problems to be incurable. I've tried to find anything to make her life worth living, but to no avail." As he spoke, his frustration and feelings of helplessness were intensifying.

"I now find myself in charge of an Erylian mission to kidnap your children, which in effect says to me and similarly affected families that our own offspring are useless. It has left me extremely frustrated and angry. It has affected my work. Many of my colleagues feel the same way. On the one hand I struggle to keep my superiors here on Erylia satisfied, while on the other I struggle against our society's belief that our problems cannot be healed. As a society we are being asked to sacrifice our genetic heritage, our bloodlines, our ancestry. I cannot imagine a greater horror. Now you say it's quite possible to overcome such a problem and I find myself suspended between soaring relief and deeply entrenched disbelief. I need time to consider all that I've heard here."

"Sir, you are quite wise in giving yourself time to digest what has been said," Nandia replied. "And there is one piece of information about healing that I believe is invaluable. Might I remind you of something Bearns spoke of during your first dreaming together?"

"Yes, please do. I find listening to you quite encouraging," the Marshal replied.

"As we have suggested, the resolution of imbalance or pain is the natural direction energy moves. However there are two choices that we can make that will quite effectively stop that natural progression. And those choices are either blame or self-pity." Nandia paused to watch Everen.

"I've found myself wondering if you and your daughter have created a deep emotional bond based on pity, in your attempts to cope with the hurt of such a horrible loss?"

"Thank you," he said. "I had forgotten that gem of wisdom. I will take time to consider your ideas and discuss them with my daughter. Meanwhile, shall we see how Hyldie and your granddaughter are faring?"

I telepathed a question to Gracie, "Would you and Hyldie feel comfortable joining us downstairs?"

"Yes," she replied. "We've been talking about the healing energy I've been giving her. She's feeling much more alive and wants to learn about telepathy and teleportation. I said that maybe you and Grand'Mere would be willing to help her."

"We'd love to talk with you," Nandia said. "Whenever you're ready, come on down."

But, just at that moment, the dream abruptly ended.

# XII

I WAS SURPRISED TO FIND myself in our suite at the Abe. Late afternoon light pierced the room — laser-like streaks that found holes amidst drawn shades. I stood, began opening the shades and said out loud, "What on God's green earth could have brought our dreaming to such an untimely end?"

"Red alert." An insistent telepathic message from Sirius was prodding at my consciousness. "Wake up you dizzy-eyed joltheads. I'm outside Nandia's cell playing silly buggers with two proctors. They're wantin' ta get in for their security check. It's a pot a' hot coffee set to boil over any second now."

"Quick, Gracie, let's away," Nandia said as she grabbed her granddaughter's hands. They closed their eyes, Nandia repeated the copper frequency and together they visualized their confinement cell. Within seconds they had disappeared.

My intense curiosity over Nandia and Gracie's dreamtime experience quickly evaporated as I found myself mired in the worry that some unknown spark had fired Sirius's clamoring proctors. I sincerely hoped that pot wouldn't boil over.

"Lovely afternoon light in this suite," El calmly said, arising from our Haida circle. Now the soft, amber rays flooding past the open shades triggering an ancient memory of a beloved, secure sanctuary from lifetimes past.

Our immortal Chambermaid quickly reminded us to refocus on our dreaming. "Let's not lose those memories," she urged. "Let me relate what Dunstan and I encountered there together."

"We found ourselves at the doorway to Everen's office. Seated at his desk, the Marshal was arguing with two officers who had taken up positions across from him. Open anger registered on each man's face.

"The elder of the pair was chastising the commander for allowing Gracie to escape. Despite his anger, Everen's protest was even-toned. He pointed out that she had been returned to custody, along with her grandmother.

"The second officer was younger and in complete opposition to his companion. He loudly challenged Everen over the abductions of Praesepian children." El paused to take a deep, connected breath, which reminded us to do the same.

"This younger officer began speaking of his own Erylian daughter, one of the countless youths diagnosed as unable to bear children. Gradually, he began to roar, protesting his government's betrayal of an entire generation of children — aghast at the idea that Erylians could be replaced with off-planet counterfeits.

"He was bold," Elli commented. "I will give him that.

He demanded that the Marshal be true to his people and not the distorted thinking of the Erylian government. He even challenged the superior officer to join in a planned coup d'état that was simmering among the proctors." El paused, tilting her head with eyebrows raised, emphasizing this new wrinkle.

That a junior officer had challenged Everen, even in the dream state, was good news. I knew that such a suggestion could help nurture the seeds of doubt within Everen's mind.

"Aye, that the Marshal, the bloody cove, didna shut that young officer down," Dunstan added. "Means he could well be leanin' our way. Back on Erylia that lad would be arrested as a traitor.

"In fact," he continued, "At the end of our dream, Everen simply nodded and then mentioned that he has a daughter in similar circumstances.

"And what news of the dreaming you visited, Lad?" he asked me.

I began preparing tea for the family and told them how Nandia and I had met the Marshal. "We followed him to his Erylian home and there met his daughter Hyldie," I explained.

"Gracie joined us and connected beautifully with Hyldie — they even spent healing time together!" I made a mental note to later ask Gracie about her experience during that dreaming.

"There was no mention of a coup d'état," I said. "We explained vibrational remedies, and Nandia told of our success at Geasa. We were talking about plans for testing Hyldie when Sirius sent the alert and the dream ended. But, we've opened a dreamtime doorway for further use. Let's plan our next dream conversations to encourage Everen to reconsider the Praesepian kidnappings."

El joined me in serving tea. As we sipped the steaming beverage, she asked Abe to arrange an evening meal to be delivered to our door. We checked in with Nandia and Gracie to hear about their abrupt return to their cell. El asked if they were hungry.

"You're going to sit down to eat?" Gracie telepathed in protest. "We'll be right there. I couldn't eat another bite of this smorgasbord fare that the proctors just dumped on us."

Within minutes of their arrival, we set about our meal with a cheerful, festive air. "Thank God for Sirius," Nandia said between bites. "We arrived in our suite to the sound of the proctor's key unlocking our door. I had fun raising my voice, feigning indignance over their intrusion into our private prayer time. I loudly demanded that the next time they wanted to check on us to please await a verbal invitation before entering. They actually apologized." We toasted Nandia upon hearing that.

"Our friend Everen's headed for stormy seas," Dunstan observed. "If he's even thinkin' about opposin' his government, he do have an imperial delegation breathin' down his neck," he noted. "You can bet he's wonderin' if this could be a good time to swing toward us as allies — or not. Lord knows he'll be needin' our help. There's Buckley's chance he'll realize that there are many ways to milfiss the balfastards without having to resort to violence."

"That's quite true," El said and then turned toward Gracie. "Sweetie, Dunstan brings up a valuable idea well worth remembering. He's referring to the principle that the only way we can effectively accomplish our mission's ideal is to use the means and methods consistent with the ideal we seek to achieve.

Looking puzzled, Gracie said, "I'm not sure I understand you, El."

It was Dunstan who replied. "Well, Lassie, we'll not be teaching the Erylians how to heal their troubles while trying to kill 'em off at the same time, now will we?" I smiled at how succinctly the Scotsman could make a point.

"I think I see," Gracie said. "You're saying that since our mission is to help the Erylians heal, we can't treat them as if they're our enemy. We have to treat them as though they're our friends, even if they don't treat us that way."

"Exactly right. And what Dunstan is also saying," El went on to explain, "is that we might need to help Marshal Everen learn that he cannot fight his government if his new ideal is to help them see the futility of their current program for dealing with the Erylian Condition.

"Which could be why Everen has been trying to hide something from us," the Royal Chambermaid continued. "If he's beginning to accept, even subconsciously, that Hyldie can heal, then he must face that he can also heal the hurts he feels. But healing puts him in direct opposition to his government's plan to replace the next Erylian generation with Praesepian breeding stock. If the Erylian youths can heal their condition, the siege of Praesepe is meaningless.

"I imagine he's hoping it would be easier not to confront the self-blame, guilt and despair he feels about his daughter's illness," she concluded. "It's understandable that anyone would try to hide this kind of emotional conflict from themselves — not to mention trying to hide it from a group of off-world healers."

"But I've been wondering if there's something else he's afraid to reveal," I suggested. "Best we keep probing to see what else there is to uncover." Nandia wrapped up the conversation by suggesting that we use our evening's sleep to ask for dreaming to help each of us grow closer to Everen.

Like kids at a carnival, we greedily polished off Abe's hot apple pie a la mode. Only then did Nandia and Gracie project themselves back to their I.C. lock-up. Sirius telepathically reported their safe return and then announced, "While I'm on guard duty here, I want ya ta be thinkin' twice 'bout havin' me spy on Everen again. I'll not be sufferin' any more abuse from Gladys and her brood. They're rough as bags with scant idea a' proper respect for my kind. Ya can bet the farm I'll be on heightened recapture alert the next time ya need me to patrol the I.C."

After praising Sirius for the dedication that took him far beyond the call of duty, El, Dunstan and I settled into a night's sleep in our rooms. Growing drowsy, I telepathically bid sweet dreams to our family in custody and asked my Inner Self to guide me into a dreaming where I might create a closer bond with Everen. I reminded myself to recall my dreaming, and soon was fast asleep.

Upon awakening the next morning, I did recall a dream involving the intelligence chief. We were in his office, where he was being argumentative and hostile. I asked if he would like to see more of the work

Nandia and I had done on our first mission together. Reluctantly he agreed to a dream journey into the past.

Placing my hand on his shoulder, I imagined the hostel in Geasa where Nandia and I had worked on many Saragalla cases. There I escorted him to the bedside of a young man whom I had helped years earlier. We found him in the terminal ward, where he lay restrained, screeching, thrashing and beyond communication — or even rational thought.

I asked Everen to sit next to me as I administered a Reiki healing treatment. This energy is magnified in the dreamtime. I do feel the flow of Reiki — similar to the awakened state — but in dreams I also experience it as music replete with a playful variety of colors as well.

It wasn't long before the young man's thrashing calmed, his ranting eased, and he was peaceful enough to begin taking deep, connected breaths. As we breathed together I found a musical tone and hummed it to the boy. He began to mimic my note and soon the ocean of muddy grey that dominated his aura transformed into bright red streaks of vitality and purple-greens of deep healing.

Then lad began to tell his tale — of the heartrending grief for a young love lost. Everen's face reflected an empathic compassion as he listened. Pale blue tones of confidence wafted through the young man's aura. The virus's vise-like grip within the lad's body further eased, and soon he was sitting up and smiling, filled with gratitude.

Quite moved by this young man's openness and honesty, both Everen and I warmly hugged him before bidding him farewell.

"I've never seen anything like that," Everen remarked as we passed through the entry of the dreamtime hostel. "It was as if I were watching a miracle."

"You don't have to work with many people in pain," I said, "before you realize that such healings are quite common. It is simply the nature of healing. Unfortunately, through the centuries, we seem to have forgotten that such recovery is the natural birthright of each one of us."

As the dream faded, I watched Everen's face relax into a look of quiet serenity. I tuned in to his mind and saw that he was imagining such healing for Hyldie.

I related this dreaming tale while Dunstan made breakfast, knowing that Nandia and Gracie were eavesdropping as usual. Elli then reported her dream with Everen. They were sitting next to a tree in Braeoon Gardens and talking about Hyldie's innate power to heal. He listened intently to El's suggestions and was excited at the idea of his daughter's presence at the next day's testing. Nandia and Gracie applauded the idea — both were anxious to meet Hyldie in this dimension.

Then Dunstan enlightened us with his Everen dream. "The Marshal and I were standin' on a rough-hewn raft, polin' our way through thick swamp. We worked well together, trustin' each other's skill as we navigated through the unknown waterway. Steadily we poled our way along a murky river channel through a dark morass a' jungle. After a while we grew relaxed enough workin' together to begin ta talk. I asked him why he had created a sub-rosa, exclusive guard within his own intelligence corps.

"He was surprised that I knew about this inner

guard, but didn't deny it. After some hesitation, he admitted that he had gathered around twenty private troops, all with children sufferin' the Erylian Condition. They're all spittin' angry over the government's abduction program."

Dunstan then shared Everen's final remarks. "I only just started gathering these men into a formal group," the Marshal explained. "I want an alliance of like-minded people who share a common concern for our children's health. This cadre of loyal people I must be able to trust — should the Imperial government turn against me."

"I told him that we might be able to help strengthen this group's common purpose," Dunstan concluded. "Aye, that was news he welcomed."

Elli nodded and added, "Let's imagine the opportunity to encourage Everen to invite his elite proctors to join today's healing session." Great idea, I thought. Why not enlarge our audience?

After breakfast, and with Abe's guidance, Elli and I collected distilled water, bottles and glass beakers from around the hotel. These supplies, to be used later to make remedies, were packed into boxes, which the front desk had delivered to the I.C.

While preparing to set out for today's session with young Erylians, Sirius announced he was staying behind. "That is, unless I get a call to join ya," he said. He wanted to haunt the Abyssinian, visit Midge at the spaceport, and check our rooms at the Vasantamos and the Don. Standing on hind legs atop a cupboard, front paws raised in prayer, he intoned, "Lord, keep me from the clutches of that grasping, meddlesome Gladyswoman." While laughing, I suspected he really wanted to hunt mice until he knew he was needed.

Dunstan teleported to the street outside, to scout for anyone who might be watching for us. "'Tis best to assume portraits of your ugly mug have now been spread far and wide amongst proctors," he said. We looked from our window as he meandered across the street and stopped at the corner. There he casually watched pedestrians for several moments before strolling back in to the lobby.

Elli helped me mount the radionics pack on my shoulders. I telepathed Duncan to see if he'd noticed anyone suspicious.

"Aye, Lad," he replied, "With Abe's help I've spotted several 'a the unduly curious hangin' about. Energy fields of currish-lookin' rogues. Appears they're waitin' for someone — 'n not ta be bestowin' a birthday blessin'.

"How about if you and Elli teleport yourselves to our grocery shop down the street?" he suggested. "I'll keep 'n eye on our suspects. No sense lettin' Everen know where we're roostin."

After notifying Dunstan of our arrival at the store, he appeared and reported that two plainclothes proctors had been watching the hotel entrance. "They got bored and are now coolin' their heels at the lunch counter across the plaza. Neither of 'em was tailin' ya yesterday.

"'Twas interestin' watchin' their energy fields," he continued. "They're hopin' one of the other teams Everen's got watchin' Braeoon's hotels will identify ya soon. These lads are bored spitless 'n in a hurry ta end this tedious assignment. They're so busy grousin' ya could a' strolled past singin' Christmas carols in July and they'd ne'er a' noticed ya." We enjoyed a laugh at that festive scene and headed toward the spaceport, eager for an update from Midge before arriving at the I.C.

We wandered like tourists enjoying a sunny day's exploration of a new-found city. Whenever a proctor came into view I ducked into the nearest doorway, shielded from sight by Dunstan and El. Otherwise, we watched people's auras, enjoyed the sunshine and commented on the shops and eateries we strolled by. We had a good half hour to spare as we arrived at the spaceport, and while avoiding the attentions of nearby proctors, made our way to Midge's information booth.

Elli and Midge took to each other like long-lost friends. "Have you heard of any more calls for additional passenger space on outgoing starships?" El asked.

Midge shook her head and quietly said, "Have heard rumors that an Imperial delegation may be arriving from Erylia. Also a starshuttle arrived in the early hours, offloading a group of young Erylians. I hope you folks find a way to end these abductions of our children. I don't know how much more we can take." She happily mentioned that Joseph, the cabbie, had overheard proctors complaining about the futility of searching for me.

"You've become Braeoon's latest needle in a haystack, and I'm right proud to know you," she smiled. "Now get to work." We laughed and wished her well.

"And, Lassie," Dunstan added as an afterthought, "if trouble comes abrewin', ye can tune in to us telepathically. Simply focus on your memory of my face and send me the mental idea yer wantin' me ta hear."

While looking skeptical, she nodded. "Don't worry," he reassured her, "I'll get yer message, ne'er you fear."

El and Midge warmly held hands, departed like sisters promising to stay in touch.

We agreed I would teleport to Everen's office alone. Elli and Dunstan thought it best to stay out of Everen's sight for as long as possible and opted to remain at the spaceport. "We'll stay tuned in to passersby here and see what more we can learn," El said, "Call out when you need our help testing the Erylian youths."

Again, I luckily arrived in the hallway outside Everen's door while it was empty. As I stepped inside, Gladys greeted me coolly and bustled me in to the inner office. There Nandia and Gracie stood waiting and hugged me warmly. Everen remained seated at his desk.

"I'm happy to see you both here," I said before turning toward the Marshal. "Sir, shall I assume that you are still comfortable with Gracie and Nandia joining today's testing session?"

"Yes," he said, sounding less suspicious than yesterday. "I think their presence will be helpful to the Erylian young people who have only just arrived this morning. My own daughter, Hyldie, is among those who await you in the conference room."

"I'm pleased that you have decided to include her," I said. "And, Sir, am I to understand that you have a small, elite corps of proctors here on Praesepe?"

"You are remarkably well informed about intelligence that my people assured me was not public knowledge," he said, his suspicions once again aroused.

"Thank you, Sir. With respect, I'd rather not divulge the source of that knowledge at the moment, but may I suggest that you invite these troops to attend today's testing session? I'm sure they will find what we discover about the Erylian Condition quite interesting."

After only a moment's consideration, he agreed to it. He mentioned the Group of Twenty in a brief conversation with Gladys and then escorted us to the conference room.

We arrived to find the young Erylians seated in a semicircle at the front of the room where the Marshal had briefed us as proctors only yesterday. Through broad windows, sunlight streamed while illuminating tall trees and lush gardens outside the building. Currently both of Praesepe's suns were overhead, occasionally shaded by the rare cloud sailing lazily across the sky.

In response to a request I'd made yesterday, the Marshal provided two tables to serve as testing stations at the front corners of the room. Toward the rear, three proctors were on duty, chatting amongst themselves. They came to attention and saluted Everen as we walked in. He told them they were no longer needed and ordered them to return to their normal duties.

Then turning to welcome the group of young Erylians, Everen briefly introduced Nandia, Gracie and me. He also announced that he had invited twenty of his chosen proctors to observe the day's session.

I thanked Everen and stepped forward to address the youngsters. They were almost evenly divided between female and male and looked to be between twelve and fifteen years old. Hyldie sat toward one side of the group, looking more vital and alert than she'd appeared during yesterday's dreaming. Without hesitation we made eye contact. I smiled, breathed deeply and then turned back toward the room.

"Hello," I began. "As Marshal Everen said, my name is Bernard. My friends call me Bearns. Please do the same, for I come as a friend. Nandia and I have been asked by the Galactic Council to see if we might be useful resolving the troubles between Praesepe and Erylia." Looks of surprise and curiosity were exchanged among the youngsters.

"A number of years ago, Nandia and I, along with Dunstan, another Council delegate, aided the city of Geasa in recovering from a fatal Saragalla epidemic. Has anyone here heard of that tragedy that took half the city's population?" I raised my hand to encourage those who knew something of the story to break the ice and speak up. Four people raised their hands. "Thank you," I said, and again breathed deeply. "Would any of you like to comment on what you know about that event?"

When a dark-haired boy raised his hand, I asked, "Would you mind telling us your name please?"

"Timothy," he replied. He was a confident lad, blue-eyed, good looking, tall and lank. His long dark hair was thinning. "I heard that some people went to Fantibo and fought with some gangsters and then discovered an herbal medicine that saved the city."

"Yes, Timothy that was part of what happened," I replied. "Does anyone else have more to add to the story?"

A young girl next to Hyldie raised her hand. "My name is Rachael. I heard that someone found a new way for healing, using energy. I don't know any more about it than that, but it sounds like a good idea to me."

"Thank you, Rachael," I said. "Yes. As I mentioned, Nandia and I worked with a musician named Dunstan. Together, we discovered herbal and energy remedies that were quite helpful in the healing of Saragalla. And Rachael, the techniques we used in Geasa were not new, but are, in fact, centuries old.

"One of these techniques is called dowsing. It's a discipline that helps identify beneficial remedies for an illness by tapping in to the inner wisdom available within the deeper reaches of the Self. Each of us has this potential and can be trained to be effective dowsers. We are here today to see if we can discover the causes and find answers for Erylia's problems." I stepped back as Nandia telepathed that she wanted to address the group.

Predictably, the young audience immediately fell in love with Nandia. She invited each one of the young people to be part of our research project. As she talked, they could hear her open heart, her abundant love. Everyone's enthusiasm grew at the chance to work with her. She added to my comments about dowsing by explaining how we use a pendulum to discover answers to specific questions that relate to a person's health.

Toward the end of her explanation, the classroom door swung open and Everen's elite group of proctors walked in. All were smartly attired in black officer's uniforms, their caps snugly tucked beneath their left arms. Nandia nodded to the Marshal, who stood, saluted and then invited the proctors to take the seats behind the youngsters. As they filed past, two young women — sisters most likely — leapt up from the front row.

"Uncle Roger, Uncle Roger!!!" they yelled as they ran to embrace a tall, grey-haired officer. The mask of stern authority that molded his features suddenly melted into a beaming display of surprised delight. With Cheshire cat grins and wide open arms, the reunited Erylians tightly hugged each other.

After introducing himself to us as Captain Whittaker, Uncle Roger picked up the two girls, lofting them high into the air. "And, how did you two demons get here?" he demanded to know. He glanced at Everen who smiled at the family interruption. Whittaker then tickled and twirled the girls before finally returning them to the ground.

"Oh Unc, I can't wait for you to hear what is happening here," one of the nieces exclaimed. "I just feel so much better knowing there may be a way to heal this sickness we all have."

While most in the room were occupied with Captain Whittaker's family reunion, Gracie quietly approaching Hyldie. She introduced herself and said, "You don't know me, Hyldie, but I am here to help. My grandmother, Nandia, has taught me a lot about helping others heal. Would you mind if together we go say hello to your father?"

At first Hyldie looked confused, until a glimmer of recognition flashed across her face. Somewhere within her subconscious she was remembering last night's dream. As the two young women drew near to Everen, he arose from his seat and extended his arms to greet them. Hyldie reached into his warm embrace and was suddenly in tears. Gracie stepped aside for a moment, watching father and daughter, before making her way back to the front of the room. There, Nandia and I reached out and held her as the two family reunions gradually came to an end.

Nandia then greeted the new group of proctors, briefly introduced us and summarized our purpose for being in Braeoon. "At the request of the Galactic Grand Council, Bearns and I," she said, "were involved in helping Fantibo's city of Geasa recover from an epidemic a number of years ago. Do any of you have any knowledge of that experience?"

Many of the proctors nodded and Nandia continued. "Similar to our work in Geasa, here in Braeoon we seek to apply the science of vibrational remedies to find answers for the Erylian Condition. Today Bearns and I will use our pendulums in a process called dowsing to determine which vibrations can clear which symptoms. The young people before you have generously agreed to be part of this research to see if we can help activate their innate healing powers by using our methods."

"We hope that you gentlemen will approach this with open minds. Our wish for you is that you willingly participate in this research." Radiating her natural magnetism and warmth, Nandia then asked, "Is there any objection to proceeding in this manner?"

Everyone within the Group of Twenty was pleased to support Nandia. She then focused on the young people and asked, "Is there anyone here who is reconsidering and may not wish to be part of such an experiment?" One hand shot up.

"Yes?" Nandia asked.

"I'm not sure about this. What I want to know is, what are the risks to me if I do decide to participate, and how long will I be away from home?"

"Thank you," Nandia said. "And your name is...?"

"Walter." Another tall lad, he had light brown curly hair, blue eyes, and a heavy body that carried significant excess weight.

"Walter, yours are valuable questions. Our first step will be to dowse to see if we can determine the causes for the symptoms you are experiencing. Next we will test those symptoms against different electromagnetic frequencies, to find the frequencies that will be useful for you to heal your symptoms. Make sense so far?"

"Yes, thank you."

"Once we've found which remedy frequencies test as being favorable for you, we will use a radionics instrument to imbue those electromagnetic energy vibrations into distilled water. So the remedies we produce will be electromagnetically structured distilled water. We will recommend dosages for each of you.

"These remedies are completely safe, free of any risk of the dangerous side effects that sometimes accompany chemical medications. But keep in mind that sometimes when people begin using vibrational therapies their symptoms can become aggravated for a brief time. That is simply the body's signal to reduce the dosage temporarily. Does everyone understand?"

There were enthusiastic nods throughout the group, proctors joining in as well.

"Walter, everyone in the room has the power to heal anything. Everyone here must make their own choices about whether or not to participate in this research. We consider you to be our equal partners in this exploration of healing. We want to find answers that stimulate healing for each individual. In addition to working with the vibrational remedies, we also work with healing energies, sounds, touch and emotions.

"We hope to apply what we learn here to all who are similarly afflicted on Erylia. We expect to begin seeing results for this group perhaps as soon as today. Certainly within the next few days. It will be up to you to decide if you want to be a part of presenting our findings to the people of Erylia. Anyone can choose to go home at any time. Marshal Everen, is there anything you might wish to add in answer to Walter's question?"

"Yes, thank you, Nandia." The Marshal stood up to reply. "I am pleased to learn that we may begin seeing results very soon. My greatest wish is for you return to your families clearly recovering from the Erylian Condition. And I also hope that each of you, once you have returned home, will help others on Erylia learn that there is hope."

"Walter, do you have any more concerns?" Nandia asked.

"No, thank you. I am happy to hear that what we're doing here could help back home. No one there wants this siege. We all have family who are deeply troubled by what is happening on Praesepe. Our healing can't help but ease these troubles. So, what's next?" he asked.

# XIII

WE ALL AGREED TO A SHORT BREAK. The Marshal had stewards standing by who wheeled in carts carrying juice, hot tea and pastries. A few people approached Nandia; most others gathered around the food carts. I took this opportunity to speak privately with Everen at the back of the room.

"Marshal, we have two other skilled friends who could be quite helpful during this stage of our testing. Would you mind if I invite them to join us?"

He raised an eyebrow skeptically and said, "I've suspected there were more of you. Someday you'll have to tell me how you've managed to evade our net." But despite his skepticism, he was agreeable to adding El and Dunstan. His energy field was reflecting more of the calming hues of greens and blue, although there were still bands of darker red-browns and blue-greys of hesitation, doubt and fear surrounding him. I telepathed Dunstan and Elli, and asked for their help testing the group.

"Aye we'll be there shortly, Laddie," the Scotsman said, exaggerating his lilt. "Bein' the only one knowin' the way, I'll be makin' sure our Royal Chambermaid arrives safely." I mentally caught her smile and I smiled myself at the thought of the two of them growing closer.

"Marshal," I said, "our two friends will be arriving shortly. Meanwhile, may I request that you provide transport for our group to Braeoon Gardens, say around mid-day? There are amazing healing properties amidst the bounties of nature. And, could we also arrange for a light picnic meal?"

Like a sudden gust of wind, my request triggered a flash of surprise on the Marshal's face. "An idea worth considering, I grant you. Give me a few minutes to check with my lieutenants. Acceptable?"

"I thank you, sir."

And, right on cue, the door opened and a smiling Scotsman and the Royal Aesirian Chambermaid stepped into the hall. I interrupted the break and announced, "Folks, I would like to introduce Elli and Dunstan, two people without whom the success of our previous missions would not have been possible. Elli is a former queen of the planet Aesir." Everyone's eyes widely appraised this immortal, for, as I've said, the woman is widely known for her own gracefully magnetic presence. She artfully curtsied and gave the room a broad smile as she stepped back, holding a hand out to Dunstan.

"And this red headed monster is Dunstan, our invaluable ally during the Geasan epidemic. Before we're done here, I encourage you to ask him to share his musical talents. Both are Grand Council Delegates assigned to our Praesepian mission."

"Aye, even Blind Freddie could see it's an unlikely lookin' lot you've managed to gather here today, Lad," Dunstan mischievously chided. The group laughed at the Scotsman's infectious humor. "And what mischief will ya be needin' us to untangle for ya, this time?"

"We'll be needing your help as soon as we begin testing these youngsters," I responded. "And I thought you'd like to hear this next part of our conversation."

"Before we begin our testing," I said, turning toward the group, "there are several questions I would like to ask. First, how many of you have spoken with Erylia's medical professionals, in an attempt to resolve your ailments?"

Almost half the proctors and all the youngsters' hands went up.

"And what were you told by these professionals?" Several hands were raised and I selected a young lady who stood and introduced herself as Margie.

"They told me that the problems I had were incurable..." a catch in Margie's throat stopped her from saying more. Tears welled up and began to flow down her cheeks.

After silently waiting a moment for Margie to recover her composure, I took her hand and helped her back into her chair. Thanking her, I then turned to the group and asked, "And how many of the rest of you have heard the same thing from other medical professionals?"

Again, all hands were raised.

"Your response confirms what I had suspected," I told them. "I am here to remind you of a fundamental law of this universe. It's a law that you can always count on. And that law is that you are beings of unlimited power and strength. Your consciousness shapes form. You and you alone, are creating every aspect of your lives merely by what you concentrate upon. As you heal the Erylian Condition you will find yourself changing and expanding your thinking in new, individual ways.

"I ask that you accept your power to heal despite what you may have heard or believed to the contrary. The real question is, are you ready to heal? Are you ready to change your thinking?" I watched for reactions and gave people a chance to absorb what I'd been saying.

Then I turned to again to Margie. "Thank you, young lady" I said, "for your courage in revealing your true feelings about being told that your illness is incurable. I greatly respect your openness. How are you feeling now?"

"A little bit better since talking about it," she admitted. She sounded relieved. Later, I noted to myself, she may want to talk about feeling afraid and hopeless.

With a telepathic nod agreeing with me, Nandia asked, "Margie, could we come back to this subject a bit later on?"

"Oh yes," she replied. "I'm happy to do that if it means getting free of this dismal future we've been led to believe we cannot escape."

"Well said, Margie," Nandia responded. "And now I would like to return to the amazing power of our consciousness for a moment.

"If you accept the principle that your projections of consciousness are shaping your health or lack of it, then you must accept that you innately carry the power to heal within you. And healing is always easier than creating an imbalance. Healing is always going on in our bodies. Healing energy surrounds us in abundance.

"Sometimes, we place health challenges in our lives because we want to grow beyond some limitation in the expression of our own creative power. Sometimes we want to recover a measure of respect for ourselves, and the only way we believe we can change destructive beliefs is to create a health crisis. Whenever we heal, our consciousness automatically grows in the process.

A proctor's hand was raised even before Nandia had finished. "Yes?" she asked.

"I'm Lieutenant Turpelo." He said as he stood. "If our children's bodies know how to heal this condition, then why hasn't it happened?"

"That's a very useful question, Lieutenant," I replied. "Whenever any of us encounter a health problem, there is always some mis-use of our power of thought. And, there are only two ways we could possibly use our power that can block our own healing. Does anyone have any idea what those two ways could be?"

"By trying to hide the problem?" the young man called Walter called out.

"Very good, Walter," Nandia responded. "Or else by trying to hide *from* the problem. And unfortunately, hiding is a very common response to health problems. Our two most common hiding places are blame and self-pity.

"Blame means we've adopted a victim's attitude. Whenever we blame, we are refusing to accept that we create our own physical, emotional or mental well-being. Blame assigns some type of judgment or punishment in response to a problem — whether by blaming ourselves or others. We refuse to accept that each of us is innately powerful, creating our lives, constructing our challenges. We each have the power to hold ourselves above violation. If you're unsure whether you use blame, get honest about any grudges you carry against yourself or others."

Another young lad briefly raised his hand and then blurted out his question, "Does that mean that hurting doesn't mean we're being punished by God?"

"There is no higher power who seeks to punish you," Nandia said quite emphatically. "That is merely superstitious flapdoodle. No one is ever punished unless they mistakenly believe that punishment is necessary to help them grow."

"The only reason for suffering is to learn that there is absolutely no need for suffering," Nandia continued lightly. "That was a great question. What is your name, Young Man?"

"Freo," came the lad's confident reply. He stood and said, "It seems as if you've just given us the answer to one of life's great mysteries. If there's no outside force trying to punish us, we must be living in a loving universe. If so, then there's gotta be many ways to recover from a mistake besides punishment. That's great!"

"Great, indeed," Nandia laughingly replied. "Guilt is a useful messenger. It helps to correct beliefs that lead us to withholding love, usually from ourselves. You crack on sharp, Freo." His smile revealed rays of a lovely inner spark.

Then Nandia turned to speak again to Margie. "And now young lady, would you mind going back to the belief that your health problems are incurable?"

Nandia stepped forward and extended her hand. Margie reached out, took Nandia's hand and then rose to stand beside her at the front of the room.

"Earlier, I noticed that you had some tears when talking about what medical professionals had told you," Nandia said warmly. "I want to thank you for your openness. It's quite courageous to stand up here and be that emotionally honest on our first morning together. Would you be willing to say more about how it felt when you heard that your body has an incurable disease?"

Margie nodded and looked down as she considered Nandia's question. "I felt really sad and hopeless," she said, as tears again began welling up in her eyes.

"Yes, I think any of us would feel the same," Nandia replied. She paused a moment before continuing. "And is there any chance you're also feeling sorry for yourself — self-pity?"

Suddenly, tears began to flow in earnest down Margie's cheeks. She nodded and slumped over, hiding her face behind her hands. Gently Nandia reached out to hug Margie, who opened her arms and fell into a tight embrace.

They held each other for a long moment as many in the room looked down out of silent respect for Margie. A golden-white light emanated from Nandia and enfolded the young woman. The balloon of light pulsed, then magnified and became brighter — the two women all but disappearing for a moment within its intensity.

The light then eased, Margie's tears soon abated and the embrace came to an end. From the folds of her gown, Nandia offered a tissue. Drying her eyes, Margie nodded with an embarrassed smile of gratitude.

"It's natural for us to feel sorry for ourselves, especially upon hearing such desperate news from a trusted authority," Nandia said, consoling the young woman.

She then turned toward the audience. "I remind all of you to consider that we create health challenges because the Inner, Eternal Self sees them as the best way to expand our conscious perspectives and way of thinking. I create my health problems for my own individual growth, in my own unique way. As soon as we accept that, self-pity automatically dissolves. We do not need to suffer in order to heal and learn.

"Simply because the medical profession does not know how a problem can be healed does not mean your body cannot heal. Each healing is an individual act of creation, which we are all entirely capable of. Every physical healing represents some way we have allowed our own consciousness to expand. So remember, self-pity blocks healing. And the remedy for self-pity is simply to trust that you have placed this exact condition on your path for a constructive purpose."

Turning back to Margie, she asked, "How are you feeling now, young lady?" she asked.

"Much better," the youngster said. "So, Nandia, you're saying it's up to me whether or not I heal this problem?"

"Exactly," Nandia said smiling. "We'll be exploring the different kinds of beliefs that cause these problems a bit later. For now, whenever you notice that you are feeling sorry for yourself, consider the idea that you have placed these health challenges on your path for a useful purpose." Smiling at Nandia, Margie gratefully embraced her again before returning to her seat.

"Obviously, the attitude of self-pity," Nandia continued, "is based on the denial of our individual power to create our own life experience. Keep in mind that all emotional upsets, mental conflict or pain are self-created messengers. No one ever has any disease, circumstance or even death thrust upon them.

"The immediate message of any discomfort is that we are in a process of healing. The deeper message is that, by allowing the process, we will discover the distorted beliefs that initially caused the problem. Once we get the message and change our thinking, the imbalance clears, or, said another way, healing happens. Healing is a constant in our lives, otherwise our bodies could not survive. The only real question is, how long will it take for you to heal? If you believe a problem is incurable, you'll needlessly suffer until you die before allowing yourself to heal."

Everen cleared his throat and then stood up. "Nandia, your ideas are quite intriguing. But, could you tell us, are you suggesting that we should ignore what our medical experts are saying about the Erylian Condition being incurable?"

"That's a very good question, Marshal Everen," Nandia replied. "It is one of the great social myths that many health problems are incurable and can only be relieved by dying. Yet there is no known disease that humans have not healed — and without intervention. We are each the ultimate authority for our own well-being. Each thought is a powerful creative action.

I recommend that you experiment and believe in your own, innate power to heal. If you find you don't experience a relief in the intensity, duration or frequency of any symptom, then you may certainly resume your belief in incurable conditions if you wish.

"If you decide that you wish to follow any medical practitioner's advice, please do so. Again, each of us is the ultimate authority for our well-being, so be cautious of those who seek to deprive you of your decision-making ability and demand that they make your choices for you."

Just at that moment, Sirius abruptly appeared and administered a whisker rub to Nandia's ankles. "Hello," she said as she reached down to pick him up. "This is another of our allies, named Sirius," she announced. "He's a creature of amazing talents, and sometimes appears out of nowhere." Proctors and young folk alike smiled quizzically as Nandia scratched his chin.

"Imperial Erylian Delegation has recently landed," Sirius telepathed. "Midge reports that immediately following their arrival, the group of a dozen or so high politicos and military brass were shuffled off in a waitin' military motorcade. Delegation is headed for the Don. All guests there have been relocated to nearby hotels."

Nandia held up her hand for a moment's silence as she considered the cat's message. "Obviously Everen will be receiving this news within minutes," she telepathed to us. "Shall we invite the delegation to observe the work we're doing?" We all agreed.

"Marshal Everen," she said, "you will very soon learn of the arrival of an Imperial Erylian Delegation. We thought it wise to inform you of the message Sirius has just delivered. Delegates have been met by a military motorcade and are being transported to the Don

Hotel. I would like to invite this delegation to join us in the work we are doing here. Does this meet with your approval?"

The intelligence chief looked bewildered. "Obviously you have communication channels far better than mine," he said. "Your group has amazing abilities, and I'm quite curious to learn how you've neutralized our zinc shielding. But first I must know, did your people arrange for the delegation's motorcade?"

"No, Sir," replied Nandia. "That was not of our doing."

Dunstan telepathically suggested that the delegation must have its own people here on Erylia, unbeknownst even to Everen. "The Marshal's caught 'n a spot a' bother, 'twixt a rock 'n a hard spot. Little good it'll do him now wonderin' who arranged for the delegation's transport.

"Very well," the Marshal finally declared, standing as he recovered a bit of his composure. "Captain Whittaker and I must excuse ourselves to greet this delegation. After they have settled into their rooms, we will return here so they can observe this testing session."

"But, before I depart, Bernard, I wish to inform you that your request for midday plans — food and transport are in place. In my absence, Lieutenant Turpelo is in command of our detail here. Acceptable?

"Yes, Sir," I said.

"Excuse me Marshal Everen?" asked an officer sitting with the proctor group. "May I be allowed to accompany you to meet the delegation? A spare set of hands might prove very useful."

"And your name?" Everen asked.

"I am Major Yellian, Sir. I, along with two aides, are here on special assignment from the head of the Defense Council, General Haplydean."

Again Everen's face registered surprise. "Very well. As we depart, Major, I'll thank you to explain how you came to be here this morning." The Marshal then scanned the remaining proctors and said, "Let us be about it then, gentlemen."

With a nod to his Lieutenant, Everen and the two officers departed. Sirius scurried out the door behind them, hot on their heels.

# XIV

AS SOON AS THE DOOR HAD CLOSED, Walter raised his hand and jumped up. "Yes Walter?" Nandia asked.

"How did that cat suddenly appear? What is going on here?"

"Teleportation is one of the human and animal kingdom's innate abilities," Nandia answered. "How many others have an interest in hearing more of what we are truly capable of?" Everyone raised their hands, save the two proctors who had been sitting next to the now-departed Major Yellian. These officers sat glumly in their chairs, arms crossed.

"The more deeply each of us heals, the more comfortable we become expressing our feelings honestly. We learn to depend upon ourselves for approval, rather than hoping to garner it from others. We realize the value in growing and using our strengths, talents and abilities. We come to trust our power to heal, and trust our power to create our individual life experiences.

"As we grow more accepting of ourselves, we come to discover and express deeper, inner dimensions of the Self. This reveals more of the true potential of our physical beings. Telepathy and teleportation are abilities that we naturally tap into when inner doorways are opened. Awareness of this Inner Self occurs as we root out rigidly held beliefs that limit the growth of consciousness. Blame and self-pity, as we mentioned earlier, are two prime examples. Fundamentally, rigorous, loving self-honesty is the primary requirement before any consciousness can expand.

"While not the complete answer, Walter, does that help you understand a bit better?"

"Yes, but how can a mere cat be capable of such a feat?" he asked.

"As we grow in learning the power of our own consciousness," Nandia replied, "we learn that all life is conscious. And consciousness, at its very core, yearns for its own growth. Humans are not the only conscious nor the most intelligent creatures alive. And here's a hint, Walter. Consciousness can be expressed as a particle, a wave or a field. Later on, you may wish to ask Sirius about how he learned the skills of telepathy and teleportation."

"Thank you." Walter said as he sat down. I mentally applauded his intense curiosity — I knew it would fuel his passion to grow.

"Now back to our discussion about healing," Nandia said. "If you will consider that we are all beings of good intent, then our creation of illness must always be for a constructive purpose. Discomfort occurs whenever we lose some measure of self-expression or self-respect. Such loss impedes the natural movement of energy that is meant to flow easily through us.

"I find it quite interesting that all healing ultimately involves emotional healing. Quite often expressing a suppressed emotion is all that is needed to heal a physical ailment.

"The most powerful choice we can make," Nandia concluded, "is to accept ourselves as creators of our hurts and illnesses and become aware of how we've compromised our self-expression and self-respect.

"Are there any questions?" Nandia silently scanned the group until abruptly interrupted by Sirius again.

"Sorry mates," he telepathed. "I'm here with Midge at the spaceport. We're watchin' an escort of armed proctors herd Praesepian youngsters into an Erylian starshuttle. Some I recognize as fellow inmates from St. Bernadette's."

Elli telepathed in reply, "Can you get aboard the shuttle, Sirius?"

"No worries. I'll follow them aboard."

Stunned for the moment, Nandia quickly excused us from our audience. We gathered in the hallway, forlornly searching each other's faces, hoping to find a way to push back the dark clouds of this grim news.

Without a comment, Nandia telepathed Sirius. "Do you think you can establish a telepathic connection with any of the youngsters?"

"I'll give it a go. There were several at St. Bern's who were close before Gracie and I got sprung. I'll find out."

"Good. See if you can find a way to keep the captain from launching the shuttle," I added. "Easier if they remain on solid ground. Do we know how many Praesepian youths are being transported?

"Somewhere around a hundred."

"Departure time of starshuttle?

"Within the hour."

"Check on level of care for our young ones, once they're onboard."

"No worries. Ciao."

Our youngsters trapped within an Erylian starshuttle was the one outcome we had most hoped to prevent. Despite Everen's support earlier in the day, it was either his misgivings or insecurities that precipitated such a drastic act.

"These plans must have been in place before the arrival of the Erylian delegation," Dunstan said. "Well, at least we've a better ken of what Everen's been hidin'."

"Or is someone else pulling the strings, working on behalf of the delegation?" I wondered. "Major Yellian perhaps? Everen didn't know about the motorcade meeting them at the spaceport. Maybe Erylian sympathizers?"

"Dear family, I hate to break up this gab-fest," Sirius again urgently telepathed. "But the captain of this buggy is not open to a chat with a cat. Need Nandia and Dunstan onboard. Put a knot in your bluey. Sending target image now."

In my mind, I caught the image of the passenger section of a starshuttle. Its aisle was lined with youngsters, its seats were nearly full. Many Praesepians were in various stages of distress. Some were in tears. Angry, tight-faced proctors stood toward the rear of the compartment, loudly berating anyone who dared lag behind.

"Sirius, can you distract the proctors while Nandia and I scurry into the captain's cabin?" Dunstan asked.

"Easy slather. More fun than a boxful of jays."

"We're on our way," Nandia asserted and then led us back into the classroom.

"People, your attention, please," she announced loudly, "We have just learned that Dunstan and I are needed to attend to a matter elsewere for a few moments.

Nandia briefly described to the group the teleportation departure they were about to witness. She turned toward Dunstan and they joined hands. "No more of yur speedin' round sharp corners, now Lassie," Dunstan quipped. She chuckled, and together, they closed their eyes, breathed, and disappeared.

I stepped up to the front of the room. "We look forward to their safe and speedy return," I said. "At that time I'm sure we'll learn more about what has called our friends away.

"To return to our discussion of our healing," I continued, "there are many ways each of us can heal any problem, and there are many ways we can stall our own healing. For many years I struggled with addiction. One deep belief that delayed my recovery was the notion that I don't deserve healing — especially after my repeated relapses. Remember, it is only our own limiting beliefs that can block the natural process of healing. I encourage each you to identify your limiting beliefs about yourself. Talk about them, question them and see if you are willing to replace them with more constructive ideas over these next few days.

"The question we want you to continue to ask yourself is: Am I ready to heal?"

Not a word was spoken, but like a nest full of chitterlings, the youngsters' energy fields reflected an eager anticipation.

"One very simple, yet effective healing tool is a series of ten deep, connected breaths." To demonstrate, I began breathing deeply. After connecting a series of full inhalations with complete exhalations three times, I continued with my explanation. "Whenever you experience a physical or emotional discomfort, experiment with taking ten connected breaths. Let's do this exercise together.

"To begin, first close your eyes, and then identify some discomfort you are presently experiencing. Even emotional disturbances have some location in our bodies, otherwise we wouldn't feel them. So take a moment to locate a discomfort's presence in your body. Where does your disturbing sensation reside?" Following these directions, the group began mentally scanning their bodies.

I gave them a few moments and then said, "Briefly nod your head once you've located your feeling." It only took a few moments before everyone, other than Yellian's duo, indicated they were ready to move on.

"Next, rate your discomfort on a scale of one-to-ten — with ten being the most uncomfortable," I suggested. After a short pause, I continued. "Now begin a series of deep breaths, connecting each full inhalation with a complete exhalation." Breathing loudly, I demonstrated this pattern of breathing and we slowly completed ten breaths.

"Now, close your eyes and locate the sensation you identified earlier. Raise your hand if you now notice a decrease in your discomfort." As usually happens with this exercise, the vast majority of people indicated improvement in their symptoms.

"Throughout our time together, we will be using

deep breathing, musical toning and energy exercises. We will also be using vibrational remedies. Ultimately you will learn that external remedies are not necessary for you to heal. Our pendulum testing will determine if there are vibrational frequencies available that can accelerate your individual healing process."

"Each of us goes through our own healing in our own ways," I concluded. "For today, use this healing exercise with your breath as often as you can — and notice the result." From watching the energy fields of the group, I knew that each person was expanding their trust in their own power to heal. I telepathed to El that now would be a good time to take the group to Braeoon Gardens for a picnic lunch. She readily agreed.

"Lieutenant Turpelo," I called out. "Can we now arrange for a lunch break at Braeoon Gardens?"

"Yes, Sir," he responded. "Transport and supplies await us at the building's front entrance."

"I thank you, Lieutenant."

I turned to the group and asked, "Does anyone here have a flying disk, which is called a Frisbee where I come from?"

Three hands went up. "Please bring them to lunch," I said. "If we can get Sirius to join us you'll be amazed at how fun it is playing with a teleporting cat." Smiles crossed the youngsters' faces as they tried to imagine a cat throwing a Frisbee.

The lieutenant proved to be quite efficient. We arrived at the gardens to find a well-furnished picnic laid out in the shade of giant fig trees. The broad lawn stretching in the distance provided a perfect place to romp and play. Blankets were arranged in a circle around trays of salads, sandwiches and fruit. Tea and juice were available. Elli sat on the nearest blanket and, together, we began passing out beverages. Proctors and youngsters alike soon settled in a circle surrounding us. We all set upon the food with a vengeance.

While eating I telepathed Sirius to see how Marshal Everen was faring in his role as host to the Erylian delegation. "No worries, Mate," came his reply. "He had an honor guard waiting at the Don as the motorcade arrived. Leaders of the delegation were most impressed. I'm sure they wondered how he knew of their arrival, but no one dared ask him. Obviously they are here to either approve or condemn the manner with which he's been carrying out his orders. They're all having lunch at the hotel now."

"We're at Braeoon Gardens," I replied. "If you can, join us for lunch and a game of Frisbee. Tuna sandwiches available."

"Too right, mate. Watch for me soon."

As I finished my meal, I listened to the lighthearted banter between proctors and youngsters. Amidst playful jokes and ribbing, many introductions passed between family members and friends. Several of the young people enthusiastically recounted how much better they felt after their deep breathing experience. Quickly these youngsters were learning that healing was meant to be accomplished with ease.

Sirius arrived in time to finish off the last of the tuna. He nestled in next to Elli where he ate and rested.

I asked El if she might tell the Erylians more about her planet, Aesir. To their delight, she regaled them with the story of how we had helped a lost soul, the former King Wilhelm. For years after his death, he stubbornly refused to release his deep grieving over the loss of his beloved wife and so, remained trapped on Aesir as a disembodied soul. With little to do without his physical body, he resorted to haunting his son, King Sabre. Wilhelm believed that harassing his son was the only way to keep Sabre from losing the royal throne of Aesir, which had been in the family for countless centuries. El, Nandia and I helped him realize that haunting his son was only adding to Aesir's problems. We then helped Wilhelm reunite with his lost love in the dreamtime. There it was that he healed his unresolved grief and began his journey onward into his afterlife.

The audience was spellbound as Elli spoke. They loved the story of a broken love affair repaired. She added much to what I already knew of the royal family's history. A gifted storyteller, El knew her audience would be captivated hearing tales of Aesir's royalty.

Ignoring repeated requests for another tale of Aesir, she stood up and asked for someone to toss her a Frisbee. She caught the bright blue disk in mid-flight and called out, "Sirius, this one's for you." Giving it a mighty heave, the disk arched high in the air heading straight for a stand of trees. Sirius leapt up into the air and suddenly disappeared.

When next he could be seen, he was riding on the back of the Frisbee, one paw lifting its left leading edge. The little sharper was steering the flying blue plastic carpet into a 180 degree turn! It gradually descended, landing in the middle of an open space. Sirius sauntered off a few paces, then sat on his haunches and began grooming his tail. Cheering youngsters raced to be the next to claim throwing rights.

I decided to get into the act and teleported to the

Frisbee, ahead of the fastest youngster. I snatched it up and threw it back toward the picnic area — where it landed in the hands of one of the proctors. Laughing, he stood, braced his stance and gave it a good, long toss. It landed in the middle of the running group of youngsters, and suddenly the game was on.

Gracie and Hyldie, who had bonded like sisters all morning, suddenly parted. Gracie ran toward the boy with the Frisbee and snatched it from his hand. She threw the disk as high as she could and El projected herself at least twenty feet into the sky to capture it.

Descending gracefully to the ground, she threw the Frisbee over Sirius's head. He repeated his earlier performance with a teleported landing on the back of the sailing disk. Suddenly two more Frisbees were launched. Sirius guided the blue one he was riding into the path of a red one and snagged the second disk with a front paw. He leapt onto the ground just as his blue Frisbee landed in Hyldie's hands, while the red one landed at her feet. He casually wandered off again.

I spend a moment considering his mid-air agility and realized he must be levitating just above the soaring Frisbees, otherwise he would be spinning madly through the air. His ability to focus so that he could to do this seemed beyond possible, but my eyes did not deceive. I was watching incredible magic.

I resorted to staying earth-bound during the rest of our play and found that a few of the youngsters could run faster than me. With three Frisbees in the air, and proctors, Elli and young folk happily racing about, it was quite a refreshing playtime. Gradually people began to get winded, the game slowed, with Walter collapsing in a heap between El and me.

"Wow!" he exclaimed as his heavy breathing began to return to normal, "I haven't had that much fun in years. While I was running after Sirius sailing through the air, I found myself wondering about how a cat can be telepathic. Is it possible I could learn to get good at it?"

"We'll be talking more about that later on," El said. "However, I will say this. Remember, Nandia mentioned the discipline of being rigorously honest with yourself? As you become more confident with that, you must allow yourself to trust yourself in your point of power — the present moment.

"Your Inner Self is continuously sending your conscious mind impulses toward action, impulses that are meant to lead you to greater and greater expressions of your life's purpose. So the next question is, Walter, can you listen to and trust those impulses in every moment? Can you learn to trust that when a destructive impulse appears, it is suggesting you examine the constructive impulses you've been suppressing? Does that give you enough to work with for now?"

"Yes, Your Highness," he replied reverently. "It's a tall order, but I know it's right." Heads were nodding among those who had gathered to listen to the former queen's sage advice.

"And now I believe it's time to return to our healing explorations back at the Intelligence Center," I announced. "Lieutenant Turpelo, would you please see to our transport? We'll collect the remains of our picnic before we load up."

"Vehicles stand at the ready, Sir," he said.

"Thank you, Lieutenant. We'll meet you at the garden entrance." I looked over our group and projected the image of us gathering armloads of blankets and other picnic debris. It did strike me that several people were at least subconsciously aware of my telepathic message for some, including Walter, headed toward the picnic grounds and got to work.

We left the place spotless.

# X V

NANDIA AND DUNSTAN were waiting for us at the I.C.'s broad-stepped entryway as we arrived in Torpelo's vehicles. We warmly greeted each other and headed into the classroom.

El, Gracie and I were anxious to hear of Nandia and Dunstan's adventure aboard the Erylian starship. I called for a fifteen-minute bathroom break and we gathered in the hallway to telepathically listen to their tale.

"The starshuttle captain, Reamer, was a right bloody hard nose, so he was," Dunstan began. "We teleported into the cockpit while Sirius distracted the armed proctors in the passenger cabin. We had ta wade through piles of Reamer's self-righteous indignation — he even accused us of being pirates hopin' to take over his craft. Nandia informed him of our Grand Council status and the Geasan mission. Finally he began to relax n' even waxed bit cadgey."

"Not only did the captain grow friendlier," Nandia

explained, "but it turns out that his own three children are caught up in the Erylian Condition. When he heard that we were exploring healing the problem, he became downright cooperative. Dunstan invited him to hold the shuttle in orbit around Praesepe, and give us a day to work with Everen and the Erylian Delegation. Reamer was willing to risk being charged with dereliction of duty if it meant there was hope for his own family. He then explained our plan to the proctors on board, every one of whom wholeheartedly stood behind him.

"Before we left, we talked with the Praesepian youngsters on board and told them of our plans. Dunstan guided them through a toning session. They're being well taken care of. Sirius will be checking in with them throughout the day. Thank God he's on this mission — what a trooper."

Relieved, El and I reconvened the classroom session. Several youngsters immediately asked questions of Elli who continued with more of our adventures on Aesir. She charmed the group with her tale of the King's falconer, who had unwittingly set a renegade Grand Council Delegate on a path of pirating Aesir's starships. She even explained how Nandia and I had befriended the falconer by finding a vibrational remedy for his birds. The remedy worked so well that the King granted us an audience, despite his aversion to Council Delegates. That led us on an adventure to a neighboring planet, where we infiltrated a warlord's outpost.

The young folk loved Elli's tale of how Nandia and I had disarmed three terrorists and so gained the warlord's good will.

Elli then talked about the community concert Dunstan had produced on Geasa, which was the best way we could think of to educate the city about the remedies we had developed.

This was a story I was surprised to hear her tell, since the Aesirian Chambermaid hadn't been in Geasa with us. Obviously she and Dunstan had been sharing their stories with each other.

It wasn't long before El had Dunstan teaching the group songs that his choir sang for the Geasan concert.

"Time to return to our healing work," Elli finally announced. "I would now like to teach you another healing process. It is called toning. It's a way to focus the natural healing energy of music."

She started with the girl named Glorya, who had earlier complained of a headache. "Are you still feeling any pain?" El asked. The girl nodded. Elli had her close her eyes and breathe deeply. After Glorya settled into a peaceful rhythm of breathing, Elli selected a single note for its resonance with the girl's body and began humming it.

After a moment or two, El stopped toning long enough to suggest, "Glorya, see if you can find a note to hum that will sound good with mine." Although initially hesitant, the girl began singing a few discordant tones. Eventually she found a note that blended well with El's.

The two toned together for only a short while before others in the group joined in. Some closed their eyes searching for a harmonic note, others simply smiled and toned the same note Elli sang. Before long the sound resonated throughout the room. Proctors who weren't singing listened with a smile. Soon Glorya's face brightened. She opened her eyes and said, "The headache is all gone. It's amazing how good I feel."

El asked if anyone else had experienced a release from symptoms. A number of people, including several proctors, raised their hands. She asked if anyone else wanted to experiment with toning. Hands went up and she repeated the process that she had just completed with Glorya. "I'd recommend each of you use this toning exercise just before falling asleep this evening," El said.

Just as El was wrapping up the toning lesson, the classroom door opened. The Erylian Imperial Delegation, led by Marshal Everen, Captain Whittaker and Major Yellian, filed into the room. A dozen Erylian political and military delegates arrayed themselves across the front of the room. Nandia and I introduced ourselves, included Dunstan and El, and briefly explained our mission as Grand Council Delegates.

"These people are responsible for the city of Geasa's recovery from its fatal epidemic of a number of years ago," the Marshal explained. "As I mentioned earlier, they are here working with this group of Erylian youngsters to see if they can find answers to the malady that has inflicted our young people back home. The proctors provide security and observe these proceedings as well."

"Would members of the delegation introduce themselves?" El asked. A barrel-shaped, graying gentleman stepped forward. At one time possibly quite handsome, his jowly face appeared to be permanently flushed. Yet, somehow he managed to look distinguished — perhaps due to the many military decorations that adorned his uniform.

"I am General Haplydean," he said. "I serve as the Commander of the Erylian Defense Council. These two officers are Brigadier Young and Major Yellian. They jointly command all of Erylia's off-world military operations." Everen looked distinctly uncomfortable as Yellian and Young stepped forward and bowed to the class.

Next in line was a tall, elegant, dark-haired woman, attired in a stylish, navy-blue suit. "I am Chancellor Branson," she announced. "I serve as Erylia's Secretary of State and report directly to the Premier, who sends his apologies that the demands of his position did not allow him to join us.

On down the line delegates introduced themselves. High-ranking men and women identified their roles within the Erylian government. All past middle age, they appeared determined and resolved as they stood before the group of Erylian youths and proctors.

"I would like to invite you to observe our work here today," I said. "If you do join us, please feel free to ask questions at any time. Since we will be discussing individual health issues, I request that you respect the confidentiality of each person's identity. Is that acceptable to you?"

The delegates gathered around General Haplydean and Chancellor Branson for a few moments, quietly discussing the terms of my invitation. Waiting in silence, I scanned the group's energy fields and noticed, almost to a person, everyone's aura displayed shades of grey revealing doubt and fear along with streaks of dark red, indicators of overwrought nervous systems. Some of their auras also displayed hues of mustard yellow, indicating craftiness and cunning, and bands of bright orange and coral pink — the colors of immaturity and pride.

Marshal Everen showed a field of red streaked with brown, indications of hopelessness and insecurity. My guess was the Marshal was quite worried over an unfavorable ruling over his command decisions.

Resolving their private conversation, the delegates reformed into their line. "We will accept your invitation, and agree to respect the privacy of each person here, as you have requested." It was General Haplydean who served as the delegation's spokesman. "However, please be aware that if at any time this delegation finds that we are wasting our time, we will order this endeavor to be halted. While we respect that you four are each Grand Council Delegates, we do claim authority on Praesepe to make whatever decisions we feel are necessary for the success of the Erylian military campaign."

"Even though this siege is clearly in violation of inter-planetary treaty and law?" Dunstan asked.

Chancellor Branson, Erylia's Secretary of State responded. "Our presence here clearly demonstrates that Praesepe is now a satellite of Erylia. If the Galactic Grand Council cannot accept that fact, then we are happy to resolve it in front of the Galactic Supreme Judicial. Meanwhile, we are in command here."

"We understand," Nandia replied. "And we thank you for your willingness to observe these proceedings. Would you mind taking seats and we will resume our work?"

The delegates filed down the main aisle and settled together in the chairs behind the proctors. The General and the Chancellor sat together and, with heads almost touching, immediately began whispering to each other.

I resumed the session by asking the Erylian youngsters to identify their symptoms. "I will ask that you speak of the physical, emotional and any mental difficulties you're experiencing," I added. "As we listen, we may suggest healing tools for you to use. For some, we'll talk about nutrition, others will be asked if you would like to receive a treatment of Reiki healing energy. We might recommend using the breathing and toning exercises that you've already learned. All these can quite effectively help your bodies unblock the inner channels through which healing naturally flows.

"Later on, we will be testing for and recommending different vibrational remedies. For the benefit of those who have just arrived, we are able to imbue electromagnetic frequencies into distilled water that, when administered orally, have proven to be not only safe but also effective in supporting deep healing. We will be demonstrating this process later today."

There were nods among the Erylian delegates so I turned my attention back to the Erylian youth.

"To you younger Erylians, if you choose to use our support, please openly share the results you get during this process. This will greatly help us in developing answers that will serve all those suffering from the health problems that are plaguing your generation on Erylia. Do each of you understand?" All of the youths nodded their heads.

"So unless there are further questions," Nandia announced, "Who would like to begin talking about symptoms you're having?"

A number of hands went up and Nandia pointed

to a young woman at the far end of the group. "Yes, and remind us of your names please. Dunstan will be taking notes so we can later refer to what you teach us about this condition."

"My name is Yvonne," the girl said. "I've been really depressed and unhappy for several years now. I'm afraid that I'm going to feel like this the rest of my life. It's a terrible burden that I can't seem to find any relief from. I've been on different medications that mostly make me feel groggy and dizzy and don't help that much."

"Thank you, Yvonne," Nandia said. "It always takes courage to be the first one to speak. Any other symptoms you want to tell us about?"

"Yes," she continued, "Despite the fact that I'm fifteen years old, I've never begun menstruating. I have no sensation in that part of my body, except kind of a heavy, dead feeling."

Nandia turned the group, "How many of you have the same symptoms as Yvonne?" All of the girls raised their hands. "And do any of the rest of you young women have any additional symptoms that Yvonne didn't mention?"

"Yes, I have regular headaches almost every day that last until I fall asleep," another mentioned.

"And how many of you girls are also having headaches?" Nandia asked. Three more hands went up. "Thank you. Are there any more symptoms that haven't been mentioned?"

"I have trouble sleeping at night," a girl who identified herself as Violet said. "I get to sleep easily enough, but wake up after a few hours and then have a hard time falling asleep after that." Again Nandia asked if others were experiencing the same problem. At least half of the girls were.

"And how about the young men, would any of you like to talk about your symptoms?"

Walter spoke up, saying, "I'm also having headaches and sleep difficulties like some of the girls, but I also get tired very easily and lose my energy about midday."

It turned out that three-quarters of the young people were experiencing exhaustion.

I pulled out my pendulum and repeated the basic dynamics of dowsing for the delegates' benefit. Asking my questions silently, my pendulum began responding with 'yes' and 'no' answers, and soon looked up to report what I'd discovered.

"After checking for the causes of your symptoms with my pendulum," I announced, "it appears that the origins of the Erylian Condition will be found within your hormonal systems. When this system is healthy, normal reproduction can occur. As we begin our pendulum testing for each of you, we will be looking to see which of these organs are weakest."

Nandia quickly described our testing process and herded the gaggle of youths into two separate groups around our two dowsing stations. After assuring that none of the youngsters had any objections, she invited proctors and delegates to observe the testing. They brought their chairs closer, surrounding Nandia and me as we set to work.

## XVI

I LOST TRACK OF SIRIUS somewhere during our return from the picnic and was surprised to see him in Hyldie's arms as she and Gracie sat at my testing table. I wondered about the fate of the young Praesepians aboard the shuttle and glanced quizzically at the cat.

"No worries, Boss," he telepathed. "The mob aboard the starshuttle is happily nappin'. Looks like yur havin' more fun here than tormentin' bugs 'n a cup. I just couldn't stay away."

I mentally thanked him. Dunstan joined me and we began to work with Walter. I explained the list of organs I was testing, as well as the dowsing process to identify the vibrational frequencies that would help revitalize the weaker areas of his body.

Walter listened carefully as I explained which organs were involved with his hormonal system. His adrenals and pituitary glands were the weakest, which explained his exhaustion and sleep disturbances. I was about to discuss the thyroid gland's role in immunity when Sirius suddenly leapt onto the table. He positioned himself right in the middle of Walter's testing sheet, interrupting Dunstan who was recording my findings.

"Sorry, Boss, another red alert," he telepathed. "I've just heard from Abe. There's a riot forming on the plaza just outside the front doors. He's concerned about the growin' crowd that's angrily protestin' the Erylian siege. They're fightin' mad over the landin' of this new Erylian Delegation and demandin' that they return home immediately."

Of course Dunstan and the rest of the family telepathically heard Sirius's message. The Scotsman jumped up and announced to the room, "Please excuse me, there is a problem I must attend to. I hope to be back before too long." Without hesitation he hurried out the door, telepathing to us that he would teleport to the hotel and report back.

Soon afterward he telepathed his news. "Midge and Joseph have alerted the underground to the arrival of the Erylian Delegation. Just outside the hotel entrance there's a nest of over three hundred angry hornets and they're turnin' ugly. Abe's jimmied his doors so most of 'em are stuck milling 'bout outside the lobby. I've got me horn, but could use some help here."

Like the rifle skirmishers who fought the barbaric battles of centuries past, Dunstan was always first on the battlefield, and the last off. This man's courage once again inspired me.

"Why don't Gracie and I leave now to join our musician?" Nandia telepathed. "Bearns and El can settle this group and join us later." Upon hearing that, a new idea came to my mind.

"How about if we invite the Delegation to observe the excitement from Abe's lobby," I suggested. "All we need is for the Marshal to assure their safety."

After everyone readily agreed, I stood and announced, "Ladies and gentlemen, a disturbance has erupted outside the entrance of the Abyssinian Hotel. Dunstan is on site now to peacefully diffuse the situation.

"Marshal Everen, might you provide an escort that would allow our group to safely observe from the hotel lobby? In that way you could all see firsthand our methods for peacefully dealing with an angry mob."

General Haplydean immediately protested, saying that any civil disturbance demanded an Erylian response. Nandia stepped forward and replied, "General, all that we ask is that you observe how we handle this situation for only five minutes. After that time, if your find our efforts unsatisfactory, we'll step aside in support of your Erylian response."

"How many people are involved in this disruption?" Everen spoke up, his tone commanding authority.

"Bearns will further explain ....," Nandia began, but suddenly Hyldie intruded.

"Papa, please?" she loudly interrupted. "Bearns and Nandia, could I join you, please?"

"Of course Hyldie," Nandia said gently. "With your father's permission of course." She turned to face the Marshal.

"This I cannot allow, my child," Everen declared. I wondered if by claiming his parental authority in front of the delegation, he hoped to add power to his command.

"Marshal Everen, please know that I will care for

your daughter as if she were my own," Nandia assured him.

A scowl of doubt hardened across his face as if chiseled into the muscles there.

"Absolutely not," his words were blunt, terse and pointed as the tip of a razor-sharp dagger.

"Sir," Nandia persisted. "This may well be the opportunity for your daughter to claim her own life, to grow in her own self-respect. She could have no greater caring support than that which will enfold her as a member of our team."

Nandia then paused and breathed deeply. She projected a brilliant white light with vibrant yellow streaks that surrounded Everen's red and dark brown aura. Their energy fields combined, the unyielding stubbornness carved across his face softened as he, at some inner emotional level, was touched by Nandia's overflowing compassion.

In a consoling voice, Nandia further assured the Marshal. "Sir, you will able to observe these events as they unfold. If at any time you wish for your daughter to disengage, we will immediately comply. Meanwhile, she may well discover more of her inner power and authority. Times of crisis are often times of growth. This could be a valuable opportunity for Hyldie to release her natural childhood dependence upon her father."

Everen looked into his daughter's face and saw a vitality and exuberance that had been missing the evening before. I watched his aura vibrate more brightly as he relaxed and decided to trust the intuitions of Nandia and his daughter.

"Stay safe, child," he said gently. "And may God have mercy on anyone who attempts to harm you."

Hyldie beamed and quickly lunged forward to hug her father. She then turned and joined hands with Gracie and Nandia.

"Thank you, Marshal," Nandia said. Turning to the Erylian delegates, she added, "May we assume that we have your consent to briefly intercede in this civil unrest before you intervene in the matter?"

General Haplydean and Chancellor Branson had begun conferring with Brigadier Young and Major Yellian during Hyldie's interaction with her father. It took a moment for the Chancellor to calm Yellian before she could respond to Nandia.

"We will agree to your request," she asserted. "Understand that we will insert our troops into the situation at any time we see fit."

"We understand," Nandia replied. "And now, we must depart." Holding out a hand to both Gracie and Hyldie, she briskly led the girls into the hallway and out of sight.

I stayed in telepathic rapport with Nandia and saw the three of them holding hands to form a triangle. Nandia said softly to Hyldie, "Darling, we're going to teleport you to where Dunstan is. Simply begin by calming yourself and breathing deeply. Close your eyes. Trust what you hear me saying as we take this journey. Remember to keep breathing deeply."

Clearly excited, Hyldie closed her eyes and began calming herself with her breath. She connected her second and third breaths. I mentally saw Nandia sending to the two girls an image of Dunstan standing calmly amidst a crowd in the lobby of the Abyssinian Hotel.

She and Gracie then imagined copper's frequency

and visualized sending a single cell from their hearts to join Dunstan in the lobby. "Hyldie, imagine a triangle of white light connecting your heart with ours," Nandia instructed.

She then suggested that waves of their energies flow toward Dunstan. Their combined energy fields vibrated within a sphere of brilliant white light. Then their bodies shimmered and faded as the vibrations intensified in frequency. The next moment, all three were gone.

# XVII

Marshal Everen quickly mobilized all proctors in the room and sent Lieutenant Topelo to arrange for the group's transport to the Abyssinian. Captain Whittaker was assigned to command an advance security detail to meet us at the hotel's front entry.

As our group of Erylian youngsters and delegates were preparing to board transport to the Abyssinian, Nandia sent an image of the lobby there, and telepathed that the three of them were standing together with Dunstan. They were watching an angry, unruly mob outside the lobby doors while listening intently to Midge and the cabbie, Joseph.

"The crowd's bloodlust is very near the boiling point," cautioned Joseph. "They're hot over the arrival of the Erylian Imperial Delegation — many sparks that could ignite a riot."

Moment by moment, more and more angry, enraged people were gathering outside the hotel's wide plaza entry. A squad of proctors stood just inside, assuring that the doors remained barred and locked.

"Me thinks 'tis time ta get ta work," Dunstan telepathed as he stepped toward the doors leading to the crowded plaza beyond. "Sirius, get ready to lead the way. And, Abe, can you open these plaza doors for us?"

"Most assuredly," came Abe's friendly reply. "I do so look forward to hearing more of your music."

Dunstan took his horn from its case and he turned to Gracie and Hyldie. "I've a feelin', Lassies," he said, "that you'll be quite useful in calming this mob. Wait here for now. I need to get outside before they start throwin' bricks and overturnin' proctors' vehicles. Watch and listen and be ready to join me as soon as my music starts to fade." He then nodded to Sirius.

The black, white-toed cat sauntered toward the door guards. They turned toward us, feet widely planted in a firm stance of resolve. Sirius deftly waltzed his way between their legs, his voice chittering a throaty gurgle. Dunstan followed closely behind. Several of the guards stepped peacefully aside and held open the doors, as if the passage of Sirius and Dunstan had been orchestrated long ago.

El and I, with the Erylian delegates and proctors, came through the Abyssinian's main entrance just in time to watch the black cat and Dunstan striding confidently out onto the crowded plaza. Once the two had stepped clear of the doors, the guards immediately slammed and locked them.

Outdoors, people nearest the doors began to notice the Erylian Delegation's arrival inside the lobby. The large security detail Everen had assigned to us took up positions along the inside perimeter. A few protestors scowled, raised their fists and began shouting, "GO HOME." Their expressions of rage were only faintly heard through the now secured plaza entry.

Out in the crowded plaza Sirius deftly darted through the angry crowd. The strobe-light effect of his dancing paws well captured people's attention. It was as if a moving light were carving a path as people began to make way for Dunstan. Only initially did he have to gently shoulder his way through the throng. Then the path widened as more people were captivated by Sirius's rhythmic prancing.

Reaching the plaza's center, feline and troubadour handily leapt up to a stone-slabbed platform where balanced a tall bronze statue of a long-past Praesepian founder. From there, Sirius gained Dunstan's shoulder and then leapt atop the statue's head. From this elevated vantage point, he scanned the plaza, gently mewed and began grooming a forepaw. People who noticed the cat stopped their ranting long enough to point him out to others nearby.

The Scotsman looked out over the crowd and spent a moment breathing deeply. Waves of people were flooding in from nearby streets — forming an angry ocean that ebbed and flowed around the plaza's hub. Dunstan's statue stronghold stood high above the maelstrom.

He set his horn's reed and softly played a gentle trilling riff to warm up. Pulling the instrument from his lips, he paused and nodded to those nearby who were now watching him. Again he put his horn to his lips, and this time blew a long, piercing note that reached far into the distance. As that sound faded he presented a loud, three-note trill of descending harmony that captured everyone's attention.

I was delighted to be listening once again to the magic of Dunstan's music as it penetrated the Abyssinian's glass-enclosed lobby. It was as if his notes had been lost to my memory and were now reawakening a deep inner trust in the sacredness of life. His music reverberated throughout the plaza and echoed off distant buildings with a startling purity and resonance. The crowd was so stunned by the Scotsman's first notes that their shouts of rage eased while their angry, upraised fists relaxed. People in the distance turned in circles, eager to spot the source of the sound.

Dunstan repeated his clarion trill three times and then descended into a lovely Chinese-sounding ballad, that was built around a lilting lullaby rhythm. An accomplished troubadour, he played with an engaging flair, dancing as his music bounced and echoed. His music sounded as if it emanated from several different points of origin.

With a steady crescendo, the troubadour's tune wafted through the arpeggios of the heart-rending melody. He then syncopated that rhythm with a few bars of a jazz beat that penetrated deep into each listener's subconscious. His ability to intuitively tune his music so that it eased the flow of angry, fearful energy was nothing short of miraculous.

The more Dunstan played, the more the angry people of Braeoon turned and faced the source of this amazing sound. Then they grew calmer. Their designs on destruction gradually began to dissolve. Faces opened into looks of amazement, smiles of delight stood alongside wide-eyed wonder.

I watched the Erylian Delegation as they observed the crowd in the plaza. Delegates with bent heads spoke in hushed tones to their neighbors. Some energy fields registered colors of orange and golden yellow, excitement and surprise, their red-browns of suspicion slowly fading. Several began surreptitiously pointing to angry individuals outside who were relaxing into Dunstan's music. One laughed heartily when shown the cat perched above the musician.

Chancellor Branson was smiling as she approached Nandia and said, "What a welcome surprise your Scotsman is. His art is a wonderful balm to many a troubled soul."

"Yes, we first met him on Geasa," Nandia replied. "He had been performing his healing music there for ten years when we met him." She then told the chancellor of the wonderful choir performance for young people that Dunstan had created — the pivotal event that had greatly accelerated healing the Saragalla epidemic.

During the time that people were growing more aware of the music's beauty, I watched the muddy red and brown colors of mob's collective aura begin to clear. People's mental and emotional fields were releasing clouds of hate and confusion. I then turned my attention to the Erylian Delegation. Lieutenant Turpelo was standing next to Major Yellian and pointed to Dunstan just as Sirius decided to abandon his high perch and go walkabout through the crowd. Yellian looked dour, the expressions on his face painted with shades of distain.

Wonder coursed through me. Again watching people's auras, I could see them recovering the sense that life was more than simply their despair over the Erylian siege. Dunstan's music awakened their natural optimism to celebrate the gift of each individual. Gradually the crowd began to grow, not with more angry people, but with more curious people. It was as if the giant troubadour's music blew away their anger and hurts as easily as the wind might bounce tumbleweeds far into the distance.

Dunstan saw that Nandia and the girls were aware of the ebbing of the mob's turmoil. He nodded to Gracie and Hyldie and played one last chorus of an eerie, gentle, riff that brought tears to my eyes.

As widespread applause swept through the crowd, Nandia, Gracie and Hyldie emerged from the Abyssinian's plaza doors and joined Dunstan. He bowed to the crowd and stepping down from his stage, softly playing his tune's reprise. Nandia mounted the statue's platform, turned and, as the music and applause faded, spoke clearly to the crowd.

"Praesepians, hear us, please." Her request was delivered with a penetrating wave of love and compassion. She stood tall and breathed deeply, quietly emanating a magnetic presence that enfolded the entire crowd. Soon silence ruled the plaza.

Nandia then introduced herself, Gracie and Hyldie. Her way of touching people was truly a miracle. They were inspired as they listened and watched her expressions of love — for herself and every other person in the plaza.

But as it turned out, she was simply warming up the crowd for the true show stopper. For then Hyldie stepped forward, nodded briefly to Nandia and began breathing deeply. The crowd's attention was riveted on this young woman who so bravely stood alone where only a moment before Dunstan had played magical music.

"Praesepians," she said loudly, "I am an Erylian. I've come from my planet to take part in a test to see if our health problems can be healed. Here I have discovered a sisterhood with Nandia and her granddaughter, Gracie. They have helped me realize that I can recover my health. With their guidance, I am healing. My emotional and physical recovery in the past twenty-four hours has been nothing short of miraculous." Hyldie paused and calmly looked out over the hundreds of people before her. Several times she breathed deeply before continuing.

"I apologize for my government's attempt to find an answer to our problems by laying siege to your home. With the healing that I and a dozen of us are now experiencing, we are confident we can take what we've learned back to Erylia. It is quite clear to me that we should now end this siege and return your children to you."

A great cheer arose through the crowd. Many were moved to tears hearing Hyldie's heartfelt revelations.

It was then that Gracie stepped forward to join Hyldie. She took her friend's hand before beginning to speak. "Praesepians, I am one of you, granddaughter to Nandia. I have been held against my will by Erylian proctors and only yesterday was released to take part in our healing research.

"I support the many people who seek an end to this invasion. I ask you to remember who you are. I ask that you accept that you alone have the power to change your thinking. I ask that you accept you can heal your deep hurts over the inequities we've endured. Consider this to be an opportunity to help another world, a world that is troubled at the moment, in learning to use the talents and abilities we are developing on Praesepe."

As the crowd's applause for Gracie's words died down, Nandia stepped up. "Those of us guiding this healing process have great faith that we are finding answers to help Erylia's young people. There is still much work to be done. The Erylian government delegation is watching us from within the confines of this hotel. We can make a change here today. We ask for a peaceful settlement to the Erylian siege of Praesepe. Many of you have aided us in what has already been accomplished. Together we can create what's needed to transfer our healing work to Erylia's healthcare system. We need your help. Those of you who can, please leave us a note at this hotel and tell us how we can reach out to you. We need your talents and abilities to restore health to the Erylian young people."

Again the street filled with applause. People gravitated toward each other animated with excitement as they considered the weight of what Gracie and Hyldie had said. At that point Dunstan began playing his music again, but quieter this time. It was a gentle rhythm that serenaded the crowd as people peacefully began dispersing — some moving into the hotel, others moving away. As Dunstan played his closing tune, Nandia, Gracie and Hyldie waved goodbye to the departing Praesepians.

And through the thinning crowd a young girl stepped forward carrying Sirius. She walked right up to the base of the statue and asked loudly, "Is my grandmother Midge here among the crowd?" Dunstan's music abruptly stopped.

"Is my grandmother Midge here among the crowd?" the slight, straight-haired blonde youth repeated loudly as she looked around the crowd. From her photograph, I recognized that this was Annie, Midge's lost granddaughter! Sirius had successfully tracked her down during his walkabout. Midge came running from Abe's crowded lobby, shrieking with delight. Their reunion was deeply touching and roundly applauded throughout the plaza. Many people left holding hands, hugging and shouting well wishes to each other.

Dunstan returned the horn to his lips and reprised his earlier Chinese lullaby. He skillfully drew in its jazzed rendition and closed with the eerie, gentle, riff that had earlier evoked tears of relief from the crowd.

As his last notes echoed away, the beloved Scotsman was engulfed in a massive hug from the family. Nandia, Gracie and Hyldie, along with Midge and Annie, jostled for position and, for quite a while, corralled the giant musician. They released him only after Sirius slithered his way in among their feet, looked up and sang out a piercing "Yeowww" that surprised everyone.

"Trouble afoot aboard the starshuttle, boys n' girls," he then telepathed. "I'll be back in two shakes of a rat's tail." Abruptly, Sirius disappeared.

As they shared looks of surprised curiosity, Nandia and Dunstan bade him godspeed. They began to make their way slowly toward the hotel, holding hands with Midge and the girls and savoring the stillness that was growing across the plaza.

Most among the proctors and the Erylian delegation applauded as the plaza doors opened and the group stepped into the lobby. Near the front entrance several Imperial Delegates, including General Haplydean and

Major Yellian stood apart from their counterparts, faces frozen and silently glum. Otherwise, the delegates were cheerfully smiling, impressed with the peaceful resolution to Braeoon's riot.

"That was a noteworthy result," Chancellor Branson said, smiling warmly to Nandia. "Perhaps now would be a good time to return to the Intelligence Center and see if you do, in fact, have the means to restore our children to health."

# XVIII

WE CAME INTO A CLASSROOM that was alive with blue streaks of exclamation emanating from the incoming clusters of Erylian adults. Delegates and proctors mingled as they trailed bubbling youngsters to seats stationed around our testing tables. Almost everyone was eager to talk of having witnessed the Abyssinian miracle. And still, orbiting around General Haplydean were Major Yellian and Brigadier Young, clearly disgruntled and wearing masks of stern rigidity.

Nandia telepathically suggested we let the talk fade before resuming the testing. It wasn't long before she loudly announced, "Ladies and Gentlemen, let us return to work. We hope that you will continue to quietly share your experience of this evening's events as testing continues."

The delegate/proctor group, with much shuffling and arranging of chairs, flowed into two semicircles around each table. An enthusiastic Walter and Dunstan sat waiting at our dowsing table — the troubadour impatient to record our findings from the boy's testing.

Dunstan pointed to my seat. "Get ta work, Laddie," he playfully crowed. "We've many a mile yet to travel this day." Nandia and El were already at work with their group of Erylian youths. I reached for my pendulum and began testing.

Using notes from our earlier session, Dunstan and I confirmed which of Walter's organs tested as having the lowest vitality readings. We then dowsed to see which of those organs correlated with the boy's symptoms. Next, using the book of radionic frequencies, we tested to find which ones would accelerate healing within the troubled areas of Walter's body.

As we worked, Dunstan fielding questions from the group. He would interrupt his responses to record a reading, and then happily return to the questioner to clarify information. He reminded his listeners that there is a unique electromagnetic vibration present within every part of the body, every substance and every pathogen. "This rate book is a mile-long list a' those vibrational frequencies."

He also further explained why we correlate each organ's vitality levels with the intensity readings for each symptom. "That way," he said, "we can easily get ta the heart a' what's troublin' ya." he said.

A proctor asked about the origins of the radionics instrument, which Dunstan explained before going on to describe its capacity to structure water with electromagnetic frequencies.

After completing Walter's test, I explained the results to him. Then a short and stocky, dark-haired girl named Alysia asked to be next. She exchanged seats with Walter and leaned forward, keenly interested in the process. She asked if she could take over Dunstan's record-keeping duties, to which we both readily agreed. As she carefully watched my pendulum, I dowsed to determine vitality levels of her body's organs and systems.

"On a scale of zero to one hundred, what is Alysia's pituitary gland's level of vitality?" was my first question. My pendulum swings sideways to my left to indicate zero percent and travels clockwise in an arc directly ahead to indicate one hundred percent.

"Twenty percent?" I asked and continued upward through the numbers in increments of ten until my pendulum stopped over the figure that represented her pituitary gland's vitality. "Sixty percent," I affirmed and nodded to Alysia. She duly noted the number next to the proper organ. I tested the rest of her hormone-producing glands and remaining organs. I also took readings for her immune, cognitive, and emotional well-being. In this way, each of the Erylian youngsters was tested, while observers, both young and old, often spoke amongst themselves. At times, someone would ask for clarification about dowsing questions or techniques.

Once we had completed our testing, we suggested a break. The family gathered around Nandia to discuss our findings. It turned out that all the youngsters' endocrine glands were sadly depleted — their reproductive organs, pituitary, thyroid and adrenals being the ones most severely affected. Many of the youngsters also tested for nervous system and cognitive difficulties, especially the males.

In our search for the causes of these troubles, we

found that chemical and metal toxins were the culprits, as well as several mineral deficiencies. Most individuals also tested for a variety of infections and parasites. We discussed which remedies tested as most useful for each youngster. After people had returned from the break, I stood and spoke to the group.

"Thank you all for your patience," I said. "Our testing indicates that many of your symptoms will benefit from vibrational remedies that will help your bodies cleanse themselves of chemical and metal toxins." I gave a few brief examples of specific toxins that were undermining the health of certain organs, and how infections and parasites were exacerbating their problems. Nandia spoke about frequency rates and remedies, answering questions along the way.

"We would like to spend a few moments demonstrating how we produce these remedies," she concluded. "I believe you will find this next process of working with the radionics instrument of great interest."

We joined the two tables at the front of the room. The group serenaded their chairs nearby as Elli and I began setting up the radionics equipment. While I gathered the water, bottles and list of frequencies we needed, El started to explain the purpose of the various dials of the instrument. This process, however, was abruptly cut short when Sirius, reprising his earlier YEOOWWW, suddenly appeared comfortably nestled in Gracie's arms.

He telepathed what he'd learned of the trouble aboard the starshuttle. There he found many upset youngsters protesting a proctor's order to remain in their seats. "I found one youngster with a Frisbee," he said. "Soon proctors were waltzin' Matilda, trying to scoop the thing out a' midair. Left the Frisbee. No worries."

"I'm just pleased that Everen or General Haplydean haven't heard that the starshuttle is still in orbit around Praesepe," Gracie telepathed.

"Me, too," Sirius replied. "But I now must rest and recover my equanimity among creatures who, with any luck, still have their wits about them."

With that, he leapt into Walter's lap, added a counter-clockwise turn, and snuggled in. The lad, beset with curiosity, asked, "Sirius, how in God's good name did you know where to find Annie?"

"Consciousness can expand to accept our greater inner perceptive senses — which include being able to recognize individuals by their energy fields." Rising onto bended haunches, the cat continued in his clear, high-pitched voice. "Each of you has this ability, but your dependence on your physical senses can obscure your inner senses. Learn to trust that your Inner Self exists and has unlimited resources. Learn to respect your conscious mind's yearning to grow." He paused to let his listeners imagine these ideas, occupying himself with more needless grooming.

"I found Annie," he then continued, "by simply asking my subconscious if she was there in the crowd. Once I felt its affirmative answer, I asked it to help me locate her.

"Then I requested that my subconscious send to my conscious mind the impulses needed to guide me to Annie. When I began my walkabout in the plaza, I stayed tuned in to my inner navigational urgings. They quite easily led me to the girl.

"Sometimes, I feel an inner nudge to turn, other

times a lighted pathway appears, pointing the way to my destination."

With that, Sirius adjusted his purr motor to its loudest setting, touched up the fur on a front paw and then returned to his nest in Walter's lap.

"Sirius, you are a wonderful teacher. Many thanks, my dear friend," I said and then announced: "I wish to suggest ways that electromagnetic frequencies can accelerate healing.

"Some researchers believe that when a pathogen's vibrational frequency is introduced into the body," I explained, "the body activates its cellular immunity on an energy level and neutralizes the destructive effects of that pathogen. This could explain how radionics rates speed up the body's natural healing processes.

"And some researchers are beginning to change deep, core beliefs that pathogens have a destructive intent. By suggesting that all pathogens are conscious, they are beginning to accept that every consciousness is ultimately of good intent.

"I quite like the idea that electromagnetic frequencies enhance immunity and quicken healing by transforming pathogens into forces that want to contribute to our well-being."

"'Tis time ta give it a rest, now Laddie, so 'tis," Dunstan chided. "We know of yar passion for healin', but your yapper's collectin' overtime." I joined in the room's laughter, grateful for how easily Dunstan restored play to our healing work.

"So, I apply the universal law of value fulfillment to radionics," I concluded. "This law states that all energy seeks to express its greatest fulfillment. So, each radionics frequency seeks not only its greatest fulfillment, but the greatest fulfillment of all life as well. The days of imagining an adversarial universe are coming to an end."

"And, with that," Nandia added, "we know that someday, enough people will come to respect the power of their own consciousness and use that gift responsibly. And on that day, dowsing and radionics will become obsolete."

With chuckles and nods, the family all agreed. Looking up from her bottle preparation, Elle chimed in, "And on that day," she chirped. "we'll all be able to heal much faster."

"Those will be the days," I agreed. I inserted a bottle of water into the well of the radionics instrument, flipped a switch and in ten seconds the water's molecules had been structured to the desired frequency.

With earnestness that comes from a shared purpose, El and I charged all the bottles we needed in a very short time. As I labeled the bottles, Elli fielded more questions about the operation of the instrument and explained dosages. She encouraged hourly doses unless symptoms become aggravated. "If that happens," she told the group, "simply reduce the dosage."

We demonstrated how to take remedies by administering each youngster's initial dose. At one point, Sirius arose from Walter's lap, leapt to the floor and sauntered over to El. With a satisfied deep-throated gurgle he elongated his body into a playful stretch. He then leapt to Alysia's lap, unconcerned about theories, or remedies, or dosages. Between pulses of his purring, he indulged her with a double chin nuzzle before slowly twirling into his newest nest.

Curious to learn more about Erylia's lifestyle and environmental toxins, Elli patiently waited for Sirius to settle before exploring more of what our testing had revealed. "It appears that there are four major toxins causing your difficulties," she began. "They are the herbicide glyphosate; a plastic-softening chemical known as phthalates, and a compound of aluminum, arsenic and mercury, often used as a preservative in medical vaccinations. Also, about half of you test positive for remedies for bacterial, viral, fungal or parasitic infections.

"We found it of great interest that so many of you youngsters test as having radiation toxicities. You've left us wondering about the background radiation levels on Erylia."

Some in the audience smiled while others frowned through their surprise at Elli's questions. Delegates, proctors and youngsters alike considered the toxin and radiation levels of their home planet. Major Yellian and several nearby officers shifted uncomfortably in their seats. Glancing at their energy fields, I caught sight of the muddied yellows and browns of doubt, anger and fear.

Yellian abruptly arose from his chair and hurried to a stop behind General Haplydean and Chancellor Branson. Crouching between their chairs, he forcefully whispered to each of them, punctuating his words with shifting frowns and sudden gestures. Their auras intensified with small clouds of muddied greys, oranges and browns. Yellian's remarks were triggering confusion in the minds of the delegate leaders.

"......ship in orbit?" the angry major's complaint was loud enough for all to hear. I wondered if he had clairvoyantly imagined the starshuttle's presence above Praesepe, or whether he had telepathically picked up on Nandia and Dunstan's earlier visit to the starshuttle.

Haplydean quelled Yellian's outburst by raising both hands, palms facing the major. The general repeated the gesture, pumping his arms up and down repeatedly. Yellian's scowl of anger faded, as did the streaks of dark red in his aura, which was now mottled with dark brown clouds of hopelessness. He nodded once, stood up and looked around the room. It was at that moment that he realized his outburst had been witnessed by everyone present. He quickly cast his gaze to his feet and, silently fuming, returned to his seat.

I decided to wrap up the radiation discussion. "Whatever the source of Erylia's radiation, there are countless remedies for these toxins," I said. "Hanna, one of my favorite teachers, often told of simply brewing a fresh willow-leaf tea to clear the problem."

El stepped forward. "Reducing exposure to radiation is of prime concern," she affirmed. "And, as radiation clears the body, healing occurs more quickly. On Aesir, we've found these remedies quite amaz...."

Alysia squealed as Sirius stood and stretched across her lap. "Sorry, Shiela, didna mean to startle ya," he apologized. He administered another double chin caress and re-nested, motor setting on high.

In a moment of inspiration, Elli asked if the two youngsters whose laps had served as napping nests for Sirius had noticed changes in their symptoms.

"Now that you mention it," Alysia said, "My tiredness lifted after a few minutes of feeling the cat's purr. I didn't give it much thought at the time." Walter was nodding, squirming with impatience for the girl to finish

"My headache had returned during lunch," he exclaimed. "But as soon as Sirius landed on my lap the pain began to recede. I feel much better now."

"Thank you, Alysia and Walter," El smiled. "Many times we don't notice when our symptoms clear.

"And, have any of you who didn't nursemaid Sirius," she continued, "noticed any reduction in your symptoms?

Several hands rose. "Thank you," Nandia said warmly. "Consider that each of us, while individual, seem to heal quicker in groups — a dynamic of healing you'll do well to remember.

"And, as Sirius makes quite clear with his attraction to you young people, cats are amazing healers," she concluded. "They are renowned for their recoveries from unbelievable trauma and illness. Like our own musical toning, cats' purring has been found to be a very effective remedy."

# XIX

AT THAT POINT, General Haplydean raised a hand, stood, and loudly stated, "Nandia and Bernard, I must ask your indulgence and excuse two of our delegation, Major Yellian and Brigadier Young." The two officers stood at attention next to their commander. "They have duties at the I.C.'s communications center," the general explained, "and will require an immediate escort."

Everen dispatched Captain Whittaker and his squad, who briskly escorted Yellian and Young out of the room.

Nandia thanked the General who had by now returned to his seat. "While awaiting their return," she calmly said, "let me share more of what we have learned.

"Minerals are a necessary nutrient for effective immunity and health of the nervous system. During our testing we also found a number of you to be deficient in several minerals, most notably calcium fluoride,"

Nandia paused, gently pacing, eyes deep in thought, her peaceful presence a study in grace. More proctors and delegates were appreciating Nandia's magical presence — the youngsters had long since joyfully accepted her.

"I do wish to learn more about Erylia," Nandia continued thoughtfully. "Since calcium fluoride so bountifully occurs in so many foods, how could this particular mineral be scarce on Erylia?"

A proctor raised his hand and said, "My name is Sergeant Hamilton. For many years my family has owned a food processing company that is under government contract to extract a number of minerals from our food chain. Fluoride is one that we've been removing from our foods because of the damage it caused to our population's thyroid glands in the past century."

"Thank you, Sergeant," I replied. "That would account for the problem. Unfortunately this news reflects a common misunderstanding about fluoride's toxicity. It is *sodium* fluoride that is the thyroid toxin — *calcium* fluoride is a necessary nutrient. Unfortunately, a derivative of sodium fluoride is often added to water supplies, with the hopes of curbing tooth decay. It is the overconsumption of sodium fluoride that weakens reproductive systems, especially among the young. Thankfully, we have a sodium fluoride detox remedy that will help your bodies cleanse this toxin."

"It's quite likely that other toxins within your environment are contributing to Erylians' ill health," Nandia suggested. "Anyone have any further ideas about how this is happening?"

Marshal Everen stood and had just begun to speak when a proctor rushed in and handed General Haplydean a note. Patiently waiting until the messenger had departed, Everen then said, "You people are quite right. Many toxins are quite prevalent in our environment back home.

"It is widely known that there has been long-term collusion between chemical manufacturers, big pharmacies and our government. One glaring example is the destructive effects of many vaccinations while government and the health care industry either ignore the problem, or quote superficial research supporting their claims that no risk is involved. There have been a number of legislative anomalies resulting in many toxic chemicals now being widely used in healthcare, food processing, agriculture and manufacturing."

A tall, heavyset delegate jumped to his feet in loud protest. "That is patently untrue," he angrily declared.

"Would you like to clarify what you mean by that?" Nandia asked calmly.

"The Erylian government has sought to create environmentally friendly laws for all of our institutions and citizens to follow."

"And how effective has that been over, say, the past three generations?" Nandia asked. "Have there been changes in Erylia's weather, reductions in numbers of animal species, and new health challenges within the human population?"

Several angry proctors began clapping in response to the question. Looking chagrined, the tall, heavy delegate sat down.

Nandia interrupted the clapping by loudly stating, "I would hope none of our discussions today would be used to chastise or condemn anyone here. Marshal Everen, did you have more you wished to say?

"Yes," he replied. "People continue to protest the building of nuclear energy generators, especially the lack of safe nuclear waste disposal. New commercial efforts to reduce toxins often collapse under the weight of tax burdens and bureaucratic red tape.

"This has been going on for so long that most of us feel helpless, believing that nothing can be done to solve the problem. As I listen to you, I'm coming to believe that it is our apathy that has rendered an entire generation infertile. It is our apathy that has led to this act of war we are currently engaged in. I, for one, am horrified that I've gone numb to the problem and enraged that we've all let it deteriorate to such an extent."

Everen's message was immediately applauded by most of the proctors and all of the young people. The room reverberated with cries of indignation mixed with groans of frustration. This new direction and tenor of the gathering had the Erylian delegates squirming in their seats.

A resolute General Haplydean jumped to his feet and announced, "I now must interrupt these proceedings in the name of this Imperial Erylian Delegation."

"Marshal Everen," he solemnly stated, "effective immediately you are relieved of your command. This is your official notice that your rank and status are under review. Please come with us to debrief and arrange for Major Yellian to assume your command."

"May I ask the Delegation's reasons?" Everen was visibly disturbed and fought to keep his voice calm.

Ignoring Everen's question, the General held up

the note he had just received and continued in a loud voice. "We have also relieved of duty Captain Reamer after discovering that his starshuttle is still in orbit around Praesepe. Failure to faithfully execute Erylian battle directives, suborning your officers — more than enough reasons to..."

"One moment, please!" Nandia's voice, though not loud, was piercing enough to stop the General in his tracks. "I request that Marshal Everen be remanded into the custody of the Galactic Grand Council Delegates who are present in this room."

We all immediately stood up in support of Nandia. A hush fell over the room. The General glared at Nandia. His mouth opened, then closed again. Abruptly, he turned and faced the Erylian delegates. At his hand signal, and they all gathered together in a huddle. Hushed talk began, rising to heated argument and falling in waves of whispered assent. In the end, the General turned and addressed Nandia.

"Marshal Everen will be remanded to your custody at the end of the day," Haplydean declared. "In the meantime, he will be debriefing with us and briefing Major Yellian to assume his command."

Led by the General, Everen and several delegates and proctors filed out of the hall. Everen walked stoically, flanked by two grim-faced proctors. His demeanor was stern — the grey, red and brown colors of his aura indicating tightly restrained hurt, disappointment and fear.

As the door closed, one of the younger proctors took the floor.

"It's quite clear to me," he loudly stated, "that something needs to be done about our lifestyle back home.

I've never before participated in a group discussion about our health problems, but now it seems inconceivable to me that anyone would sit still for so many years when our children's health has been so compromised. "

Another proctor stood and said, "I'm spittin' angry at what we've allowed to happen, not only to our planet, but even more to our own loved ones. I've been listening today to many new ideas and am just now realizing how I truly feel. I'm more than angry. I'm feeling like taking up arms and chasing the damn government off the face of Erylia. I know it's mutiny, but that's how I feel."

The remaining delegates, now led by Chancellor Branson, sat silently stone-faced and rigidly erect in their chairs.

Other fired-up proctors stood and registered frustration and fury. There were calls to lead a full scale armed revolt, calls to organize Everen's elite corps into squads of firebrands to inspire Erylia's one million-plus military to overthrow the government.

"The intensity of your feelings is admirable," I said after the proctors' wave of anger began to ebb. "It's a natural reaction to lash out, especially when hurt. But I've found, time and time again, that my desires to attack are my way of trying to ignore my own hurts. If I pursue those desires, I always end up — and I mean always! — regretting it."

Elli stepped to the front of the room. "And yet, expressing our pain is a very wise choice," she said. "As we express our hurts, doors open to healing them.

"Perhaps, some here today could use some help in expressing their feelings of hurt, upset and disappointment," she suggested. After intently gazing into each person's eyes, she quietly announced, "It is safe."

She then turned and simply said, "Sirius?"

At that invitation, the cat began a low-pitched YEOWLL that slowly rose in intensity. Dunstan and I added our voices, the rest of the family right on our heels. Soon most people were standing in a room that loudly reverberated with the feeling-tones of collected anguish and rage.

I was reminded of the emerging roar of an earthquake, or a string of diesel locomotives, drawing its train ever closer and painfully louder. The cacophony went on a minute, then two, over three, and only then began to wane. At that point, most of the Erylians in the room and all of the Praesepians were exhausted and in tears.

Nandia began to breathe deeply as the roaring wave of sound ebbed. The rest of the family joined in, followed by the youngsters and then many of the delegates and proctors.

The firebrands were all breathing calmly now. I could see the tension and hurt easing from their auras and their bodies. As I scanned different energy fields, I could see a number of people had recognized their own blaming and self-pity. Some realized that they had projected their own hurts onto their government, which had fueled their desires for punishment and revenge.

"Part of every healing's message," El stated, "is a reminder that we all create the common events in our lives for a constructive purpose. At times that purpose may seem obscured by the hurts of disappointment and failed expectations. But whether realized at the time or not, the outcome we create together will ultimately prove to be beneficial to our individual and collective growth. Keep in mind we have all contributed to the Erylian Condition. I suggest its healing will reverberate far beyond the symptoms of these young people."

The classroom door swung open as proctors escorted Everen, Haplydean and Yellian back into the room. Yellian ordered Everen and his guards to take a seat toward the back.

Yellian and the general then stepped to the front of the room, where Haplydean announced, "I am pleased to inform you that Colonel Yellian is now commander of Erylian operations on Praesepe. Colonel?"

"Thank you, General," Erylia's newest military commander beamed, having risen to the rank of Colonel within a very short time. Then his smile turned into an authoritarian mask.

"As of this moment, I am ordering that all Grand Council delegate healing work with Erylian citizens will immediately cease." He gave us a moment to digest his decree before he turned to us to say, "Please submit written proposals for any further work you wish to undertake directly to my office."

"Not to worry," Nandia telepathed to the family. "I imagine Yellian's tyranny will open new doors for us."

"I also order that Nandia and her granddaughter be immediately returned to Erylian custody," Yellian's expression bordered on a sneer as he issued this latest decree.

"You've made your wishes clear, Colonel Yellian," Nandia calmly replied. "Of course Gracie and I will return to your custody.

"However, with your permission, Colonel," she continued, "I would now like to address the Erylian Delegation."

Yellian scanned the delegation, and seeing no disagreement, nodded his head.

"I would like to suggest a group resolution process tomorrow morning, at the entrance to Braeoon Gardens," Nandia stated, in an even, yet warmly inviting tone. "The Erylian Delegation and everyone here today should be in attendance."

"And what is the nature of this process?" Chancellor Branson asked.

"It is called a Resolution Walk, a process which has been used since ancient times on Praesepe," Nandia responded. "Two opposing groups involved in a conflict engage in a guided walk in nature together. Thereafter I will lead a brief, eyes-closed process for all to participate in, amidst the natural beauty of Braeoon Gardens.

"I would also ask that afterwards we share a meal outdoors in the gardens and discuss our experiences of the Resolution Walk. The intent is to discover what options we can create together so that everyone's wants and needs are addressed. As a conflict mediator, I can assure you that every conflict contains many solutions that will allow all opposing parties to win."

Everyone in the room, save Yellian, Young and Haplydean were openly interested in Nandia's idea. "And what conditions and terms are attached to your request?" Chancellor Branson inquired.

"I ask that we undertake this Resolution Walk tomorrow morning, after a brief session here," Nandia responded. "Then together we'll travel to the Braeoon Gardens and begin the process."

"Sounds reasonable," the Chancellor said. "Any other requests?"

"I ask that the Praesepian children aboard the Erylian starshuttle be returned here so they can participate in the Resolution Walk," Nandia had pitched her voice to a gentle assertive intensity that penetrated each delegate's sense of humanity.

"Absurd," General Haplydean exploded. "Why should we include legitimate hostages of war when it was you who encouraged the starshuttle commander to disobey his direct orders?"

"General, we encouraged Captain Reamer to remain in orbit for exactly this purpose. You have not lost custody of your hostages, we merely ask that you allow them to be a part of the Resolution Walk."

The man blustered, turned his back and conferred with his tightly knit group of disgruntled delegates and proctors. An argument ensued. I watched their auras shift from muddy brown darkness to the warmer empathic tones of jade green after Chancellor Branson quietly intervened. I began breathing deeply and then joined Nandia, El and Dunstan as they began humming healing tones so quietly as to be nearly inaudible.

After Branson had concluded her quiet comment to Haplydean and his cronies, Hyldie approached the delegates. "Honored Erylians, I humbly ask that you to allow the Praesepians aboard the shuttle to join us tomorrow. Keep them in protective custody if you wish, but we need them with us during Nandia's Resolution Walk. These are young people we've imprisoned in the hopes of a future for Erylia. If ever they are to be used for such a purpose, they must have their say.

"You've seen what these Grand Council Delegates accomplished during a near riot. You've heard of the health benefits we twelve guinea pigs have been experiencing. It is time to trust that this crisis surrounding our Erylian Condition can be peacefully resolved. You have nothing to lose."

"Thank you, Hyldie," the Chancellor said. "What you say does make sense." Most among the delegates, including General Haplydean, nodded in agreement.

But, then one of the younger delegates objected, "If such an action were to become public knowledge back home, I'm afraid my reputation among my constituents would be irrevocably tarnished."

Nandia stepped forward. "And if so, is that not worth the possibility that an entire generation of unhealthy Erylians can heal?" she asked, gently and softly this time.

The young delegate looked down at his feet, as a grimace ran across his face. Finally he looked up and somberly replied, "I beg your pardon Madam, it most certainly is."

Seeing no further objection as he scanned the delegates, the General directed Yellian to order the starshuttle to return to Praesepe. Gracie asked if Captain Reamer could be invited to be a part of the Resolution Walk.

"Aye, that youngster has sand," Dunstan acknowledged telepathically. "No wonder we've been blessed with her. Imagine the wee lass as a Grand Council Delegate." Gracie looked startled while the family chuckled at the idea.

"General Haplydean and Chancellor Branson?" Nandia asked, "Could the entrance to Braeoon Gardens be cordoned off for our use by 9 A.M. tomorrow?"

Branson and Haplydean only briefly conferred. "As it is key to your Resolution Walk, most assuredly," the Chancellor agreed. "Colonel Yellian, please arrange escort for this contingent of youngsters." Despite his apparent disapproval of the Resolution Walk, he nodded to the chancellor.

"Many thanks," Nandia smiled. "I appreciate the opportunity your delegation is providing us." She then turned to the Erylian youngsters.

"You young people who are leaving with remedies from today's session, please remember to take them several times this evening and tomorrow morning."

Although dismayed by Yellian's dismissal of our healing work, after hearing this encouragement from Nandia, their auras lit up with confident light blues, healing purples and the bright reds of vitality. Noting the absence of any delegate objections, they happily stood and applauded.

Nandia, along with the rest of the family, responded by applauding the youngsters. She then turned to Colonel Yellian, "Sir, is it safe to assume that Marshal Everen and his daughter will remain under the custody of the other Grand Council Delegates?" Scowling, he glanced at General Haplydean, who looked to Chancellor Branson. She nodded to both officers.

"Very well," the Colonel grunted, visibly unhappy about the decision.

"Thank you," Nandia replied. Sirius appeared and leapt up into Gracie's arms. "Now Gracie and I are prepared to return to Erylian custody."

Colonel Yellian signaled for Captain Whittaker's squad to escort the three to their lockup. El, Dunstan and I made a show of being distressed as El telepathed to the prisoners an invitation to share our evening meal in our suites at the Abyssinian.

Immediately following Whittaker's escort, the unhappy Colonel stalked out of the classroom. Next, another contingent of proctors departed, accompanying the Erylian youths to their quarters. Haplydean took his leave only after he had walked the line of delegates, shaking their hands and expressing his appreciation to each of them. He was the last of the Erylians to leave.

## X X

Everen and Hyldie were quite pleased to be sharing our suites at The Abe. During our ride to the Abyssinian — graciously arranged by Lieutenant Tupelo — Hyldie comforted her father over the loss of his command. He calmed her by explaining that although he felt some hurt, he also felt relieved. "I quite expected it darling — more and more I've been doubting the wisdom of this siege."

She hugged him and sat back satisfied. But after a moment's thought, she moved forward and exclaimed, "Oh, how I wish Gracie and Nandia weren't locked up."

"Aye, Lassie, ya never know. Ya might see them sooner than ya think," Dunstan's eyes twinkled. El and I simply smiled. Then Hyldie realized they could teleport from their confinement at will and giggled with delight.

"You must be quite proud of Gracie," Everen said. "For her age, she's quite marvelous. She has been treating Hyldie with healing energy. It is true joy to see the two of them growing closer and to watch my daughter recovering her happiness and vitality."

After congratulating Hyldie on the speed of her recovery, we spent a quiet time considering the passing view of Praesepe. The evening's darkness was being held at bay by charming arrays of gas lighting, while the city's sidewalks carried more people than usual. I wondered aloud about that.

"Perhaps the manner with which you so peacefully disarmed that Abyssinian mob has something to do with it," Everen noted. There followed a round of congratulations — after which each of us returned to a satisfied silence, recalling our own memories of the crisis and its unforgettable resolution.

After a time, I noticed that Everen appeared to be grappling with some hidden puzzle. "Bernard," he suddenly asked, "Nandia and Gracie aren't truly imprisoned are they? I've had a feeling all along that putting them in a locked room was an exercise in futility."

"Aye, ya could be right, so ya could," Dunstan mirthfully replied. "But I've been wonderin' if Sirius hasn't been arrangin' things so that neither Nandia nor Gracie are doin' their fair share of the chores." At that, we enjoyed a playful laugh together.

"Nandia?" I then telepathed, wanting to check in.

"No problems going to jail. Same cell, same guards," was her immediate reply.

"We're on our way to The Abe. Marshal Everen and Hyldie are with us. Will you and Gracie have dinner prepared by the time we get there?"

Chuckling she responded, "So you want us to escape and cook dinner? That will cost you big time. On our way now. Sirius will remain to monitor guard activities.

Gracie's looking forward to the evening with Hyldie."

Upon walking into our suites, we found fresh fruits and vegetables, a potato leek soup warming on the sideboard, and hot, sprouted, freshly baked bread laid out for us. Our guests were delighted at the sight of Nandia and Gracie. After enthusiastic greetings, we all dove into the fare that the two escaped captives had prepared.

"Our zinc shielding never really did slow you folks down, did it?" Everen asked after savoring the soup and declaring it good. "You've been free to teleport since you got here, haven't you?"

We all laughed out loud and returned to devouring the wholesome and delicious fresh, live food. At one point, El congratulated Dunstan for the music he had played downstairs in the plaza.

"But, I noticed during that gorgeous Chinese lullaby," she continued, "that you played an F-sharp, rather than the F-natural in the seventh bar of the bridge. No big deal, just wanted you to know that it hadn't gone unnoticed."

Dunstan threw a bread roll at El, who calmly watched it sail over her head. I could have sworn it changed trajectory mid-flight. I then went back to enjoying the food and began watching our auras, noting how the chance to relax and nourish our bodies had brightened our energy fields.

While I set about preparing a pot of tea, Everen pushed back from the table with a warmly satisfied golden glow in his energy. "I so appreciate the comforts and warmth of being surrounded by a loving family. You all have helped me forget my worries over what could be the loss of my career."

"Well, Sir, perhaps all is not lost," Nandia offered. "I will say that the Resolution Walk tomorrow morning will very likely shine a new light upon the siege of Praesepe."

"I'm coming to trust your confidence, young lady," he replied. "But just recently, I've been wondering if I chose a military career to try to prove myself to the world. I believed that if I could become a high ranking officer, no one would ever dare doubt me or dismiss me."

That revelation moved El into a wonderful tale of attempting to prove her worth as the young bride of a past Aesirian king. "The sad part was, it never seemed to work. It took me decades to learn that it was my job, and my job alone, to approve of myself."

I told a similar tale of the same lesson while a student studying with Agoragon. As they listened to our stories, Gracie and Hyldie were quietly attentive. We sat enjoying our tea, surrounded by the warm glow of simply being together. Hyldie pointed out the outdoor balcony, now brilliantly illuminated by the nearly full moon rising just above the trees.

With wonder and awe, we lined the balcony and watched Praesepe's moon —the first time for most of us. I felt as if I were seeing a newborn child arriving into the world. It was a rosier color than Earth's moon, and at least three times as large.

As is common in the camaraderie that comes of sharing a new natural wonder, we gathered closer to each other. Elli asked Everen if his home planet had a moon. "We have seven moons," he proudly replied. "A small one in the far distance that appears only as a bright star. Our largest, while as big as this one here, is not tinted as is this beauty above us. We celebrate several natural holidays each year as multiple lunar eclipses succeed each other."

"Aye, that would be a sight to behold, so 'twould," Dunstan mused aloud. "Marshal, I'm wonderin' how much do your ocean's tides rise and fall with havin' so many moons?"

"It would be lovely to study their orbits," Elli added. "The mathematics involved must be intriguing."

I enjoyed letting my mind gnaw on that puzzle as we stood bathed in the rouge moonlight of Praesepe's moon. Everen seemed to have drifted off into his own private world, oblivious to questions about Erylia's tides.

"We call our moon Iounn," Nandia said, "after the ancient Praesepian god who activates healing, nurtures fruit orchards and watches over the young. It progresses to full tomorrow — which I'm quite pleased coincides with our Resolution Walk. It is the most favorable time to have dreams realized.

"Iounn does have an amazing effect on Praesepe's tides," she continued. "Especially during the two weeks of every year when it's at perigee and closest to Praesepe."

I could easily have spent the rest of the night standing on that balcony in the moonlight had it not been for the growing cloud of drowsiness that descended upon us — a warm, silent fog that beckoned us to sleep. Before heading off for bed, Nandia suggested that we focus our dreamtime travels on an effective Resolution Walk in the morning. She and Gracie then teleported back to their cell in the I.C.

A firmly cushioned couch warmly welcomed me as

I snuggled under blankets. Just as I was drifting off I heard the far distant roar of ocean waves. Then I remembered I hadn't even glimpsed a Praesepian sea. Relaxing into the rhythm of the waves, I wondered if the rosy hue of Iounn rendered these nighttime seashores far different from those back home. With that question I fell asleep. The next thing I knew, I was standing once again under the full bright light of Praesepe's moon.

I was in an open space of Braeoon Gardens and noticed I was holding a staff in my right hand. Examining it, I realized it was my t'ai chi staff, a six-foot-long stave worn quite smooth through years of practice. T'ai chi was the one discipline I had maintained since my early adulthood, studying with many teachers and marveling at how the practice enhanced my connection with the realms of energy. I hefted the staff, felt its familiar length and girth and posted it in the ready position alongside my body.

Away in the distance illuminated by Iounn's warm moonlight, I noticed that one side of the parkway was lined with the Erylian delegates and proctors, while opposite them stood a line of Praesepian and Erylian youths. Everen, his Group of Twenty proctors and Hyldie were standing in this second line. Everyone seemed to be frozen in time — and no one seemed to notice me.

I decided to practice my staff form and let myself enjoy the sensations of energy coursing through my dream body. I stood erect and slowly began the form I had learned in my youth — a choreography of ancient flowing katas designed to open the body's inner doorways to unlimited power. I executed the flowing motion called 'Break Open Temple Gate, Left,' turned and deftly flowed into 'Break Open Temple Gate, Right,' basking in the growing intensity of energy flowing through my body. As I began the move 'Cover the Pate,' Dunstan stepped next to me and matched my form, move for move, using a staff of his own.

So elated was I to find another person trained in Miss Chin's staff form that I nearly faltered. Doing this ancient art with others magnifies the physical body's delight at being so uniquely suited to this realm.

And then El and Nandia stepped into formation behind Dunstan. Both carried staffs as well. The flow of energy intensified as the four of us continued with a precision and synchronicity I'd never before experienced. Light began flowing between our energy fields and radiating out into the gardens. As we glided through the moves of the form, I became enfolded in a soaring sense of joy and delight.

In the face of such intensity, it was all I could do to continue breathing and focusing on T'ai Chi. The field of energy surrounding us began to pulse with gold and green colors. I realized a new-found depth to my desire for loving play. I was immersed in deep gratitude when I heard Elli invite Gracie to join us.

"But I don't know how…," the girl protested.

There followed wise counsel from Nandia, "Trust, Gracie, simply trust your body. Use your thoughts to transform the energy within your doubt into an expanded ability to trust."

Gracie began to relax and let her body flow. A staff appeared in her hands. She stepped into formation breathing deeply. After a few tentative moves, her staff began mimicking our moves. The more she relaxed, the more she was able to meld into the form with ease. Soon we all were in perfect sync. I abandoned my need to follow the remembered form and simply let my body move with the energy of T'ai Chi.

It seemed to me that our combined energies began melding with the light of Iounn. I was mesmerized by the elongated and synchronized shadows that we cast across the moon-lit lawn. Then a most unusual bit of dream magic occurred. Our shadows moved across the open space and enfolded the two lines of Erylians and youngsters! Both groups began moving in perfect harmony with us — everyone was doing Miss Chin's staff form! I imagined that the form was emanating from each person's moon-shadow and being perfectly replicated in their dream body.

It was truly a marvel, the joy and wonder we shared as we created this flowing landscape together. I felt a new inner doorway opening to even greater love. Continuing through the form, I noticed that our energy field's pulsations of green and gold started to wane as Iounn began its descent in the sky. Just as it touched the horizon, we came to a stop, staves vertically nested along each person's left side.

And then Nandia's clarion voice rang out, clear as a bell.

"And so, as clouds become the winds and skies become the seas, together we create a cosmos from the chaos."

Slowly, the dream melted away, like a spring frost on a sunny morning.

# XXI

THERE WAS VERY LITTLE chat the next morning — the Everens, El and Dunstan all radiated a warm glow of peace as we prepared breakfast and ate in silence. It was taking some time for the joy and magic of last night's dreaming to percolate through to our daytime consciousness.

Abe arranged for a hotel transport to carry us to the I.C. We warmly greeted Gladys and helped with last minute preparations for the classroom. Soon the teens began to arrive, many of whom were quite early. The crowd grew as we welcomed a small group of proctors. More young folk arrived, some in small cadres, others alone.

Colonel Yellian appeared, escorting Nandia, Gracie and Sirius. "Ya did well in the dreamtime last night, Boss," the cat acknowledged as he leapt into my arms. "Ya didn't see me, but I was there." He tucked his head inside my elbow and fell into a loud purr.

Marshal Everen coolly, yet cordially, greeted Yellian,

who, in response, was abruptly curt. The new Colonel still carried some of yesterday's scowl, leaving me to wonder about some unspoken animosity there.

Finally, the Erylian Delegation arrived, and milled about the front of the room until Nandia asked loudly, "Colonel Yellian, would anyone here object if we spend a few moments listening to how the young people are feeling this morning?" He quietly conceded to Nandia's request. Proctors and delegates took the seats immediately behind the youngsters. Nandia quickly recapped the accomplishments of yesterday's session and then asked the Erylian young people to report on their symptoms.

Hands thrust into the air enthusiastically — a virtual stampede to share their appreciation for their improvements in health since yesterday. Nandia intervened after a cacophony of responses and asked that youngsters be brief in describing their healing and expressing their gratitude. Excitedly optimistic, most spoke of a newfound confidence in their power to heal.

Almost all reported sleeping deeply and awakening with more vitality. Several initially noted headaches, which quickly waned after dosages were reduced for a short time. Walter thanked Gracie for her answers to yesterday's questions about remedies and healing. Nandia recapped how to deal with aggravated symptoms by reducing dosages.

Several told of using El's breathing exercise and Dunstan's toning to great advantage. Others, including Hyldie, mentioned dreams in which healing had occurred.

The mood of the room brightened with each successive story. Occasionally one of us would interject a question, but otherwise the sharing moved apace, unimpeded. As individuals reported their healing insights, the whole group moved into deeper levels of healing.

The Erylian Delegates listened intently. The bright oranges, reds and purples in their energy fields reflected their growing amazement at what they were hearing.

As the pace of storytelling began to slow, Nandia stepped forward and said, "To begin this morning's Resolution Walk, I would like to briefly revisit yesterday's exploration into issues leading up to the siege of Praesepe. Please remember that our intent is a mutually beneficial resolution, and refrain from using this forum to invalidate any individual or their point of view. Any comments or questions?" She looked around the silent room for several moments before resuming.

"To those of you who believe a violent overthrow of Erylia's government is your only option, let me remind you of a long-proven dynamic of effective change," she began. "Effective change always begins with a small group of dedicated people — a group committed to its purpose. And from our work accomplished yesterday, there's more than a slim chance that this group of Erylians here today is quite capable of sparking such a change, yes?"

Again nods around the room. Suddenly a boy's hand shot up from the front of the room. "Yes, Walter?" Nandia asked.

"What has me puzzled is how anyone might think that we can change our world for the better by going to war. I know that violent overthrows have occurred in our history, but it's never made sense to me."

"Walter, that took courage to say. Thank you." Nandia's acknowledgment evoked a proud smile on the boy's face.

She let Walter's challenge to violent overthrow hang in the air for a few moments — giving the delegates and proctors a chance to respond. While considering Walter's message, the auras of the firebrand proctors swayed between bright and murky yellow as their thoughts bounced between confidence and doubt. The young proctor who yesterday had advocated a coup d'état raised his hand.

"Yes, Sir?" Nandia asked.

"That idea sounds credible in theory, but if we don't overthrow the sons of bitches and start over, how in the hell are we going to effect such a momentous change? Given the determination of our government and industry leaders, a peaceful possibility seems but a forlorn hope." Anger and frustration clearly reverberated in the proctor's tone. Many other proctors nodded, vocalized approval and applauded.

"Thank you, Sirs." Nandia's tone was gentle. "You present valuable perspectives and objections worthy of note." She moved across the front of the room and paused there before continuing. "It is quite obvious that among us there are conflicting points of view. For any lasting resolution, it is imperative that we air these differing perspectives.

"Each point of view has something to contribute to this resolution process. Our willingness to listen to each other with open minds, without judgement and without condemnation is key to the creation of a workable solution to this crisis."

She answered a few clarifying questions and then

announced: "I believe now would be a good time to undertake our Resolution Walk. Colonel Yellian, are the arrangements we decided upon yesterday still agreeable to you?"

I had been watching the Colonel to see how he was reacting to Nandia. His anger seemed set to slow simmer as he stood at the back of the room. After grimly nodding to Nandia he signaled to Captain Whittaker, who briskly departed to look after our travel and meal arrangements.

Within minutes we all were aboard transports heading toward the Braeoon Garden gates. Right on our heels were another two buses, loaded with the Praesepian youths, recently off-loaded from the Erylian starshuttle. Overhead, the westernmost of Praesepe's suns, Njoror, was above the eastern horizon, lending a warm maroon tint to the morning light.

As we unloaded at the entry to Braeoon Gardens, the youngsters who had spent a day aboard the starshuttle looked quite happy to be standing on their home ground. Several recognized Gracie and Sirius and lined up to hug the pair. They were being closely guarded by proctors wearing side arms, whose watchfulness waned after seeing the number of troops Colonel Yellian commanded.

Proctors had cordoned off the area as requested by Nandia. A few Praesepians stood at barricades, openly curious about what was happening.

Nandia called out for everyone to gather together just inside the garden gates. The bright orange blossoms that blanketed the entry's archway reflected an unusual tint in the early morning light. The air held just the slightest of chills. Leaves of distant fig trees seemed somehow more vibrant, almost as if they were reaching out to capture the light of Njoror — a light still untainted by the golden rays of its companion, Freyr, still resting below the horizon. A few stray clouds drifted across the maroon-blue sky.

After acknowledging the beauty of the day, Nandia explained the Resolution Walk. "People, this exercise is a silent process," she said, pitching her voice to be heard by those at the rear of the gathering. "Please refrain from speaking until we gather at the end of the walk.

"I ask that each of you participate fully and pay close attention to your inner feelings and ideas. We will divide into two groups, those in support of the Erylian government's siege of Praesepe and those who wish the siege to soon reach a peaceful conclusion. We each have our own hopes and fears over the possible consequences of these outcomes. But for this morning, please set those aside and allow yourselves to be fully open to your own experience of the Resolution Walk.

"The group supporting the siege will be headed by the Erylian Delegation. You will begin your walk here at the entrance to the gardens. The second group will begin about a quarter-mile into the park, where Bernard will be standing. Upon hearing a musical signal from Dunstan, each group will begin walking single file as you pass the opposite group. Please do not hurry, but proceed at your own pace, without crowding or passing the person in front of you. Once everyone has completed the walk you will then be standing in the position formerly occupied by the opposite party. Does everyone understand these instructions?"

People nodded. Nandia had the crowd separate into

their respective groups. Those who supported an end to the siege — the firebrand proctors, the recently kidnapped Praesepians and the Erylian youngsters all followed me, El and Sirius to the far terminus of the Resolution Walk. There we stood silently awaiting Dunstan's signal.

The moment the minstrel's characteristic three-note riff pierced the air, El, as first in line, began walking toward Nandia's group. She was followed by Hyldie, who was followed by one of the kidnapped youths. Initially, some in our group were hesitant to begin moving toward the Delegates' position, but after watching the youngsters that led the way, they stepped forward with more confidence.

Dunstan and Gracie had remained with Nandia to lead the delegate group. They were followed by General Haplydean and Chancellor Branson, then the delegate party and the proctor group moving single file toward us. By now Njoror's warmth had melted the edges of the chill in the air. The clouds seemed motionless, the air as still as if time had frozen. We watched in silence as the two groups gradually began to pass each other. Some people looked at their counterparts walking in the opposite direction, others looked away, preferring the natural beauty that surrounded us. A few looked down at their feet. As I watched peoples' auras, the dark browns and greys of fear and insecurity dominated both groups.

It took ten to fifteen minutes, maybe a bit longer, for the last members of each group to pass each other. It took another few moments for the groups to reassemble, now opposite their starting point. Once that was accomplished, Nandia telepathed Dunstan who then repeated his clarion-like call. I noticed the faintest of breezes as I nodded to Dunstan. Nandia gestured to El and the process was repeated.

During this segment of the walk, more people looked at their counterparts with open curiosity. Some recognized those they were passing and nodded or smiled to each other. Overhead, a few more clouds were gathering, the air had begun to move. I enjoyed watching the participants' energy fields changing, the darker browns, greys and blues of uncertainty yielding to brighter oranges and warm golden-yellow tones of curiosity and openness.

This second walk took more time, as people slowed in recognition of each other and tuned more deeply into their own feelings. Some proctors and delegates were beginning to shed their masks of authority. Colonel Yellian, however, walked rigidly, bringing up the rear of the delegate group. This segment took at least twice as long as the first walk before both groups had passed each other and reassembled in their original positions.

Then, for a third time, Dunstan's musical riff signaled the final encore of the Resolution Walk.

During this walk, the energy intensified as more people chose to look at each other. Distant leaves rustled in the intermittent breezes that returned a slight chill to the air and left people mildly windblown. Some folk sought to calm their locks, but abandoned this vanity as the walk proceeded. At one point, Chancellor Branson slowed to a stop as she gazed at a Praesepian child — one of those who had been held captive aboard the starshuttle. Finally the Erylian leader moved on, with tears in her eyes.

Many deep connections occurred as the two lines passed each other. The mood was somber and subdued as each group reassembled for the last time. An east wind kicked up as more clouds began to appear in the sky's distant edge. It was then that the morning light from Freyr, still below the horizon, tinged the clouds overhead with its golden hues. The colors intensified, as if the manes of flying white lions had been set afire. People from both groups turned their attention to the skies as the overhead drama unfolded. Gradually, the colors faded. Freyr tipped its golden head above the horizon and Praesepe's sky slowly assumed its tint of natural daylight.

Nandia returned us to the Resolution Walk by telepathing that she wanted the two groups to meet in the middle of the walk. We led our respective groups toward each other, stopping as we met.

"I would now ask that you all form a circle around me," she announced. "Please remain silent as we complete this process. We prefer that you position yourselves between people you do not know." Everyone readily complied with these instructions, save Colonel Yellian and his two dour allies. Standing off to one side, they auras reflected coral pinks of dismissal and dark reds of anger.

Once Nandia's circle was formed, she directed people to lie on their backs on the lawn with their heads pointing toward the center of the circle. It was there that the family gathered with Nandia.

When everyone was in position, she loudly announced, "I will now guide you through an eyes-closed exercise. This will take only a few moments. Again, I ask that you listen and observe your subjective feelings, thoughts and attitudes. There will be a time to discuss your experiences at the end of this process."

Nandia directed people to begin breathing deeply, each full inhalation followed by a complete exhalation. She invited them to notice the clouds floating above them and Praesepe's two brilliant suns piercing the skies overhead.

"Now I would like you to close your eyes," she said noticing that people were now breathing in harmony. "Please continue this deep breathing pattern through-out this exercise." The five of us at the center of the Haida Circle breathed loudly together to help the group maintain its rhythm. Nandia proceeded slowly, with extended gaps of time between directions.

"I ask that you begin to recall the faces of the people you passed during our walk together... Notice your thoughts and feelings about the individuals that come to mind... Recall any worries you may have had about how you may have appeared to them... Let yourself honestly acknowledge whatever experiences you were having during this walk. Breathe...

"Recall the impressions you had about the sun and the wind... Notice any positive or negative judgments you had about the individuals you passed... Become aware of any emotions that are attached to those judg-ments... Be honest about any feelings of guilt, anxiety or resentment you felt during the walk...

"Notice any attitudes you hold about the Erylian presence on Praesepe... Acknowledge any attitudes of blame or pity you've imposed upon yourself or others... Take your time."

Again, Nandia interspersed her instructions with

long pauses, breathing deeply and in concert with the family.

"And finally, I ask each of you to spend a few moments and visualize your most preferred outcome for Erylia's presence on Praesepe... Set aside any doubts you have about your outcome happening and simply imagine the one you would most like to see happen... Visualize this outcome vividly, in color, with the people involved actively engaged in some kind of action... Again, I ask that you let this image unfold with ease... Experience your emotions and feelings during this process.

The four of us continued breathing together and telepathically shared our own preferred outcomes as we stood in silence surrounding Nandia.

"Focus on the feelings you have associated with your preferred outcome..." she said. "And once you are at peace with those feelings, please slowly bring your awareness back here into our circle... Take your time, listen to the sounds around you... feel the ground below and the slight breeze above... Whenever you are ready, open your eyes and sit up."

Upon concluding, Nandia sat cross legged upon the grass, with the four of us seated around her facing outward toward the people at the circle's circumference.

We waited in silence, breathing deeply, until everyone had opened their eyes and returned to the natural world. There were those who sat up almost immediately; others took longer.

After everyone had fully recovered their awakened state, Nandia signaled to Colonel Yellian. He nodded and in turn signaled Lieutenant Turpelo. A group of proctors with trays of steaming hot beverages, croissants, fruits and nuts stooped to offer their fare. People began serving themselves, sipping their drinks and quietly talking to their neighbors.

"As you enjoy this food, I would ask that you share with each other your experiences of the Resolution Walk and the meditation we've just completed," Nandia announced. "Later, after we have returned to the Intelligence Center, and with the Delegation's permission, we will be resuming our discussions about the conflict that has brought us all together."

Here Nandia paused and looked to General Haplydean and Chancellor Branson. Both nodded their agreement. Nandia continued. "So, for now, please limit your discussions to recounting your own personal experiences of the Resolution Walk."

People enjoyed the fresh air and sunshine as they sipped hot tea and cocoa, nibbled at food, and continued talking amongst themselves. Initially some spoke only to people they knew, but as the suns moved across the sky, even they timidly reached out to strangers. Praesepian youngsters talked with proctors; Erylian delegates spoke with Praesepian youngsters. Some stood and stretched, and then resumed their discussions. As the sounds of people talking began to settle, Nandia invited those who wished to share their experience to stand and clearly address the group.

Hyldie was first to begin. "Thank you Nandia and fellow Council Delegates for your continued efforts on our behalf. As I walked past our Erylian Delegates the first time, I noticed the vast physical differences between individuals. Then during our second walk, I felt as if I could sense some of their individual feelings and thoughts. During the final walk, I began to realize how much their points of view reflected my own."

She turned and spoke directly to a group of delegates nearby. "I began to see our common experience as humans, each living our own individual lives. At that point I found it quite easy to change my thinking from making you my enemy to seeing you as people with whom I share a common goal. We all want to rid our planet of the sickness that shackles my generation."

Some youngsters, proctors and delegates applauded, some waved and some smiled at Hyldie.

Walter stood next, eager to share. "I also must thank the Grand Council Delegate family. I realized that my healing was being blocked by me blaming my parents and their generation of leaders for my generation's troubles. It has kept me from even imagining how we could work together."

Next, one of the firebrand proctors came to his feet and immediately apologized to the Erylian delegates. "I have been guilty of not maintaining my duties as an Erylian officer and blaming you for poorly managing our troubles back home. While unable to imagine an outcome at this moment, I can now begin to entertain that a favorable solution can and does exist for Erylia."

Many people stood and told of their new insights and dreams as a result of the Resolution Walk. It was amazing how many spoke about having a deeper appreciation of the beauty and importance of each individual. A number of the kidnapped youth specifically apologized for their anger, blame and resentment over their incarceration. Many expressed gratitude for their new relationships with proctors and delegates — relationships that could lead to even more solutions to the Erylian Condition.

For over an hour we listened, before Nandia asked Colonel Yellian to bring his transport vehicles to the garden entrance. Soon we were again settled into our classroom at the I.C. The Praesepian kidnapped were delighted to be part of the session and filled most of the chairs at the back of the room.

Nandia again took the lead and asked, "Erylian Delegates and Colonel Yellian, is there any objection if we engage in a creative brainstorming process to identify options to Erylia's siege of Praesepe?"

The Delegates gathered together and quietly conferred, mostly trying to calm down Yellian. He seemed to be objecting — loudly at times — to any threats to his new command and the military presence on Praesepe. Finally, General Haplydean firmly ordered the new colonel to stand down. "We are happy to see where this leads, Nandia," the General announced and both officers returned to their seats.

"I welcome all the new people with us today," Nandia began. "I especially appreciate the open-heartedness of you Praesepians who have joined us this morning. By now I imagine that you've come to understand that we seek to mediate a peaceful resolution to this siege on Praesepe — the planet Erylia's attempt to resolve a debilitating epidemic that has descended upon their planet.

"But today, we also seek to promote the effective healing of what has come to be called the Erylian Condition. I ask that you listen carefully, ask questions freely, and join in the conversation wholeheartedly." Nods and smiles spread across the crowd of youngsters — the Resolution Walk had been their first ray of hope since their incarceration.

"In the spirit of creative play," Nandia said as she scanned the room, taking in the entire audience, "let's openly express any and all possible options to the Erylian siege. Please express those preferred outcomes that you imagined after the Resolution Walk. A brainstorming session is meant to be playful, so let's set aside criticisms and work to encourage a free flow of ideas. Any questions?" Seeing that everyone, aside from the Yellian exception, was clearly on board, Nandia continued.

"In every conflict," Nandia said as she resumed speaking to the entire gathering, "there are times when a favorable outcome looks to be a forlorn hope. Feelings of powerlessness, hopelessness and helplessness are widespread. This does not mean that favorable solutions don't exist, it simply means that the conflict has not matured enough for us to see how an ideal resolution can be realized.

"When things look hopeless, when I am feeling powerless, I simply remind myself to stop, take time for breathing and to heal my hurts. I set aside any impulses I have to make hurried decisions or to force a hasty resolution.

"There is one last resolution principle that I ask each of you to keep in mind. And that is that no option we consider need undermine the ideal that we share — that the healing of the Erylian condition and the cessation of the Praesepian siege can nurture the well-being of all life, both individually and collectively, on each planet. So, as we set out to brainstorm options why not set aside the belief that the ends justify the means?

"With that in mind, I request that we all refrain

from suggesting any options that include acts of violence or the taking of a life."

A proctor raised his hand and asked, "But Nandia, why such a request? It seems quite obvious to any number of us that our only option is to force the Erylian government to step down. That may well require harsh means to accomplish those ends."

"Throughout history, many governments have resorted to or been replaced using violent measures," Nandia said. As she moved across the front of the room, her grace and charm naturally drew the audience in. "Centuries ago on Earth, a country called India freed itself from imperialist oppressors by using simple acts of peaceful non-resistance. People spoke out against tyranny and put their economic might behind their protests. Similar examples, though much rarer than war and violence, dot history's landscape throughout the ages.

"What I am suggesting," Nandia clearly stated, "is that to effectively bring about the ideal outcomes you wish for Erylia, you cannot use a means that is not ideally suited to that outcome." Nandia was clearly challenging many of the proctors to re-think how they might accomplish their ends. Hearing this challenge, most of the Erylian Delegates appeared visibly relieved.

"So how might the change you wish to see on Erylia come about?" Nandia asked.

Marshal Everen's hand went up. Nandia nodded and he stood and addressed the room. "When Nandia suggested that the ends do not justify the means, I began considering just what kind of government I most want to support. And I found that beneath my doubts and all my military training I want a government that recognizes each individual's innate value. In realizing that, I must admit that I would accomplish very little by wanting to kill the individuals who don't agree with me.

"This has forced me to change my thinking about our Praesepian siege. After seeing how quickly my daughter has been healing, it seems to me that one thing we must do is train these young people here to teach others about healing."

One of the delegates began to raise his hand when suddenly an Erylian youngster jumped up and suggested media involvement — publicizing the favorable results of our healing program. Then followed a barrage of ideas: one officer offered to fully fund a concert for Erylia's capital city, to be organized by Dunstan. Our troubadour nodded eagerly as he recalled the joys of our similar event in Geasa. The previously interrupted delegate suggested local gatherings back home where proctors and youngsters could speak to their families, neighbors and local politicos. As options flowed it was clear there was no shortage of individuals who were passionate to seed ideas into fruition.

"I certainly recognize these ideas as powerful," said another Erylian delegate. "But I seriously doubt that we can send a delegation that the politicians, military and corporate leaders will listen to."

"It is widely known," Nandia responded, "that within any individual's talent there innately exist many means for that talent's expression. The same holds true for a society. As change appears, the abilities, ideas and resources needed to support that change appear — usually unexpectedly. This we can learn to trust. All acts of creation hold the potential to manifest in a state of ease. This, also, we can learn to trust. If this were not true, there would be no growth in our knowledge, our technologies, or our institutions."

While listening to Nandia's wisdom, the delegate's face transformed. It was as if a dark cloud that had been trapped within the strata of his face had suddenly been released, letting light return to his eyes. "So we need to find a way," he exclaimed, "to show the drug manufacturers, the plastics manufacturers, the chemical manufacturers and the government that it is economically viable to look after the well-being of each and every individual. That's a tall order, but not impossible for the land of Erylia. Perhaps that's the true purpose of 'tribal loyalty above all.'"

"So you have spoken of educating your news media," Nandia summarized. "You have floated ideas to educate your legislators. You wish to reach into your families and reach out into your communities. You are wise to consider how to change the industries that are toxifying your homelands. And some of you, quite naturally, have expressed doubts about some of these options. I recommend that you consider doubting your doubts as you ask yourselves, "So what's next?"

Immediately Chancellor Branson stood and said, "The ideas being generated here today are all quite wonderful. I'm wondering if there are people here who would be willing to be a part of a delegation to visit Erylia's World Council?"

Virtually everyone in the room stood up and, with cat calls, cheers and applause, loudly asserted their desire to be a part of such an action.

I did notice, however, that Colonel Yellian's energy field was growing darker and murkier.

# X X I I

AS THE APPLAUSE FADED and people returned to their seats, General Haplydean stood and surveyed the room. His was an imposing presence. "I propose we end the Erylian program on Praesepe today," he stated. "Right now I am rescinding the order to detain Praesepian youths. Officers, please be in Colonel Yellian's office at 0900 tomorrow to present written plans for the return of your commands to Erylia."

At that moment Colonel Yellian stood. Shrouded in an energy field shot through with dark browns, angry reds and fearful grays, he scowled as he gave voice to his objections. "I for one, must protest, General Haplydean. The activities that have been condoned by Marshal Everen are of dubious result. Furthermore, he has allowed the direct orders of the Imperial Command to be countermanded. The very presence of these Praesepian youths, who have been ordered to Erylia, speaks to his malfeasance. These are treasonable acts, General. I cannot not stand by and watch such a wholesale betrayal of the Erylian high command's authority. I will not betray my homeland."

The General looked as if he had expected such an outburst. "Colonel, do you have any family members who have been affected by the Erylian Condition?" he quietly asked.

"No Sir, I do not. And I fail to see what relevance that has to my duty as an officer."

"Quite right you are, Colonel," Haplydean replied evenly. "However, I trust that while on duty in Praesepe, you acknowledge that you fall under my comm..."

"Please excuse my interruption General," Dunstan interjected as he stepped forward. "I d'na wish to intrude upon your command, but, might I speak to the Colonel?" With a nod and a wave of his arm, Haplydean stepped back, and gave the floor to the troubadour.

"Colonel Yellian, each of us is solely responsible to maintain our own self-respect." Dunstan spoke in a tone that asked to be heard. "No order issued to an officer has ever had the power to force that officer to abandon his own integrity. If yours guides you to oppose our direction, fair enough. Some may call these ideas treason. Again, fair enough. All I ask is, that for a few moments, you honestly explore your deepest feelings about what is occurring here. Discover if you are at truly at peace within yourself continuing the Praesepian siege."

Yellian's brow clouded. He angrily opened his mouth, about to object to the implication that he wasn't at peace with himself, when some seed of self-doubt suddenly sprouted. Looking confused, he quickly clamped is mouth shut, reconsidered and re-set himself to bluster when Nandia stepped forward.

"Colonel, your devotion to duty is certainly a measure of your integrity and loyalty to Erylia. Would you be willing to be a part of today's process of creation, without believing that such an act would compromise your dedication to duty?" With this Nandia paused, letting her gentle words sink in.

Suddenly Yellian's shoulders slumped. He buried his face in his hands; his body began heaving with silent sobs. In response to the man's pain, Nandia began breathing deeply. All the family immediately came to our feet and followed her lead. Soon the entire room was taking deep, connected breaths.

The Colonel took time to regain a measure of composure before he spoke. "While it is true that I have no family affected by the Erylian Condition," he said after lifting his head from his hands, "I lost my only son and his beloved mother nearly twenty years ago. Had my son survived, he most certainly would have been affected by this malady." A torrent of tears again streamed down his face, which again he hid behind his hands. His energy field was aswirl with bright colors emerging from deep within the muddy hues that had been his norm.

Nandia was watching Yellian's energy field. As his brighter colors intensified, she quietly asked, "Is it possible, Colonel, that you've been blaming yourself for the loss of your family?"

Her question triggered a wail and a renewed flood of tears. Everyone in the room resumed breathing deeply until, at last, the Colonel's pain subsided and he could speak again.

"You are quite right, Nandia," he said quietly. "As a

young married officer on a limited budget, I sought to make ends meet by replacing the sensor controls on our family vehicle myself. I tested my work and was satisfied with it. Later that same day, my wife and son were travelling to visit her family when one of the sensors I had installed failed. The vehicle fell from the sky. It was entirely my fault."

As he revealed this great shame, a blush of deep scarlet raced up his neck and flooded his face. Breathing heavily, he dropped his head and closed his eyes. Yellian had finally allowed himself to admit the anguish of loss and shame that he had been hoping would stay hidden for life.

Gently, Nandia moved close to Yellian and spoke softly yet clearly. "Colonel, please consider that we each are far more than physical beings. As beings of energy, we sometimes choose events that, while great challenges at the time, are selected because of opportunities for our healing and growth." Again Nandia hesitated, as if listening to her own inner impulses, before she continued.

"Sir, would you be willing to consider that your family did not have that tragedy thrust upon them? Perhaps, at some deep level, each member of your family willingly took part in creating those events. Perhaps each of you knew that event was the doorway that could best lead to the growth each of you fervently desired."

The Colonel looked up, brow raised in surprise. "But we loved each other so much," he cried in protest. "Why would we have created such a tragedy?"

"I'll wager it was *because* you loved each other so much that such a tragedy occurred," Dunstan offered from the front of the room. "It was ta aid each one of ya — aye, there's nae doubtin' that Lad, rest assured.

"Colonel, please d'na stop lovin' 'em simply because they nae be here showin' ya the light 'n their eyes. They're around ya now lad, just imagine it so, 'n you'll sense their lovin' presence."

After listening to both Nandia and Dunstan, Colonel Yellian looked around the room. His eyes came to rest as he gazed out the broad window, watching sunlight as it bounced off trees and danced through windswept leaves. Suddenly a surprised look of delight lit up his face. Turning toward us, his energy field flashed with vibrant intensities of violet and gold, the hues of exhilaration and spiritual love.

"You are quite right," he exclaimed. "I do feel my family's presence for the first time in twenty years. I cannot thank you enough for such a magnificent gift." He turned toward Nandia and fell into her outstretched arms.

The room was abuzz with excitement and broke into spontaneous applause. El, Gracie and I stood with Dunstan, breathing deeply with broad smiles of joy beaming across our faces.

After Nandia and Yellian drew apart, Chancellor Branson rose to her feet. "I and the other delegates have been observing these proceedings. We have come to several conclusions that I have been asked to share with you.

"Ours is a world of despair," she began, looking out at everyone in the room to make they were included. "Our own growth has been stalled for generations. We are a people who have come to believe in our own delusions — that torturing people and disregarding our responsibility to live on life's terms is the only way our survival can be assured.

"We are a people afraid. Afraid that our problems are insurmountable. Fearful that we are powerless to change our world. We have become mired in our distractions of greed, blame and revenge. For generations we have disregarded our home environment. We have polluted our foods with the toxins you describe. We have imposed upon our own offspring the job of cleaning up our messes. And now we face an entire generation that is unable to bear children. Our answer to this self-created problem has been our military takeover of Praesepe.

"It is obvious to us today that such a course has been a grave mistake. We have seen how your gentle listening and wisdom have helped these Erylian children recover their passion for living. The healing they have accomplished in such a short time, your peaceful handling of yesterday's near-riot, and your Resolution Walk are each powerful inducements for this delegation to change its thinking. We do not know if you can produce these same results for an entire generation of our children. However, it is clear that taking that chance is far preferable to abandoning our own youth in the hopes that we could force Praesepians to become our new breeding stock.

"It has become very clear to us what it has cost our children to even imagine such an outcome. On behalf of Erylia, this Imperial Delegation presents a most humble apology for our actions. As of now, we cease and desist in our siege of Praesepe. All the kidnapped youths will be returned to their homes.

"We humbly request that the four Grand Council

Delegates, along with any Praesepians who are of like mind, journey with us to Erylia and help us heal. It is time to change our world. We will put the full might of the Erylian government toward enacting such a change.

The chancellor stepped to the front of the room and stood next to Nandia. "I believe our next course of action is obvious," she said. "Marshal Everen, at the suggestion of this delegation and with the full support of General Haplydean, you are ordered to return to your command on Praesepe. This includes overseeing the Erylia's disengagement from this siege. Your reinstatement also includes a promotion.

"We must immediately send a delegation to the Erylian World Council," Branson continued. "Colonel Yellian and Marshal Everen would you two accept the duty of leading this delegation?"

Obviously surprised to be offered such an opportunity, both officers, whose auras were glowing vibrantly bright, replied most enthusiastically.

"I trust our four Grand Council Delegates will accompany us?" Everen asked as he turned toward us. "Will you accept our invitation to be part of the delegation to our World Council?"

The family had telepathically touched on this idea right after breakfast. After all, it only made sense. We knew of the healing results achieved. El had pointed out that arriving on Erylia with a group of healthy youngsters recovering from the Erylian Condition would pose one gigantic social problem.

And that problem was, would the society deal with a large surge in teenage pregnancies? That possibility alone would capture widespread attention from the media and the masses. It would quite quickly change the direction of social thinking and policy making.

Elli laughed lightly in response to Everen's offer and said, "We Council Delegates will be quite happy to accept your invitation. Of course, we'll include Gracie for the adventure. I trust you will also include these Erylian youths in your World Council delegation?" Everen and Yellian quickly nodded in agreement.

"But you now have a much larger problem," Aesir's immortal queen loudly asserted as she smiled broadly with delight.

She paused and enjoyed watching the Erylian delegates and officers as they puzzled over her riddle. Then she looked squarely at Everen and said, "Marshal, are you prepared to deal with the sexual revolution that is sure to occur as more and more of your young people heal?" Everyone laughed at the question — it revealed a delightful reality that few, if any, had even considered.

"Are all of the young people here today prepared to be a part of a delegation to the World Council?" Everen asked.

Walter raised his hand and stood tall. "I am very happy to be a part of such a delegation, but am in a bigger hurry to get to the sexual revolution part of this idea."

This brought cheers from around the room. As the din died down, Marshal Everen spoke up, this time to Colonel Yellian.

"Colonel, would you assign an officer to immediately contact all Praesepians who left contact details with the front desk of the Abyssinian? I would like them to be at the hotel at 0900 to begin outlining their duties for joining us on our return to Erylia."

"Certainly, Sir," Yellian replied. He quickly turned and nodded to Captain Whittaker who immediately headed out the door.

"And, Marshal Everen," the Colonel then continued, "might we work together to coordinate plans to return the Praesepian teens to their homes?"

"Absolutely," Everen responded. "And, I appreciate your request, Colonel."

I mentally cheered Yellian's wisdom to team up with the Marshal in the task of releasing the imprisoned teens. I dearly wanted to watch both of them looking into the faces of Praesepian families as their kidnapped youths were returned to their homes.

# XXIII

Early the next morning an officer from Yellian's command knocked on the door to our suite. The Colonel needed our help in sorting the two hundred-plus people who were lined up outside the Abyssinian's front entrance. All were eager to assist in either dismantling the Erylian presence on Praesepe, or somehow serving the Praesepian delegation to Erylia.

For over an hour, we helped organize the Praesepians into logistics, staging, transport and nursing crews. Then someone recognized Gracie, and suddenly she, Dunstan and Nandia were mobbed by a crowd, wanting either autographs, hugs or a musical performance. At that point, our presence became a hindrance to the work at hand, so with Sirius perched on his shoulder, Dunstan played a few tunes in the plaza before we retreated to our suite.

Midge and Joseph stopped by later in the day, and thanked us for our help in finding her granddaughter,

Annie. Sirius accepted their accolades with his usual dignified humor, all the while pretending to be mute. I later learned that Midge and Joseph had taken command of the Praesepian logistics team on Erylia and had received commendations for their brilliant leadership during the three-month campaign.

Little more is there left to tell of this tale. Of course we did accompany Everen and Hyldie and the rest of the Erylian youths to their home planet. Daily, they continued making remarkable progress in their recovery, and were soon being hounded by a boisterous group of paparazzi who took vids of their every move. We stayed on for more than a month, the last few weeks being entirely devoted to training Erylian healers.

Members of the Erylian World Council were greatly inspired, mostly by the young people in the delegation. It took only a single session for legislators to recognize the dry-as-rain futility of their plans to seed their younger generation with kidnapped Praesepian youths. They couldn't help but recognize our youngsters' vitality and could not afford to ignore the clamors of amazement from their medical community.

The night before our departure to Erylia, while still on Praesepe, we had the great joy of witnessing the wonder of a one-and-a-half solar eclipse. Nandia told us it happened only once every eleven years, and that birthrates always climb at least thirty percent for the following twelve months. Little wonder that the ancients on Nandia's home planet had long ago ascribed sexual vitality as one of the attributes of their sun Freyr. El wrote a year later that there were three Erylian youngsters from our testing sessions who gave birth to babies about nine months after that eclipse.

Interestingly, in the next few years, thousands of teens from Praesepe decided to visit Erylia. Hundreds stayed on to live there. Hundreds of others visited often. Needless to say, thousands of young Erylians also travelled to Praesepe. Initially receiving a cool and dubious reception from Praesepians, over the years they came to be regarded with great respect.

Elli and Dunstan stayed behind to educate Erylia's health care hierarchy about the use of vibrational remedies. Dunstan was asked to host a concert, like the one he had put together on Geasa. It was attended by tens of thousands of people, most of whom were under twenty-five years of age. It wasn't long before the Aesirian Royal Chambermaid and the red haired troubadour were running tours from Erylia to Praesepe. I'm told their lunar and solar eclipse excursions were widely and enthusiastically received.

The secretary of the Erylian World Council invited Nandia and me to speak at a conference about the coming sexual revolution, which we did. I mentioned to the lads that a mark of maturing as men was the ability to accept "No" with peace and grace. Some were surprised to hear that "No" didn't necessarily mean "Never" — it just meant, "Not Now."

Nandia was inspiring when she talked about the fact that each of us is ultimately responsible for our own sexual well-being. She was quite humorous describing the many ways we tend to give that responsibility to our partners, a dependency destined to create conflict, not satisfaction. There were huge sighs of relief from many women in the audience when they saw men listening intently to her message.

We shared tales about the sanctity of every individual. Having unprotected sex meant, at the very least, a positive, albeit subconscious, desire to parent a child as it matured to its full adult potential. "But, if you're not willing to accept that responsibility, don't have unprotected sex. You certainly have many other options," I told them. Some in the audience groaned, others chuckled. After our talk at the behest of the World Council we visited the galaxy-renowned Cratered Canyons of Erylia before continuing our travels.

In time, Dunstan and Elli moved on to Aesir. I heard stories decades later about the sprinkling of red-haired musicians born to the Aesirian royal family.

Before she returned home to Praesepe, Gracie instituted a Healing Walk for young people there who were deeply impaired and believed their ailments were incurable. She modelled the walk on her grandmother's Resolution Walk — a line of the infirm moved slowly past a line of youths who had recovered from the Erylian Condition. It seemed obvious to me that the energy exchanged during Gracie's walks accelerated healing. Like Nandia, Gracie had her walks repeated three times. Gracie's Healing Walks were clearly quite effective — the practice spread across the planet.

And after her return to Praesepe, Gracie went on to become the youngest person ever to be named to an administrative cabinet post. She was selected as their Minister of Well-Being, charged with educating youth in the skills of telepathy and teleportation. Last I heard, she was training dozens of students to accept responsibility for their own well being. I'm told she's a master at helping them learn to effectively listen to their own bodies. True progress on any planet.

Sirius stayed on Praesepe with Gracie and visited Annie and Midge quite frequently. He was often seen scampering down the halls of the Abyssinian and befriending those who were most in need of healing. It was said that he even took time to travel to Erylia and visit Everen's secretary, the groping Gladys, whenever she was feeling poorly. Last I heard, she was one hundred and two years old and going strong. Like Dunstan says, that cat has sand, and I still hold out hope for another mission together.

And Nandia and I? After our departure from Erylia, we had quite a memorable time touring the wonders of the planet Praesepe. Nandia's husband petitioned her to dissolve their union, saying that their children had grown and he had an itch to lead a colonizing expedition to a far-off galaxy. After spending three lovely months together, Nandia and I settled in a home nestled high in Praesepe's northern mountains. There we raised Gracie's younger aunts and uncles. More about those days I will not comment, other than to say they have been the happiest of my life.

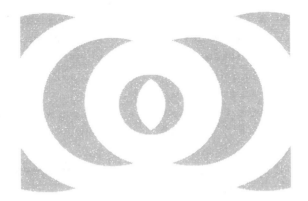

# AFTERWORDS

AT THE RISK OF REPEATING MYSELF, all healing abilities and modalities used in *Nandia's Children* are well within reach of human endeavor today. In truth, each of us heals in our own unique ways, and each act of healing is, in itself, its own unique creation.

The names of people and locales in The Nandia Trilogy were chosen for their specific meaning to the tale of which each is a part. While I have attempted to replicate certain characters' dialects as faithfully as possible, any failures in the accuracy of idioms and cultural expressions are mine, and mine alone. For those I apologize.

My heartfelt thanks go out to the many beloved friends, family and supporters who have made the publication of The Nandia Trilogy possible. Especially to Mary-Ann, your joy and encouragement have been an ongoing inspiration. Hajo and Kate your editing wisdom has long served to strengthen my skills and vastly improve the final result. To Erik, of Longfeather Book Design, I so appreciate your creative talent. Your design of The Nandia Trilogy has greatly made my work easier and more fun. Wendy, your artistic creativity has, once again, given Nandia an eternal beauty. Collaborating with you to arrive at this latest cover has been most rewarding.

And, my heartfelt gratitude goes to sister Margaret, as well as Jerry, Joanna, Renee, Kristen and the many others who offered welcome encouragement and support throughout the many renditions it took to breathe life into this tale.

To all of you, may you know this is only one of many expressions of my deepest gratitude for your support. Together we have brought Nandia and Bearns to life. And, we have now brought an end to The Nandia Trilogy. But, with every ending a new door opens, and I've the feeling these extraordinary healers will find a way to travel the many worlds of adventure again.